Book 2 in the Dearly Departed Series

DOUBLE CROSS

A different kind of ghost story

M. LARSON

ILLUMIFY
MEDIA.COM

Published by
Illumify Media Global
www.IllumifyMedia.com
"Let's bring your book to life!"

Paperback ISBN: 978-1-959099-32-1

Typeset by Jen Clark
Cover design by Debbie Lewis

Printed in the United States of America

This book is dedicated to my amazing Granny.
She was always the safe place to land for many of us.

Acknowledgment

Karen Scalf Bouchard, my perfectly wonderful editor.

Prologue

October 2002

The sun peeked over the Eastern horizon as a Suburban stopped in front of cabin number 6 at the Bear Creek Hunting Lodge. The new sheriff of Elk City, Colorado, pushed up his Ray-Bans, slipped a miniature recorder in his jacket pocket, and adjusted the silverbelly Stetson on his head before stepping out of the rig. He had been hunting for two missing teenaged girls for several hours, ever since being rousted out of his nice warm bed by the night shift deputies at the sheriff's office.

Damn telephone anyway.

He sauntered over to the rustic cabin door and banged on it with authority. He could hear the rustle and scurry of the occupants and a feminine squeak. He dipped his head and studied the dust coating his highly polished Tony Lama boots while listening to the voices.

First, he heard a sleep-graveled "What the hell?" Then a different male voice said, "Answer the damn door." More rustling and the metal clinks of a belt buckle before a disheveled man with a pronounced five o'clock shadow yanked the door open. He looked confused and hungover as he dragged a hand through the top of his black hair. "Yeah, what?" he barked before even looking at the man

1

standing on the stoop. As soon as his brain registered the uniform and badge, his tone changed.

"Uh, sorry, man. What can I do for you, Sheriff?"

The sheriff tugged his sunglasses slightly down his nose with one finger so he could peer over the top rim.

"I'm looking for these two girls." He produced two photos.

The man's eyes skittered away. "Why are you looking for them? Did they do something wrong?"

"Well, you see, their mommas are worried about them. They didn't make curfew and haven't been seen since eleven o'clock last night."

"Curfew?"

"Yeah, curfew. I think I better come inside."

Looking stunned, the man stepped back and waved the lawman across the threshold. Inside the hunter's cabin, a small deer head hung above the west window and full-size bunk beds were tucked into an alcove next to a bathroom door. A sitting area sported garage sale finds for furniture, and there were a few metal cabinets in a small kitchenette. The main room reeked of alcohol. Empty bottles and cans littered the tops of every flat surface.

The sheriff surveyed the other occupant of the room, who hurriedly yanked his pants up. Smirking, the lawman walked directly to the bathroom door and pounded on it with the side of his fist. "You two might as well come on out and face the music."

The door opened just a crack.

"Come on out of there now! Both of you."

The door squeaked as it opened wide, and two girls shuffled out. Heads down, shoulders slumped forward, they moved out of hiding. Sheriff Garrison pulled his sunglasses off his face and pointed toward the small sofa. "Sit down while we figure out what's going on around here."

ONE

Present Day

wins Lisa and Lillian Garrison sat in a corner booth in The Diner and waited for their younger sister to arrive. The wall clock above the cash register showed four minutes after eight.

"If Meg doesn't get here soon, we'll be skipping breakfast and ordering afternoon tea," Lisa grumbled.

"Relax. She's only a few minutes late."

The front door flashed open. Meg waved and headed their way. One arm hung in a sling, and bruises covered the side of her face. She was still healing from the rollover crash a couple of weeks ago that had totaled her cherished Jeep.

As she scuttled toward her sisters, Meg drew greetings from some of the other diners. Much to her chagrin, she had become a bit of a celebrity since helping solve the deadly virus mystery that had rocked their small community and cost the lives of several friends and loved ones—including Grams, the girls' beloved maternal grandmother.

Fortunately, as the girls were discovering, "dead" didn't always mean "gone."

"Sorry I'm late," Meg rattled as she slid onto the seat next to Lillian. "I had to get a ride from Jace."

"I didn't think you would ever get here. I'm starved," Lisa snipped.

Lillian grinned. "Don't mind her, Meg. She's 'starved.'" She flashed air quotes with her fingers.

Their waitress, Alice, glided past the table, loaded with a five-person order stacked up her arms. Her steps were sure. The woman was ageless. She had been working at The Diner for as long as the girls could remember.

After effortlessly delivering the food to a nearby table, Alice pulled her order pad out of her pocket and slid over to greet the sisters with a smile. "Hey girls, how are all of you? I heard Jessica had twins," she said, referring to the fourth and oldest Garrison girl who lived with her husband on the front range. "Meg, you're looking better every time I see you."

"Hi, Alice. I feel better every day. And my bruises are turning lime green—which I think goes better with my hair—so I can't complain. How about you?"

"I'm good too, honey. What'll you have?"

"I don't know about the Leg sisters, but I'll have a bacon-and-egg sandwich with a large cranberry juice."

Lisa scowled. The "Leg sisters" was a childhood joke that still got her goat.

"Switching it up. Good for you," Alice said as she jotted it down.

"That sounds good," Lillian added. "I'll have the same."

"Fine, make it three." Lisa slapped her menu closed and replaced it in the sliver rack attached to the napkin dispenser.

The sisters had been squabbling over the Legs moniker since they were kids. Meg, then seven, had just discovered that the initials of her full name—Madison Eileen Garrison—spelled Meg and refused to answer to anything else. When Meg realized the twins' initials were both L. E. G. and began calling them the Leg sisters, or sometimes Left and Right.

Lillian, then nine, had been easygoing about the whole thing. Lisa, not so much.

Nearly two decades later, Meg still liked to use the nickname to push a few buttons.

Alice grinned at the three girls before taking their order to the kitchen pass-through.

Meg turned to her sisters, too curious to wait any longer. "So . . . what's happening? Have you gotten into the house yet? Have you uncovered any clues about the Grandma Willie mystery?"

Lillian shook her head. "Not yet."

"Have you talked to—" Meg lowered her voice and looked around. "Grams?"

At the time of Grams' unexpected death from a mysterious virus, Lillian and Lisa had been out of the country. Both nurses, they had been serving in a remote village with Doctors Without Borders. It took several weeks for the news of their grandmother's death to reach the village, and another two weeks for the twins to travel home. By then, Meg had helped solve the origin of the deadly virus that had killed Grams.

Of course, she hadn't done it alone. Sheriff's Deputy Jace Taggerty had stepped in just when she needed him most—just like he used to do when they were kids—and in the process, the former childhood sweethearts had managed to fall back in love. Wedding bells were on the horizon.

But Meg's main crime-solving partner had been none other than Grams herself, recently deceased but still as feisty as ever.

The first time Grams had appeared to her grieving granddaughter, Meg thought she was going crazy. To make matters even more interesting, Grams had introduced her to a colorful cast of deceased friends and kinfolk that included Meg's great-aunt Ethel.

Grams had two sisters: Esther, who was as alive and grouchy as ever, and good-natured Ethel, who had been "gone" three years now. Apparently, in the afterlife Ethel and Grams were as thick as thieves, just like before they died.

Meg—assisted by her ghostly "support group"—had helped stop

a group of greedy malcontents from using the good people of Elk City as a science experiment gone wrong.

In the process, she had solved the mystery of Grams' death.

But as one mystery was resolved, another emerged.

Shortly after the death of her husband, Frank, the girls' paternal grandmother—Grandma Willie—had disappeared. That was ten years ago, but in all that time, none of the support group had spotted Grandma Willie "on the other side."

Which begged the question, was Grandma Willie dead or not? And if not, where was she—and why?

It was a mystery that Lillian and Lisa had vowed to solve.

All four Garrison girls had been close with both sets of grandparents. After the untimely death of their parents, the four girls had been raised by Grams and Grandpa Mike. Willie and her husband, Frank, had played a big role in their lives as well, which meant they'd spent a lot of time at the Garrison family ranch—co-owned by Frank Garrison and his brother, Big John, who was married to Esther.

Big John and Esther had never taken too kindly to the four Garrison girls.

Which was probably why Aunt Esther hadn't been returning their calls.

"No." Lillian shook her head at her sister's question. "I haven't talked to Grams in a couple of days. I'd love to know what she would suggest we do next."

"We haven't been able to do the *first* thing she suggested, which was to talk Aunt Esther into letting us visit Grandma Willie's old house so we could search for clues," Lisa grumped.

"How can we? Aunt Esther is stonewalling us. She won't even answer our calls. And without her help, I don't see how we're going to get onto the ranch and into the house."

Lillian looked at Meg. "Can you get in touch with Grams, or do you just have to wait until she shows up on her own?"

"You know Grams." Meg sighed. "She still does what she wants when she wants."

The girls sat quietly for a few minutes, considering their next steps.

Alice appeared and placed orders on the table. "Need anything else?"

"Nope! It all looks good," Lillian answered for the three.

"Enjoy. I'll check back in a little bit." She smiled and swished off to take care of her other customers. As usual, The Diner had filled to capacity for breakfast, with old ranchers who came in to catch up on gossip and drink too much coffee.

The women tucked into their breakfast. The Diner served food that was the definition of comfort. Conversation deviated to small talk while they ate. Just as Lisa took the last bite of her breakfast sandwich, the scent of Charlie perfume permeated the booth.

"Hi, Auntie Ethel," Meg whispered toward the now-familiar scent.

Aunt Ethel shimmered into view for the girls. No one else in the diner could see the fourth soul at the Garrison girls' table. "Hello, girls. Got some information for you."

"Is it about Grandma Willie?" Lillian lowered her voice even further.

"Yes! We've been checking through the grapevine, and not one of my contacts remembers seeing a person of her description cross over at least as far as Monarch Pass to the east and as far to the southwest as Ouray, and we have quite a network going."

"Network?" Lisa frowned. "You have a network?"

"Still not a morning person are you, sweetie?" Ethel looked kindly at her great-niece.

"No, Auntie, she's not," Meg confirmed.

Lillian cleared her throat. "So, you're pretty sure Grandma Willie didn't die?"

"That's what we're thinking right now. Your Grams said she would check in with you later after she's done with her training."

"What training?"

"If Eloise wants to stick around for a while before going on, she has to know all the rules for her post." After finishing her statement, she disappeared.

"I will never get used to this," Lisa muttered.

"I thought the same thing at first," Meg said. "It gets easier."

Lillian shoved her plate to the middle of the table and tidied her spot. "I think we should take another run at Aunt Esther today."

"She's not even answering our calls." Lisa frowned.

"Then let's stop calling." Lillian had a new pluckiness to her voice. "Let's drive over there and just show up. She'll *have* to talk to us then."

"Sounds like fun." Meg pulled a ten out of her wallet and dropped it on the table. "But you'll have to count me out for the rest of the week. My future mother-in-law has an entire wedding planning schedule, and apparently, I will *not* be excused."

"Ha, sucks to be you," Lisa said.

Meg had wanted to exchange vows at a family BBQ right here in Elk City, but Jace's mom wanted to help so badly, Meg had agreed, and Mrs. Taggerty had jumped in with both feet.

Meg stood up, dug her cell phone out of her hip pocket, and headed out the front door.

"Tell me why we asked her to breakfast this morning," Lisa complained. "She's no help."

"Oh, hush, grumpy. She's our baby sister, and I enjoy being around her. Besides, she knows the most about the support group." Lillian tidied up Meg's area and started to do the same to Lisa's until she saw her twin's raised eyebrow and returned her hands to her lap.

After paying their tab, they headed to the parking lot, toward the black four-door Chevy Colorado that had belonged to Grams before she died. Lillian tugged the keys out of her front pants pocket, and Lisa climbed into the passenger seat and buckled in.

The two hadn't even reached city limits when the distinct scent of sunshine-fresh laundry permeated the interior of the Chevy.

"Grams!" Lillian said as Eloise shimmered into visual range. "We're so glad you're here!"

"Hello, my darlings. Where are we headed?"

"The Garrison Ranch. We need your help, Grams. Aunt Esther is always too busy to talk to us, so we're going to try just showing up at her door."

Eloise leaned her ethereal form between the front bucket seats. "Sweeties, glean any information you can from Aunt Esther, and—if you can—find a chance to poke around any of Willie and Frank's stuff. There must be some of their things left in the old house. And watch and listen to me for clues—I'm getting very good at reading emotions from the living."

Lisa frowned. "I think all this cloak-and-dagger stuff is ridiculous. Grandma Willie and Grandpa Frank left us their house—and everything in it. We shouldn't be playing footsie with Aunt Esther. We should be hiring a lawyer."

"You girls were so young when Frank died and Willie disappeared." Grams clucked her tongue. "It was downright sinful, Frank's brother and my sister taking over everything like they did. But right or wrong, she's not gonna let you two waltz in there like you own the place—even if you do."

Lisa felt a feather-light brush of energy slip over her cheek. She had come to know that sensation as a kiss from her late grandma.

"The first thing we gotta do is find out if your Grandma Willie is dead or alive."

A few minutes later, Lillian guided the Chevy down the access road toward the massive arched gate heralding the Garrison Ranch. Since Big John and Aunt Esther had taken everything over, the original simple wooden crossbeam with the ranch's brand had been replaced by a fancy wrought iron structure with an electronic gate and call box.

Lillian pulled the truck up to the gate, lowered the window, and pushed the button on the call box.

"Yes," came the tinny voice of Great-Aunt Esther.

"Hey, Auntie Esther, it's Lillian. Lisa's here, too."

"What do you want?"

The twins exchanged looks. They'd spent a lot of time on the ranch when they were growing up. Now they were outsiders.

Grams rolled her eyes. "That woman is such a trial. Just tell her you need to visit with family."

Lillian turned back to the little speaker. "We just want to visit with family. You know, what with Grams gone, and we didn't even get back in time for her . . . her funeral." She added a little break in her voice for good measure.

"Oh. Well then, I suppose, but I don't have all day."

The large gates swung slowly open. Lillian eased her foot onto the gas pedal and aimed the car down the wide dirt road as the gate clanged shut behind them.

Chapter Two

Fifteen minutes later they parked on the hard-packed driveway just south of the kitchen door.

"Okay, girls, keep playing the 'grieving relatives' card. My sister doesn't have a sympathetic bone in her body, but she is full of duty for appearances' sake."

"We will, Grams," Lisa said as she tried to arrange her face to suit the mood.

The girls popped open the doors of the Colorado as Eloise floated through the side panel. During this egress she changed her appearance from the comfy appearance of faded jeans and athletic shoes to a more buttoned-down look of an oxford shirt, dark western slacks, and boots.

"Um, Grams," Lillian said quietly, "Did you just change . . . clothes?"

"Thought I better dress for battle just in case."

"All righty then," Lisa whispered.

When the girls reached the screen door to the kitchen, the wooden door was standing open. The girls exchanged looks as a brusque voice from the kitchen called out, "Well, come on in. Don't dawdle. I have things to do."

The twins stepped into a kitchen that smelled like apple pie and, of all things, bleach. The kitchen should have smelled homey with the apple pies baking, but there was that underlying scent of sterility in the updated kitchen.

Lisa remembered how welcoming the big house used to be. The big house was a short walk from Grandpa Frank and Grandma Willie's house. Frank and Big John's mother—the girls' Great-Grandma Garrison—always gave them fresh-baked sugar cookies and glasses of cold milk.

But with Esther at the helm of the family estate, nothing was comforting or homey, and sugar cookies were clearly out of the picture.

"Hey, Auntie Esther, thanks for seeing us today," Lillian said charmingly. "It means a lot to us."

Lisa stayed quiet with the silent comfort of Grams at her elbow.

"Well, don't just stand there. Come on in and sit down. It's my one day at home, so I need to get things done while we visit." Esther never stopped wiping the clean counter as she spoke.

The two young women found places at the kitchen table that still existed from cozier times. It was a yellow Formica-and-chrome job with yellow Naugahyde-and-chrome chairs. Lillian found it curious that Auntie Esther had replaced everything in the kitchen except that table and those chairs.

Esther wiped her hands on the hand towel tucked into her apron before picking up her coffee cup, walking to the head of the table, and sitting down.

"What can I do for you?"

"We were missing Grams and Grandma Willie this morning, and we're hoping you could share some memories with us," Lillian wheedled.

"I can't imagine my memories of those two would be a comfort to you."

Grams whispered into Lisa's ear, "Why, that old goat."

Lisa coughed to cover a laugh.

Lillian didn't give up. "Don't you have any pictures we could look at or things like that?"

"Not that I can think of. I think Eloise kept all the family pictures from *that* side of the family, and Willowmina, and Franklin's pictures are probably stored in the second story of Clint's house."

"Clint's house?" Lillian asked.

Aunt Esther looked uncomfortable. "After Willowmina disappeared, Clint moved in there to keep an eye on the place since you girls were too young to take it on. John thought it was best."

"So, all of Grandma Willie's and Grandpa Frank's stuff is still in their house?" Lisa said, trying to keep them on the subject at hand.

"Well, yes, it is. We moved it all up into the two big rooms upstairs. To keep it all safe, of course."

"She's very uncomfortable, girls," Eloise said, then drifted to the head of the table and hovered in front of her sister. She turned up the glow and waved a hand in front of Esther's face. There was no reaction. "No surprise. She could never see or hear me even when I was alive either."

At that moment, Eloise started messing with Aunt Esther's cup, moving it a few centimeters at a time. Lillian spoke quickly.

"Auntie Esther, do you think it would be possible to get a few things from the house? Like pictures and mementos?"

"What? I don't know. Clint is out of town at a conference, and I don't think he would want you in his house."

"*His* house?" Lisa repeated.

Lillian kicked her twin under the table just as Esther reached for her cup. It was several inches from where she had left it, with the handle turned the wrong direction.

"*Harrumph*," she grunted, surprised. "I keep putting things one way and they end up another these days."

Eloise smirked.

"Couldn't you take us over there just long enough to get a few old photos?" Lillian's sweetness-and-light act was getting on her own nerves.

"Well . . . I don't know . . . everything is in boxes, you know."

Lillian interrupted. "We'll be really fast. I promise. In fact, we'll take boxes with us and look through them at home to take up less of your time."

Esther twisted her pursed lips to the left and squinted her eyes at the girls. "Let me get my pies out of the oven first. But understand me—I don't have all morning for you to ooh and aah over every little thing. When Clint gets home, you can talk to him about picking up more of the things—although I can't imagine why you would want it —but I warn you, he's a very busy man."

Lisa and Lillian nodded, but it was hard not to be distracted by Grams. She was leaning one elbow on the table next to Esther.

Lisa stared. *Is Grams making faces at her sister?*

Their great-aunt suddenly slid her chair back as if in discomfort. "Sit still, the timer is about to go off and then we can leave." She stood up and literally walked through her sister with a little shiver. "I don't know where the cold drafts are coming from in this kitchen. There isn't even a breeze blowing yet this morning."

She wasn't the only who shivered. Eloise shivered too.

"I hate when she does that," Eloise said. "It sure discombobulates a person."

The girls didn't dare respond.

Aunt Esther set the pies on the counter and pulled off her oven mitts. Grabbing her car keys, she said, "I know it's a short walk, but follow me in your car and then you can head home as soon as we're done."

Chapter Three

The drive to their grandparents' cozy little house only took a couple of minutes by the back road. The July temperatures were moderate, and the girls lowered the windows to enjoy the soft summer morning. They raised them back up quickly as the dust from the dirt road roiled inside.

"Great," Lisa said. "We're going to need a date with the car wash when this is over."

They pulled up to another electronic gate and fence surrounding the little house and yard they had played in when they were children. That was new too. Aunt Esther pulled in behind them, tooted her car horn, and motioned to the girls to get out of her way so she could pull up through the gate first.

Eloise gave an inelegant snort. "She always did need to be first in line."

Once both cars were inside the fence, the gate quietly eased shut behind them.

"Don't get out yet," Esther hollered. "Got to get the dog put in the dog run."

"Talk about security overkill," Lisa muttered.

Lillian didn't answer. She was staring, speechless, at the yard. All of Grandma Willie's beautiful flowers and gardens were gone. All she could see was a very precise green patch of lawn clipped short and bordered with rock. The trees she had nurtured were gone. The raised flower beds were gone. The yard looked like a military compound complete with a tidy dog run and a camouflaged parking area with two four-wheelers painted to blend into the landscape—a green four-wheeler to blend with the summer foliage and a white-and-grey vehicle to blend in with winter's hues.

Esther waved the girls to follow her into the house. "Had to put Brutus up. He doesn't like strangers." She pulled a key out of her apron pocket when they reached the front door. "Let's be quick about it."

She unlocked the door and it swung into, for lack of a better phrase, a man cave. Gone were the quilts from the walls and the cozy overstuffed furniture. The old treadle sewing machine was not to be seen nor were any of the family pictures. This room housed a giant flat-screen television, surround sound speakers hung in various corners, and the furniture was all leather and all male. Lillian looked over to the dining room and almost lost her composure. Her chin wobbled and tears stung her eyes. Grandpa Frank had built a sunroom off the dining area. Grandma Willie had turned it into a fairy land with all kinds of plants and flowers. She had snuggled with her granddaughters on the wide white glider Grandpa built for her, reading stories and laughing with them.

It was all gone. Now, inside the sunroom sat a massive hot tub that smelled like chemicals. Lillian looked at Lisa and saw anger smoldering in her blue-green eyes.

Oblivious, Aunt Esther led the way to the stairs.

Shimmering at the top of the stairs, Eloise studied her grand-daughters' dismal expressions. "Chin up, girls. I'm as perturbed as you at what's been done to this home. It looks like a bachelor pad. But stay focused. Look for anything that might help us understand what happened to your Grandma Willie. It will all come out right in the long run. I am very sure of that."

She drifted backward as Esther and the twins reached the top of the stairs.

The second floor had, at one time, been one large room before it was divided into two rooms with oddly angled doors facing each other.

Eloise was hovering in the room to the right, near a neat stack of clearly labeled boxes. Thankfully, Esther walked to that room first, and the girls gravitated toward the area where their grandmother was snooping around.

"The photos and albums should be in this room, the furniture in the other." Esther peered through the bifocals of her glasses at the bold black letters on several of the boxes.

"I think the photos are over here," Lillian called out.

"Good, be quick about it. I've got things to do."

"Yes, ma'am," Lillian replied with syrupy sweetness coating her voice.

Lisa wanted to smack her twin and say, *Gag me*, but she kept that thought behind her teeth and pulled a box off the stack to take with them. Lillian followed suit. They made quick work of pulling boxes and stacking them by the door.

They had at least six of the cartons stacked when their great-aunt asked with impatience, "Have you found what you're looking for? Do you have enough to get started?" She was shifting her weight from foot to foot and checking her watch.

Lillian looked over at her, pasted a smile on her lips, and said, "Oh, Auntie, there is just so much, and we don't want to have to be a bother and come back in a day or two."

She turned back to perusing the boxes and reading labels carefully, looking for anything that might include a diary, financial records, or something more than pictures that might give them a clue as to Grandma Willie's past. The family seemed to know nothing of her life prior to her marriage to Grandpa Frank.

Eloise had been drifting from stack to stack silently pointing out a possibility here and there. As the girls continued their treasure hunt, Esther's fidgeting became more pronounced, and Eloise was mumbling under her breath about overbearing nincompoops.

"Okay, girls, I really have to go, and it's been fifteen minutes and you have eight boxes stacked up to take with you. I'll try to find more time next week, but no promises." She gave the girls a stern look. She turned and marched from the back of the room toward the front, stopping about halfway to her goal and bending to look at one of the boxes on her right. "Lisa, come here and get this one. It has her garden journals in it. You know how she loved all those messy plants. You would think a redheaded freckle face like her would avoid being outdoors all of the time."

Lisa had just stacked another box on the growing pile and turned to frown at her aunt.

Lillian swiftly moved from the back of the room to Aunt Esther's side. "I'll get it, Lisey." She moved three boxes from the top of the stack, pulled out the box marked "Garden Notes," carefully set it aside, and restacked the others. "Thanks, Auntie. This should be enough."

They didn't waste any time hauling the boxes down the stairs and out to their truck. Once the cartons were stacked and secured in the back of the Colorado, the girls jumped into the front seats and Grams drifted into position on the backseat. As they buckled in, they watched Esther secure the front door and let scary-looking Brutus out of the dog run.

They didn't talk until they were off the ranch.

Lisa was the first to break the silence. "Can you believe what *he's* done to that house?"

"It was very unsettling to find the gardens gone and that stupid hot tub in the sunroom," Lillian muttered.

Eloise leaned between the seats as was her habit. "Girls, I know that wasn't easy. I had a hard time with that myself. Just take comfort that they packed everything up and stored it safely instead of dumping it somewhere."

"Small favors," Lillian agreed.

"Let's hope there is something usable for our search in what we have." Lisa shifted in her seat as far as the seat belt would let her so she could face Grams and Lillian. "Does anyone know where Grandma Willie came from or who her family was?"

Eloise knit her eyebrows in thought. "I've been trying to think if I ever heard even one thing about her past. I don't think she ever talked about her life before she met Frank. Nothing earlier than the first time they met when he pulled in behind her broken-down car. Not one thing about when she was growing up or her school days. None of that."

They rolled along the blacktop road in silence, everyone lost in their own thoughts for the rest of the drive.

They arrived at Eloise's condo ten minutes later. Doctor Meeker and her Centers for Disease Control friends had been staying there while helping Meg solve the virus mystery, but they had cleared out three days earlier, taking their makeshift lab with them.

Lillian parked the little truck inside the garage and turned off the engine. "Well, we're here. Let's get the boxes inside and then have lunch. I'm starving."

"I'm going to get Ethel while you girls have lunch," Grams announced. "We're going to need all the help we can get." Then she was gone.

It took very little time to get all nine boxes stacked by the dining table.

The women found bread, deli meat, chips, and olives, and made quick work of lunch. They were just cleaning up when Grams and Ethel popped in.

"Hey girls," Ethel chirped.

"Hey, Aunt Ethel," the twins said in unison.

"What did you have for lunch?" Grams said wistfully. "Tasting things is the one thing I can't seem to stop missing."

"You'll get used to it soon enough, give it time," Aunt Ethel said matter-of-factly.

"Humph," Grams retorted before she changed the subject. "You girls ready to get started digging through these boxes?"

Lisa dried her hands on the seat of her pants instead of waiting for the hand towel Lillian was using. In turn, Lillian snapped the towel at her sister. Grams and Aunt Ethel laughed.

The two young women tackled the boxes while the two spirits directed the operation. After opening the cartons, Lisa and Lillian arranged photo albums and framed pictures on tables and couches, attempting some semblance of chronological order, at least as well as they could with their great-aunt's and Grams' guidance.

The four women studied the photos looking for any clues about Grandma Willie's past—after all, she might have left Elk City and simply returned to her family. But the earliest photos were black-and-white images of her and Grandpa Frank doing the silliest things, with broad smiles and love shining in their eyes.

Lillian laughed out loud when she found a picture of their father when he was eleven or twelve. He was up to his knees in a shallow river, his skinny bare chest truly sunburned, with a long string of trout proudly raised up in his left hand and a small fishing pole slung over his right shoulder. His smile was so proud.

Lisa sighed a few times looking at the family history unfold before her eyes. Occasionally, she would ask Grams or Aunt Ethel a question about their dad when he was young. They had so few memories of their parents because they died when the girls were seven. Sometimes it felt intrusive to be looking at all of the photos without one of them there to narrate the picture story. In all the pictures, there was so much love.

After six hours of looking through memorabilia and sharing memories, Eloise and Ethel were running out of juice and were fading in and out as well as having trouble moving pages. They weren't any closer to finding a place to start the search for Willie, and it was dinnertime. The girls were hungry as well as discouraged. They had been through every photo album and framed picture, checking for anything tucked behind a picture or in between pages, and there just wasn't one thing.

"I don't know how we are ever going to find out what happened to her. There isn't one blasted shred of anything. We don't have a clue where to start," Lisa agonized.

"There are still a lot of boxes over at the house," Lillian countered.

Lisa got up from her cross-legged position on the floor and put another album back in a box. "Grams, would you and Aunt Ethel be able to go through boxes by yourself at Grandma Willie's house? You know, in a secret way?"

"Sorry, girls, it doesn't quite work like that." Her voice quavered in and out as she spoke. "And now Ethel and I need to go rest, so to speak. You girls get some dinner, and tomorrow we'll think of another way to look at things."

The girls each felt a feather-light brush across their cheeks, and they knew their two helpers had gone.

"Ugh," Lisa groaned, "my back and neck are stiff from sitting on the floor and pouring over all of these pictures."

"It was a big project but . . . I don't know, seeing the old photos was nice," Lillian responded as she closed the last carton. "Wow. We went through all eight boxes. No, make that seven—I think I see another one."

She lifted one more box onto the dining table. "It's the one with Grandma Willie's garden journals."

"I don't think I can sort through anything else tonight. It's after seven and I'm starving," Lisa said.

Lillian fiddled with a little edge of tape on the box before she said, "Me too. Where do you want to eat? I don't have the energy to fix something."

"Diggers," Lisa said.

"Perfect! We won't even have to get out of the truck."

"My turn to drive." Lisa grabbed the keys.

With that, they were through the kitchen door as the garage door hummed open.

Chapter Four

———————

*L*isa nosed the small truck into the busy parking lot. Diggers Drive-In had twenty carhop slots, plus parking places for folks who wanted to grab a bite inside and sit on the chrome-and-plastic-molded stools around the plastic-molded tables —and right now everything looked full.

Lisa spotted white backup lights on a one-ton truck with a lariat swinging from a gun rack in the back window. A moment later, Lisa swung the little Colorado into the vacated slot, cut the engine, and popped her seat belt loose. Both girls leaned forward immediately to study the large menu hanging from the rafters.

They were debating the merits of the Macho Nachos with jalapeños versus the large chili cheese fries when they heard a tapping on the window.

Lisa and Lillian looked over and saw their baby sister standing at the window with a grin on her face. Meg's arm sling sported a bright yellow mustard stain. Jace's truck was behind her, parked in the spot next to theirs.

Lisa powered the window down.

"Hey, Meg. Foot-long chili cheese dog with mustard and onions for dinner tonight?"

"Hello to you too. Hi, Lill." Meg switched her gaze back to Lisa. "How do you know what I ate for dinner?"

Lisa grinned and pointed at the bright yellow spill.

"Oh crud. Last night it was soy sauce and now this. I will be so glad when I don't have to wear this stupid thing anymore."

Jace leaned across the center console of his truck. "Hey, Left and Right, how are things?"

Lillian took the conversation to keep her twin from going off on him. "Hey, Jace. Things are okay."

Lisa shot her a look. "No they aren't."

Meg immediately asked, "What's wrong?"

Lisa frowned. "We finally got into Grandma and Grandpa's house to get a few boxes of photos and things, but we haven't found anything to help us figure out what happened to Grandma Willie."

"But the shocker is what we found at their house," Lillian interjected as she leaned forward to see Meg and Jace better. She pulled her reddish-blond hair over her right shoulder so it wouldn't swing in front of her face. "All of Gramma's little gardens are gone, and her sunroom is now home to a hot tub."

Meg groaned. "Clint is such an ass."

"No doubt," Lisa snorted. "Let's change the subject before I lose my appetite. How was wedding planning today?"

Meg laughed. "I'll show you." She whirled around, leaned into Jace's truck, and began digging around in a large tote bag. It didn't take long for her to whip out a handful of turquoise fabric swatches and turn back to her sisters. "Say 'Thank you, Meg, for not letting the bridal attendants be dressed in orange.'"

Lisa and Lillian shuddered at the thought. With their red-gold hair, fair skin, and blue-green eyes, orange made them both look jaundiced. Meg pushed the swatches through the window and dropped them in Lisa's lap. "You guys figure out which one of these you like best and let me know."

"Megs, it's getting late, and we need to get to the airport," Jace interrupted.

"Airport?" Lillian asked.

"Yeah, we're picking up a friend of Kai's who's flying into Gunnison," Meg explained. "He's an acupuncturist, like she is. He's also a nutritionist and naturopath. He doesn't know if he'll stay long-term, but he's agreed to help Kai out for a few months. He's taking on all of Jack's clients."

Kai and Meg worked together at Altitude Adjustments, a wellness clinic Kai had founded several years earlier. A few short weeks ago—as the virus scam escalated to a climax—Kai had taken a bullet in the arm. She also was grieving the recent murder of Jack, a practitioner at the clinic, the man she loved, and the father of their precious unborn baby.

Lisa and Lillian hadn't met Kai yet, but they knew of the traumas she had gone through.

"I'm glad she's taking some time for herself," Lillian said.

"Me too," Meg said with a note of sadness in her voice.

"Hey, if you two aren't busy tomorrow night, meet us at the Powder Keg," Jace said. "We're going to take him out for a beer after dinner."

"We might do that," Lillian said. The twins waved as Meg climbed into the truck and Jace backed out of his slot and turned the truck toward the parking lot exit.

The twins shared a messy dinner of chili cheese fries and loaded Macho Nachos washed down with Dr Pepper. Napkins littered the dash by the time they finished. There was nothing tidy about eating in a vehicle with your fingers when everything is drippy delicious.

Groaning with full satisfaction, Lillian said, "I've missed yummy junk food."

The girls had been traveling for four years. They'd worked all over the United States as traveling nurses before signing up with Doctors Without Borders. They'd each been able to save a chunk of money to add to the inheritance they received when their parents died. It seemed a good time to take a break and stay Stateside for a while.

Plus, it felt good to be home, good to be with Meg—and with

Grams and Aunt Ethel, in a fashion. Lillian felt that way and knew that Lisa, despite her grumpier disposition, felt that way too.

When they walked into the kitchen of Grams' condo, Aunt Ethel and Grams were visible again and waiting for them.

"Hey girls," Grams greeted them.

Ethel gave a cheery wave. "Eloise and I have been thinking about Willie's garden journals."

"We spotted them earlier but haven't gone through any of them yet," Lillian said.

"Aren't they just about gardening stuff, like which plants did well, which ones sucked, and what to plant next year?" Lisa asked.

"Could be," Eloise replied, "but I think there were times she used them more like regular journals, like when your mom and dad died in the avalanche."

"Really?" Lisa hung the ring of keys on the hook by the kitchen door.

"I think she did," Grams said.

"Well, looks like there are several years' worth of journals." Lillian walked to the last unopened carton and hefted it up to the kitchen's breakfast bar. Pulling the packing tape away, she unfolded the flaps of the box. "Why don't we team up? Lisa, you and Grams take a few of these, and Aunt Ethel and I will take some."

Ethel shimmered over to a place at the dining room table and moved a chair out without touching it.

"Show-off!" Eloise scolded with a haunting rendition of her once-warm laugh.

Each duo picked up a few journals to start the process. On the first page of each fabric covered book there was a date written in delicate script. The journal covers were works of art in their own right, but as soon as the girls opened the first journals, they gasped at the intricate drawings and miniature watercolor paintings of flowers and plants.

"I didn't know Grandma Willie was an artist," Lillian murmured.

"She said she 'dabbled' with paint on odd occasions. This is so much more than dabbling," Eloise added with a sigh.

Once their initial astonishment waned a bit, the foursome set to the task of reading entries. Grandma Willie had written mostly about plants and wildflowers, but there were occasional notes on things happening in her daily life outside the gardens. It was fascinating reading her thoughts on everything from the joy her granddaughters brought her to laments about dealing with Esther and Big John.

Eloise, Ethel, Lisa, and Lillian read, laughed, oohed and aahed, teared up a bit. But by midnight, after pouring through the most recent journals, they had yet to find a single clue to help them learn more about their mysterious grandmother.

"Maybe we started at the wrong end of time." Eloise drifted back to the end of the table where the box sat. "Maybe she had more to say about her extended family when she first started writing. What's the date of her earliest journal?"

Lisa collected the journals they had already gone through and slid them aside while Lillian rummaged through the remaining books.

"Either we're missing a box of journals or"—Lillian paused to swallow— "she didn't start keeping these until Momma and Daddy died."

Lisa squeezed her eyes shut a moment and swallowed the lump in her throat that always arose at the mention of their parents. Then, with an efficient tone she used in her work as a surgical scrub nurse, she replied, "Well, this is all we have right now, and I seriously doubt we're going to get Aunt Esther to open up the house again in the middle of the night."

Lillian stretched her back and leaned just a little to the right so she could see the clock on the microwave. "Ladies, it's just past midnight. I think I've got another hour in me for this, and then I'm going to need to sleep for a while."

The girls selected two more journals each and sat with their ghostly partners, turning pages and reading the entries.

"Look," Lillian whispered. She pulled a folded sheet of paper from the middle of a journal dated 1994. Carefully pressing it open one fold at a time, she gave a startled gasp. Eloise was already at her elbow, and if spirits could cry, she would have. Lisa moved to her other side, and Aunt Ethel floated next to her sister. Together they stared at the colored-pencil portrait of Jessica, Lillian, Lisa, and Meg when they were little girls. In the drawing they were sitting around the dining room table at Grandma Willie's house. It was clearly winter because they wore bibbed snow pants and woolly sweaters. Stocking caps hung on the wooden drying rack in the sunroom just behind them.

"Look at the detail. She really captured that moment," Ethel whispered. The small group fell quiet, each lost in her own thoughts.

Eloise broke the silence. "Let's finish the journals we've started and then call it a night, girls."

In the journals from 1995 and 1996, they found nothing that might help solve the mystery.

"Well, my darlings, it is bedtime for you," Eloise said as she bussed each of her granddaughters' cheeks with a kiss.

"Night, Grams. Night, Aunt Ethel," the twins said in unison as the two spirits shimmered out.

"I'll repack the box with the ones we've already read," Lillian offered. "You organize the others for us to read tomorrow."

"Can't we just go to bed and take care of it in the morning?" Lisa whined.

Lillian ignored her twin and began boxing journals.

Lisa stuck her tongue out at her sister and reached for the stack of journals they would peruse tomorrow. As she did, three of the journals slid off the table and hit the floor. As she picked them up, a small envelope fell out of one of them. Lisa glanced at the date of the journal—1997, the year their parents had been killed in the avalanche. Then she scooped up the envelope. It was sealed.

"Lill? Come here and look at this." She turned the envelope over. It was addressed to a Mr. Thomas Putnam in Boston, Massachusetts. "Have you ever heard that name before?"

Lillian shook her head. "Should we open it? It's kind of like invading someone's privacy. I mean, it's sealed."

"Of course we're going to open it," Lisa snapped.

Lillian gave her sister a look of exasperation. "You're really crabby when you're tired."

Lisa stuck her finger under the flap and ripped it open. It was a Christmas card with a letter tucked inside. The card was signed "Your loving sister, Willie.

All thought of sleep fled.

With trembling fingers, Lisa unfolded the single sheet of paper and began to read aloud:

Dear Tommy,

Once again it is Christmas, and I am missing you. I hope you are well. It is hard to think of the many Christmases that have passed since we last spoke. Every year, I write to you about the joy and pain that life has brought me, and I so wish, dear brother, that you would do the same. I'm not nagging, and I understand the way things are, but I can't help my wishes.

I'm assuming you received my letter about the tragic loss last month of my son, Peter, and his beautiful wife. I wish you could have met them, Tommy. I like to think you would have loved them.

We have four beautiful granddaughters. Jessica is almost ten now and takes after you in so many ways. She has an affinity with numbers and gets really good grades. The twins, Lisa and Lillian, are seven now, and they have the most beautiful red-gold hair and unusual turquoise eyes; they are so happy and smart as whips too. The youngest, Madison, now this one is a true spitfire! She is five and so much like our mother in temperament. All of the girls are amazing little people.

I hope one day you might visit us. You would love it here. I know you would. The wide-open spaces, the high mountain valleys, and oh my, you would love fly-fishing on the rivers around here. They are so different from the rivers back east.

I long to hear about your life. Do you have children or grandchildren? How is our uncle? Has he turned the reins of the family business over to you as he promised?

I love you, Tommy, no matter what.
Willie

Lisa carefully laid the letter down and looked at her sister. "Wowzer."

Lillian stared at the Boston address on the envelope. "Now what?"

"I don't know, but I can't even process this right now. I need to go to bed." With those words Lisa stood up and left the room without looking back.

Lillian gently replaced the card and letter in the envelope and tucked it next to the stack of journals.

What in the world had been happening in their family?

Chapter Five

By seven o'clock the next morning the twins were sitting at the dining table. Over toasted bagels with cream cheese, they studied the three pieces of paper they had discovered last night: the Christmas card, letter, and envelope addressed to a great-uncle they never knew existed.

Could any of this help them track down what had happened to Grandma Willie?

"Let's call Meg," Lillian suggested. "She might have a fresh perspective."

"She does have a devious way of thinking about things."

Lillian sighed with exasperation.

Lisa picked up the second half of her bagel with her left hand, her phone with the right, and speed-dialed her baby sister. After all, it might be fun waking her up from a dead sleep. Unfortunately, Meg answered on the third ring sounding wide awake.

"Hey," Lisa greeted her sister, "since you're bright eyed and bushy tailed, head over to Grams. We have something to show you."

As Meg responded, Lisa took a bite of her bagel. She coughed before responding.

"Wait, you're *where*? How long have you been there?"

After more listening and chewing, Lisa said, "Okay," and ended the call. She turned to her twin. "She's been hiding out at the Golden Bear since six this morning. She wants us to come there."

Lillian's brows knit together. "Why is she hanging out in that dilapidated rattrap?"

"Apparently, she needs a break from the wedding hubbub. Oh, and she says, would we please hurry up and pick a dress fabric."

"What if I don't feel like hanging out in a haunted bordello?" Lillian asked. "As kids, we were terrified of the place. For decades, nobody has been able to walk onto that property without bad stuff happening. At least until Meg started traipsing around in there."

"Maybe it's because we're related to Bridget, the madam, although I haven't figured out how yet. And you're right, Meg has been all over that place, with nothing but dust and dirt to worry about, I might add. Besides, we've already met the inhabitants and know they don't want to hurt us."

"I get the feeling we haven't met *all* of them."

Thirty minutes later Lillian pulled the Colorado over to the curb in front of the Golden Bear. She stared at the broken windows and weather-beaten façade looming over the front yard, which was consumed with trash and weeds. A few straggly lilacs hung on for dear life, surviving on the bit of rainwater that drained off the steep pitch of the leaky roof. The attic of the place had to be a moldy, spongy mess. It gave her the shivers.

"Well," Lillian said, "let's get in there before I chicken out."

The girls opened their doors and hopped out. The scent of sunshine-fresh laundry surrounded them. Eloise shimmered into view. "Hi, darlings. How are you this morning?"

"I'm fine, but Lill is not sure about this rendezvous."

"Oh my. Lilly, there's nothing to worry about."

Lillian gave a little shudder. "I know that. It's just . . . I don't know . . . it feels like there's something or someone staring at us all the time."

"Ah, well, don't worry about it. You are perfectly safe here as long as you don't fall through a rotting board."

Eloise turned and drifted back toward the sagging porch, the twins following close behind. As their grandmother shimmered through the siding of the old house, the twins worked to yank open the squeaking, squawking double front doors far enough to squeeze through.

"Next time just use the left door," Meg called down to them from the second-floor balcony. "It's not as stuck as the right one." Dust floated down from where she leaned against the banister. Cobwebs shivered in the vibrations caused by her movements.

Lisa and Lillian began their hazardous climb up the once beautiful and ornate staircase. They stepped carefully and progressed single file to miss the warped and crumbling treads.

When they reached the top, Meg led them toward the small parlor they had visited before.

It was filled with dust but somehow didn't feel as abandoned as the rest of the house.

The furnishings must have been very expensive in their day. Now the once-plush upholstery was worn and slightly mouse-chewed. The ornate trim around the room appeared to be cherrywood—but then again, who could tell for sure with all the grime.

As the girls settled themselves on the aging settee and wingback chairs, Eloise called out for Ethel to join them.

"Where are the others?" Lillian asked.

"Jack is spending time with Kai," Meg explained. "He's a bit of a helicopter dad-to-be, hovering around, making sure she's okay. Of course, he's *literally* hovering, now that he's dead. And Doc Lindsey is working on some things, and Bridget is busy with other things." Meg glanced at Grams.

Lisa caught the look. "What's going on?"

"Nothing you need to worry about, sweetie," Eloise said. "So, what did you find?"

Walking to the library table, Lisa produced an envelope out of her hip pocket and laid the contents flat on the table.

The others gathered around.

Meg picked up the letter and gave it a quick read. "Grandma Willie had a brother? Do you think he's still alive?"

"We don't know yet. We just found that last night." Lillian stuffed her hands in her sweater pockets. "This morning we googled Tommy Putnam and found out he is some muckety-muck in Boston. Or at least he was. We found some newspaper articles about his retirement from the family firm in 2011, but nothing since."

Meg replaced the letter on the tabletop. "Now that we have a name, you know who could dig a little deeper, don't you?"

They all crowed in unison, "Jessica!"

"Of course," Ethel said when she shimmered into visual range. "That girl's been interested in family genealogy for years. She would love researching Willie's mystery brother."

"Do you think she will have time with the new babies? Her twins aren't but a few weeks old," Lillian said, worried.

"Only one way to find out." Meg pulled her cell out of her front pocket, put it on speakerphone, and dialed their oldest sister.

"Hello," Jessica answered, her voice sounding teary.

Lillian immediately took charge. "Hey, Jess, it's Lill," she said in her most soothing voice. "We thought we should check in with you. Meg and Lisa are here with me."

"Oh, I am so glad you called." The sound of nose blowing came through the speaker.

"What are the tears for, Jess?" Lillian gently asked.

Meg and Lisa looked at each other. They weren't very good with the touchy-feely stuff. Thank goodness Lillian was there.

"Oh, it's these darn hormones. The babies are just . . . just perfect." The tears were coming in earnest with a couple of hiccups in between. More nose blowing. "How are all of you?"

"We're all fine. Did you get the boxes we sent for the babies?"

"I did, and everything was just perfect." The last word came out on a wail.

Lillian continued to soothe the distraught new mom. Before long she had Jesse laughing and telling them all about the twins.

"Patrick and Merry are such easy babies. They only wake up a couple of times at night for feeding and changing. They are just little angels."

"That's what people thought about us until we got mobile," Lisa quipped.

"I kind of remember that," Jessica laughed.

"Hey, Jess." Meg interrupted the small talk. "Do you think you have time to work on a little piece of family genealogy?"

Lillian glared at Meg. Meg squinted her eyes and wrinkled her nose at Lillian.

"That actually sounds fun." She thought a moment. "I bet I could do it during nap time."

Meg shot her sister an "I told you so" look.

"What've you got for me?" Jess sounded like she was practically rubbing her hands together.

The sisters explained their goal of finding out what had happened to Grandma Willie, then told Jessica everything they had discovered about Grandma Willie's mysterious brother, Tommy Putnam. Jess promised to see what she could find out. Before hanging up, the four girls sent kisses back and forth.

"I think Jess is homesick." Meg returned the phone to her pocket.

"I'm sure she is," Lisa responded. "I'm glad we called her and very glad we had something for her to do. She needs to feel connected with us. Things are all mixed together for her. First Grams dies, then Meg almost bites the dust at the hands of a crazy woman, and then something wonderful happens . . . she has the twins. That's got to be emotional gobbledygook."

"So what now?" Lillian asked.

"I'm going to stay here and take pictures as the light changes. Then Jace is picking me up for dinner with Kai's friend, and then it's off to the Powder Keg. You two are joining us, aren't you?" It was more of a command than a question.

"Don't look now, Lill, but I think our baby sister is trying her hand at matchmaking."

"I am not," Meg huffed. "I just thought it would be nice to hang out since we're all in the wellness biz—not Jace, of course—but the rest of us. Strictly platonic." Then Meg gave a wicked grin. "Although he *does* have a very sexy accent."

The twins laughed at that and agreed they would be there at eight that night.

"As for our next steps," Lillian said, turning to their grandmother, "there may be another box of earlier journals at the house. Grams, do you think Esther will let us back into the house?"

"I can't say, kiddos."

Lisa looked mischievously at her twin. "Lill, didn't Aunt Esther say Clint was out of town until next week?"

"Lisa Emma Garrison," Lillian said sternly. "Don't even *think* about breaking in and having your way with the house. I'm going to talk us in. I sweet-talked her last time, didn't I?"

She reached for her phone. Her great-aunt answered on the second ring.

"Hey, Auntie Esther, it's me, Lillian. How are you this morning?" She listened and rolled her eyes. "Really, that does sound like a jam-packed day." More listening. "I can see that. Actually, we're hoping to come by for a few more boxes." Lillian started pacing. "I under-stand. Well, I'll let you go now, and maybe we can get together for lunch one of these days. Thanks, bye." She thumbed the phone off. "That woman is a sociopath!"

"Breaking in is sounding better and better, isn't it, sis?" Lisa goaded.

Lillian turned to her grandmother and great-aunt. "You game?"

Ethel cracked her knuckles and stretched her cherubic, translu-cent face into a conspiratorial smile. "Girls, stealth is my middle name."

Meg chimed in. "She's a regular Nancy Drew."

Through this little exchange Eloise watched her granddaughters' faces. The twins seemed determined. "Well, Chickies, I think we need to come up with a plan if we're going to get away with this." She drifted over to the crumbling fireplace without looking back.

The girls followed, with Ethel bringing up the rear.

By the time Grams turned around, she was ready with a plan.

"The first thing we have to do is get our hands on Esther's schedule today. Then we need to make sure Big John and the ranch hands aren't around the house or the main gate."

"Well, when she was talking my ear off on the phone just now," Lillian remembered, "she said she has a hair appointment in town, and then a meeting of some sort after that. Oh, and she said that John was in Gunnison for the day. Something about an auction."

"Lillian, that's a great start!" Grams exclaimed. "Ethel, can you zoom in on our sister and see if there's anything else you can learn?"

Ethel popped out of the room, displacing energy and causing the dust to puff up around the room.

"She only does that when she's excited," Eloise assured the girls as they fanned dusty air away from their faces with their hands.

"What about the electronic fence and cameras?" Lisa coughed.

"Oh, I've gotten pretty good interfering with electronics. I can bring them down long enough for everyone to get in and out."

"What about the dog?" Lisa hadn't liked the looks of Clint's guard dog.

Meg raised her hand as if she were in grade school and blurted, "Aunt Ethel was a whiz calming dogs when she was sneaking me through the back alleys to the Golden Bear."

As if summoned, Ethel popped back in, stirring up more dust around the girls. Her face was arranged in her best clandestine-spy expression, but her hands were clasped at her waist like an excited pixie.

"Okay, here's the scoop." She jumped into the conversation immediately. "Esther won't be home until five this evening. She's got bridge club this afternoon, and since Big John will be eating supper with his cronies in Gunnison, she is eating with the ladies of her social circle." This last part came with a phony, snooty tone of voice to mimic her oldest sister. "Her words, not mine. I overheard her bragging to her hairdresser. So, what else?"

"Can you get a guard dog into its kennel?" Lisa asked.

"Course I can. Didn't Meg tell you how good I am calming animals?"

"Well, it seems we have everything settled except the ranch hands," Eloise announced.

"Oh, oh, I almost forgot!" Ethel squealed. "The ranch hands are moving cattle into the high country. Esther was complaining because she didn't have anyone to mow her lawn this week."

"Then we're all set. Are we all going?" Eloise looked at Meg.

"I'm not quite ready for another adventure where I might have to move fast," Meg said apologetically. "I'm still bruised and stiff. I think I'll just stay out of your way and keep taking photographs here. I even brought my lunch."

"Speaking of lunch, we shouldn't take the time to eat until *after* we pull off this little heist, but I sure could use a snack." Lisa looked at Meg. "You could share. What did you bring?"

Meg narrowed her eyes at her sister. "A tuna sandwich with pickle relish."

Lisa shuddered. She'd gotten food poisoning once from a tuna sandwich. With pickles. She'd hated them ever since. "Really?" she said with a grimace.

"Don't blame me," Meg shrugged. "I didn't know you were coming."

"We're burning daylight, ladies." Lillian stood up. "Let's git 'er done."

After the others had gone, the scent of lavender permeated the room. Bridget shimmered into view. "Did you really bring a tuna sandwich for your lunch?"

"Nope." Meg turned to the former madam of the Golden Bear and smiled.

Chapter Six

With Lisa behind the wheel, the twins and Eloise and Ethel pulled up to the main gate of the Garrison family ranch. Eloise drifted out of the truck and hovered next to the little control box. A moment later, the gate swung inward.

They spent the next twenty minutes driving slowly to keep the road dust down. No use announcing their presence to the whole county. They crept along until they were idling in front of the gate to the little house Clint had taken over.

"It still burns my hind end that he moved in so soon after Willie disappeared," Eloise huffed as she floated out of the Colorado. She worked her magic on the second gate and it slid open.

As Lisa eased the truck into the yard, Ethel was already out of the truck throwing old tennis balls to Brutus, who retrieved the balls and dropped them at her feet. With his ears perked and bobbed tail wagging, he didn't look vicious at all. After a few tosses, Ethel had the guard dog behind the locked gate of his kennel.

"It's okay, Brutus. I'm staying here with you." Ethel soothed Brutus with the kissy voice people use for their babied pets.

Eloise disappeared through the front door of the house, then swung the door wide and waved the girls inside.

"We need to move fast," she said urgently. "This alarm is tricky. It's motion and sound activated, and I'm not sure it doesn't do some other things, so I need to keep my energy attached to it. Hurry upstairs. The box we're after is in the far-left corner near the window."

The girls darted up the stairs. They spotted the box in no time. Lisa snatched it up, and they scrambled back down the stairs. Just as Lisa was about to step into the living room, Grams' voice halted them in their tracks.

"Don't come in here yet. I'm having a little trouble with this system. There is something else humming on the circuits, and I think it has to do with the little red light that just came on in the upper-right corner of the room."

Lillian looked up. "Grams, I think it's one of those nanny cams."

"Give me a minute to see if I can't connect with it too."

The girls held perfectly still. The only sound in the stairwell was their breathing until Lisa whispered, "I bet he has the camera connected to his smartphone."

"And the security system too," Lillian whispered back. "Grams, can you fry all the circuits?"

Eloise caught the drift of what the girls were saying. "Do you mean he can monitor the whole place with his cell phone? I'll bet that's why I can't get control of the camera."

Ethel popped her head in through the door panel. "Hey, did you know there are cameras under the eaves of the house?"

Eloise moaned. "Now what are we going to do?"

Lisa got that "what the hell!" smirk on her face. "Well, Grams, do you think you guys show up on video?"

"Meg tried to take pictures of me once, and they just came out as light bubbles in the photos."

"Well, how about you two put on a show for our watcher. You know, make things float around in front of his very eyes, and then, if you can, fry the camera circuits so we can get out of here."

"We don't need to put on a show. Although . . . that might be fun," Ethel said.

Eloise appeared to bite her lip. "But if I let go of these circuits, the alarms are going to go off."

"So?" Lisa was a woman of action and didn't like cowering in the stairwell. "We'll be outta here before anyone can show up, and with the cameras down, no one will be able to say who was here."

Eloise narrowed her eyes and her energy. "Ethel, get the rest of the way in here, and let's get the show on the road."

Ethel drifted through the door and into the living room. She picked up a pillow and started pitching it in the air and catching it. "Did you girls know that I used to do a little juggling?"

After Eloise fried the alarm circuits, she lobbed the television remote through the air to her sister. Ethel wiggled her fingers at the other two remotes sitting on the end table.

The girls watched in fascination as the ghosts continued tossing things back and forth. Around and around they went, right in front of the camera.

"I wonder what the sheriff thinks of that." Lillian snickered.

Next, Grams floated over to the nanny cam and stuck her hand all the way into the little device to connect with its circuits. "There, got it. This one is now dead. Girls, get to the door and wait for my signal. I'm going to check out the outside cameras. Ethel, stop juggling and help me out."

Ethel let the items drop, one, two, and three, to the floor as she shimmered out of visual range. The girls moved quickly to the door. Lillian couldn't help but look back to the camera.

"Stop looking at it. What if it comes back on and he sees your face?" Lisa snapped.

Eloise stuck her head through the door. "You two get into the truck. And don't forget the box of journals!"

Lillian's palms were sweating, and she was sure her heart was going to hammer out of her chest. Lisa flipped the box into the bed of the truck and jumped behind the wheel. Lillian vaulted into the passenger seat. As the gate began to open, Lisa started the truck and peeled out as soon as there was room to pass though.

Their grandmother popped inside. "Don't speed. We still need to keep the dust down just in case."

"What about Aunt Ethel?" Lillian worried.

"She'll be fine, my darling girl. Ethel said Bruno is quite lonely and sad. She thinks it would be wise to hang out with him, see what happens next, and report back."

Lisa kept the truck at twenty miles an hour. As the main house came into view, they heard the faint sound of sirens. "Do you hear that?" Her voice raised three octaves.

"Calm down. I hear it. Turn left and get behind the main barn." Eloise popped out.

Lisa wheeled the Colorado to the left, defying the urge to stick her foot down hard on the accelerator. The siren sounds were getting more distinct. She followed the road to the barn, pulled in behind it, and killed the engine.

The silence inside the truck was marred by the tiny pings of the cooling engine and the sirens coming closer and getting louder by the second. The girls held their breaths. They spotted a dust cloud roiling up from the road leading to Grandma Willie's old house. Lillian wrung her hands, and Lisa's knuckles were white from crushing the steering wheel.

As Eloise popped in, both girls let out short shrieks.

"Calm down, girls, it's just me."

"What's happening over there?" Lillian asked.

"The deputy is going to check out the house. But don't worry. What could he possibly find?"

"We probably left prints or something," Lisa warned.

"That wouldn't mean anything," Lillian pointed out. "We left prints the other day when we were there with Aunt Esther."

Eloise leaned between the front seats. "Look, I'm going to pop back over there. You two sit tight until I get back." Then she was gone, leaving the scent of sun-dried laundry in her wake.

"I really hate it when she does that," Lillian whispered.

Lisa peered in the rearview mirror. "I hope we find out what happened to Grandma Willie, and I pray she's still alive. What do you think the odds are on that, sister mine?"

Lillian started tracing patterns in the dust covering the dash. Without looking up, she said, "I believe God answers prayers."

There wasn't any more conversation. They just sat in the tense silence waiting for their deceased relatives to return so they could get off the ranch before they got caught.

Time ticked on, and the girls felt like they had been there for an hour, though it had been less than twenty minutes. They spotted dust clouds on the road between the houses, but no sirens pierced the air this time.

The girls waited until Grams and Aunt Ethel shimmered back into the truck.

"The officer is on his way back to town." Eloise looked like she was trying very hard not to burst into laughter. "Oh my. That poor man didn't know what to think."

"What do you mean?" Lillian shifted in her seat to face the back around the side of her seat.

"Well, as soon as he opened the front door, everything electrical was turning off and on in random patterns. The poor man had to shut the electricity off to the whole house and gate."

Lisa glanced back into the rearview mirror. "Are you telling us that even the gate was opening and closing?"

Ethel just beamed. "Yep, and I did that one."

"He called Clint and told him what he'd found. Apparently, Clint told him about the remotes because he walked to the table and said 'Well, they're all on the table and the pillows seem to be on the couch.' The young man looked horribly confused by whatever he was hearing. Then he said, 'There aren't any other vehicles around, and I didn't pass anyone on the way out here.'"

"Do you think he might wait down the road to see if anyone comes from here?" Lillian asked, twisting her hair around her finger.

"Good question, Lill. Grams, do you remember the back way off the ranch?"

She did. The back road was little used and a mess. When they pulled into town two hours later, they were dusty, hungry, and driving on fumes.

"Better feed the truck before we feed us, or we may spend the rest of the day on foot." Lisa drove to the nearest gas pumps. She ran her credit card and started pumping. It took 17.9 gallons of gas to fill the nineteen-gallon tank.

When Lisa slid back into the front seat, their grandmother and great-aunt had departed. "Where is everyone?"

"Grams said she was about out of 'juice,' and Aunt Ethel said she had to check on some things. Oh, and we're supposed to give each other a hug and get something to eat."

Lisa pulled the seat belt across and buckled up before she restarted the truck. "I'm starved. Where to?"

Lillian chuckled. "Let's hit Diggers. I need sustenance and then I need a shower."

Two Diggers cheeseburgers and fries later, the twins felt much better. At the condo, they took showers and naps before Lisa retrieved the box from the bed of the truck.

As Lisa set the box on the dining room table, Lillian checked her watch. "We have about three hours before we meet Meg at the Powder Keg. Do you think we should start now?"

"Can't hurt. Set the alarm on your fancy watch so we don't lose track of time."

As Lillian set her watch, Lisa opened the lid of the box.

Chapter Seven

The girls worked through about one-third of the journals before Lillian's watch alarm went off.

"This is amazing stuff," Lillian said. "Her illustrations are beautiful, and some of her side notes about family are deep and hilarious. So far, nothing more about brother Tommy. I've gone through the journals from 1971 through 1976. She even goes into historical detail about Colorado being the Centennial State and the celebrations the family attended then. She was so much into the spirit of the times she planted a full red-white-and-blue flower bed in the shape of the American flag."

Lisa leaned back in her chair in an attempt to alleviate the tight muscles in her neck. "I've gone through the rest of the '70s and started on the '80s with the same kind of stuff. I did find out that our grandmother loved disco music and made her cowboy husband and son learn how to do the hustle."

"No way!"

"Can you see Grandpa Frank in his cowboy boots learning to disco?"

Punchy from the two hours they had spent pouring over the journals, both girls burst into uncontrollable laughter. They couldn't even look at each other without the hilarity ratcheting up another notch.

"Stop! My stomach hurts!" Lisa finally blurted, holding her sides, which only set off another round of belly laughs.

THE GIRLS DRESSED and headed to the Powder Keg to meet Meg, Jace, and Kai's friend. When they walked into the local dimly lit honky-tonk, they spotted Jace easily, since his height made it easy to see him above the crowd. Not that there was much of a crowd, since it was a weeknight and there wouldn't be a live band. The jukebox wasn't even fired up yet.

They wended their way through the tables acknowledging friends and acquaintances who had stopped off for a beer after work and hadn't headed home yet.

Meg and Jace were sitting with a man. His back was to Lillian and Lisa as they approached, yet the closer they got to the table, the quieter Lisa became. Before long she seemed to be practically dragging her feet.

Lillian stopped when she realized her sister was falling farther behind. She walked back to where Lisa was standing still as a statue in the middle of the dance floor. "Lissy? What's wrong?"

"Please tell me that isn't him," Lisa whispered.

"Him who?"

"Ian Connors."

"Hey, you two, what's the hold up?" Meg's cowgirl boots clicked on the wooden floor as she approached.

"Who's that?" Lillian pointed to the man chatting with Jace.

"Who? Oh, that's Kai's friend, Ian. He's going to—"

Before Meg could finish, Lisa shook off her frozen mode and stormed to the table. Picking up a random glass of wine on the table, she threw the cabernet into the man's face before turning on her heel and stomping out of the bar.

Lillian was torn between following her furious twin and smacking the wine-drenched man on the head. She scowled at Ian. "You, you . . . *ass!*" she said, gritting her teeth, and turned on her heel and left. When she got to the truck, she saw the fury and pain on Lisa's face.

Meg was right behind them. "Somebody want to fill me in on what just happened in there?"

Lisa shook her head and held her hand out to Lillian.

Lillian pulled the keys out of her front pocket and clicked the door locks open. "I'll drive. Meg, I'll call you later."

"Lill, what's going on?"

Lillian reached for the door handle and stopped. She turned her face to her baby sister. "Ask him what he has to say about it. I've got to get her home and give her time to calm down. I'll explain it all to you later."

Meg nodded and headed back the way she had come, gravel crunching under her boots with purpose and arms swinging in angry time to her stride. The last thing Lillian heard before she fired up the engine was their baby sister yelling Ian's name as she flung open the door to the Powder Keg.

She turned to Lisa, "You gonna be all right?"

"Working on it."

The rest of the short drive to the condo was in silence.

In the house, Lisa had just slumped into a chair at the dining room table when Meg came bursting through the front door.

"How did you get here so fast?" Lisa asked. Her tears hadn't started yet, but she could feel them gathering like clouds behind her eyes.

"Jace tossed me his keys. He probably saw murder in my eyes and wanted to get me out of there before I killed someone. I'm dangerous now. In case you hadn't noticed." She waved her left arm up and down. "No sling."

She stood hands on hips, arms akimbo, breathing hard, and battle clearly in her eyes.

Suddenly the twins laughed, and the tension in the room broke. For the past five years, Meg had buried her legendary temper beneath a protective layer of control—but not anymore.

"She's baaaaack," Lillian sang as she headed into the kitchen to put on a pot of tea.

Meg pulled out the chair next to her angry, forlorn sister. "What's going on?"

"I knew Ian at one of the camps in Mogadishu," Lisa said with a sigh. "He was there with the nutrition program."

"And?" Meg encouraged.

"And nothing. We started seeing each other. I thought he might be *the one*. Turns out, he's married."

The tea kettle tore into the silence with its shrill whistle.

Lillian spoke from the kitchen . "You might as well tell her the whole story, Lisa."

"Look, Meg, it felt serious, you know? We spent every available hour together. Then one day I'm waiting for him in the surgery center and this pretty, blond woman comes in looking for Ian. I tell her he was expected soon, and she could wait for him. She thanked me and then someone else asked who she was, and she said she was Ian's *wife*."

"His wife . . ." Meg trailed off.

"I hightailed it out of there and refused to speak to him again. He kept tracking me down and saying he wanted to explain, that it was complicated, but I told him to stay away from me and to go home to his wife because I didn't date married men. He finally got the message. Or I thought he did until tonight."

"Wowzers." Meg let out a deep breath. "Kai never mentioned anything like that. In fact, she spoke highly of him."

Lillian carried brewed tea into the dining room on a tray. "Well, she probably only knows him as someone with skills in the medical field."

As Meg started to say more, her cell phone jangled. She looked at the caller ID. "It's Jessica." She thumbed the talk button. "Hey, Jess . . . Uh huh, yes. They're right here." She listened more and said, "Sure, just a sec." She keyed the phone to speaker and laid it on the table. "Go ahead."

"Hey, sisters," Jessica said before jumping right to the point of her call. "So, I found a lot of information on Thomas Putnam." She barely took a breath before continuing. "He's a big muckety-muck in Boston. Apparently, he headed up some family-owned corporation that has its fingers in all kinds of things. Anyway, he *is* still alive. Parents died in some kind of an accident in the '50s. He was raised by an uncle who was a confirmed bachelor and Thomas's predecessor in the family business. He resides near Boston. There's also some sort of apartment in the city proper. I emailed all of you the addresses I dug up on him."

She took a deep breath. "Oops, gotta run. One of the babies is awake. Love you all. Chat soon. Bye."

Meg ended the call. "Well, that was a whirlwind!" She smiled at the thought of their oldest sister running off to do anything. This was the first time she had known Jessica to not be in methodical and complete control of her entire world.

Lisa retrieved her laptop from the couch and opened it on the table. "I think we need to head to Boston sooner rather than later."

Lillian and Meg glanced at each other, the same thought in both of their heads. Lisa needed to get away from Elk City.

"We can fly out in the morning. There are several early-morning flights to choose from."

"Not me." Meg shook her head. "I've got a dress fitting tomorrow."

Lisa raised an eyebrow at her twin. "You?"

"Hey, I'm game."

Meg pushed her chair back from the table and stood. "You two have fun. I need to get back to the Powder Keg and retrieve Jace— and probably that *snake* too, if he's still there."

Lillian nodded. "I'll walk you out, baby sister."

Lisa muttered, "Like I don't know you're going to talk about me."

Once they were outside, Lillian said, "I'm not sure exactly what's going on, but I think there's more to the story than what we know. Maybe more than what Lisa knows. See what you can get from Ian."

Meg huffed out a breath. "If he lies to me . . ."

Lillian put her arm around the spitfire of the family and gave her a little squeeze. "Don't make Jace put you in jail."

Returning to the condo, Lillian immediately saw Eloise hovering next to Lisa. She was being politely quiet as Lisa booked two plane tickets out of Grand Junction first thing in the morning.

"Our flight out is at six o'clock. That means we need to check in by four thirty at the latest. If we head out tonight, we can stay at a hotel close to the airport." She stretched her arms over her head with a self-satisfied look on her face.

"Hotel reservations?"

"Already done at the new Holiday Inn." Again, that self-satisfied smile lit her face.

"I just popped in to make sure everyone was all right," Grams said. "It appears you have things well in hand. Do you think this Thomas Putnam will have any helpful information?"

"We won't know until we corner him."

"Are you sure he's even there?"

"He'll be there. Lill and I stalked him online, and he's supposed to be the guest of honor at a party taking place day after tomorrow in his honor."

"Be careful, my beauties. Keep Meg posted and she'll keep us informed. Okay?"

Lisa agreed and Eloise faded out.

The night in the hotel was short, and the flights to Boston were long. On the first flight from Grand Junction to Houston, Lisa found herself stuck next to a heavy smoker whose jacket reeked like a dirty ashtray. After rubbing shoulders with said jacket for the better part of two hours, Lisa was sure she would smell like an equally dirty ashtray when it was finally time to change flights to Logan International Airport.

Lillian didn't fare much better in the second leg of their flight journey. A sullen, freckle-faced boy named Davis kept kicking the back of her seat. Lillian knew the boy's name was Davis because his eight-year-old sister, sitting next to Lillian, told her. Actually, Angie —spelled A-N-G-I-E—was the princess of TMI, and before long Lillian knew that Davis was ten, that their two-year-old baby brother was an accident and ate his own boogers, and that Angie's best friend, Kate, had red hair, freckles, and owned twice as many Barbies as Jennifer, Angie's last-year best friend.

The kids' grandmother was sitting next to Angie in the window seat, looking tranquil despite the nonstop chatter. Lillian wondered how she looked so relaxed, until the plane began its descent into Logan International Airport and the older woman reached up and turned her hearing aids back on.

After finding each other in the stream of disembarking passengers, Lisa turned her head to sniff at the shoulder of her hoodie. "I can't wait to clean up. I smell like a dirty ashtray."

"And my ears are bleeding," Lillian quipped.

An hour later, their cab pulled up to The Langham, a posh number downtown. As the girls took in the shiny chrome doors under red awnings, Lillian raised an eyebrow at her twin. "Wowzer, sis! What's this going to set us back?"

"Don't worry about it, Lill. It comes with a chocolate bar."

Their boot heels rang against the shiny lobby floor as they approached the front desk. After they checked in, a well-dressed clerk reminded the girls, ever so politely, that they were in a nonsmoking establishment. Lisa couldn't help but sniff at her jacket sleeve.

As the girls waited for the elevator, they noticed a few startled stares and whispers behind hands.

"You'd think they'd never seen a couple of country girls before," Lisa whispered to her sister.

Just then, the heavy doors slid open and a young, well-dressed woman walked out of the elevator. As her eye caught Lisa and Lillian, her gait slowed and her mouth dropped open. After a not-so-discreet study of the girls, she hurried toward a tall, ginger-haired man in an expensive suit who appeared to be waiting for her. The young woman gestured as she tried to surreptitiously point at the girls with her pinky finger.

Lisa and Lillian entered the elevator and pushed the button to their floor. The young woman was still quietly talking to the ginger-haired man as the steel doors whispered closed and the elevator began its quiet ascent.

Lisa broke the silence. "What the hell was that all about?"

Both girls retreated into their own thoughts for the rest of the short ride.

When they unlocked their hotel room door, they were surprised at the luxury they found inside.

"Why are we staying here, Lisa? I mean, we're kind of used to the camping version of the world."

Lisa walked the rest of the way into the room before answering. "Because this hotel is where Uncle Tommy's award celebration will be day after tomorrow. I figure if we can't get him to see us before then, maybe we help him celebrate." She winked at her appalled twin.

"What do you mean 'help him celebrate'?"

Taking a turn around the room, Lisa ran a single finger over a chair, an armoire, and the granite top of a small wet bar before flopping down on the nearest bed arms flung wide. "Oh, this bed, it's pure heaven. Come on, check it out. Sit by me and I'll tell you what I've come up with." She patted the mattress next to her.

Lillian smiled at her conniving twin, then joined her on the comfy bed. "Okay, so what do you have squireling around behind those eyes?"

"Today we're going to pay a call on our long-lost uncle. And if he won't see us before his party, he'll see us during his party."

"But we're not invited to the party. How in the world will we get in?"

Lisa pursed her lips. "Still working on that. Right now we're going to check out the two addresses we have for Thomas Putnam and see if we can arrange a conversation with the man."

Lillian closed her eyes. "Not until I get a hot shower and clean up a bit."

While her sister showered, Lisa rang the concierge to arrange for a rental car for the day.

Chapter Eight

They only got lost twice. Lillian, behind the wheel, finally found the apartment building owned by Thomas Putnam and pulled the rental car to the curb. As the girls approached a snappy uniformed doorman, the man smiled at Lisa. When he spotted Lillian, his smile faded. "May I help you?"

Lisa's mouth tightened as a storm brewed in her eyes.

Lillian spoke quickly. "Yes, thank you, I hope so. We're here to see our uncle, Thomas Putnam."

The doorman said frostily, "You will need to check in at the desk."

Lisa planted her feet and opened her mouth. Before she could speak, Lillian grabbed her sister by the arm and yanked her into the lobby and toward the front desk.

The greying clerk behind the counter shot them a friendly smile before a confused frown pinched his oversize forehead.

"May I help you?" he asked in a very formal manner.

Taking note of the name on the man's badge, Lisa leaned assertively across the counter. "Mr. Weaver, we just flew into town to attend a party for our uncle, Mr. Thomas Putnam, and we would like to speak with him now." She spoke just above a whisper and gave him a laser stare. Seeing Lisa's face reflected in the mirror behind the front desk, Lillian hoped the clerk didn't call the cops on them.

Mr. Weaver pulled himself up to his full height and looked down his nose at the two girls. "And you are?"

Lillian smiled sweetly at the man. "Lillian and Lisa Garrison."

The man consulted his computer. "I don't see you on the guest list. I suggest you call his personal assistant and find out why you aren't on the list."

As Lisa opened her mouth, Lillian thanked the clerk and dropped her arm tightly around her sister's shoulders. She guided Lisa away from the front desk and didn't let go until they were a half block from the parking lot and their rental car.

Neither of them spoke until they were in the car and buckled up. Then Lisa shifted in her seat belt, angling to face her twin. "Lill, something's going on."

Lillian started the car and backed out of their parking spot. "Right? But you don't help matters when you look and sound like you're going to tear their heads off."

"It doesn't matter." Lisa shrugged. "Putnam's probably not at his hotel anyway. He's probably at his estate. Which means we can still get to him."

"Maybe." Lillian hedged.

"Turn right at the next intersection."

They only got lost once this time before pulling through the open gate of the estate of their great-uncle. Large oak trees lined the long driveway, throwing dappled shadows across the rental car as the girls approached the impressive brick house at the end of the lane.

Lillian parked in the circular drive that fronted stone steps leading to red double doors. The steps were flanked by matching planters spilling riots of colorful flowers. Both girls leaned forward and peered out the window at the impressive mansion.

"Well, Lill, let's stop gawking like a couple of country bumpkins and go meet the relatives."

A moment after they rang the bell, one of the red doors opened wide. A matronly woman wearing a grey dress and white apron smiled at Lisa. "Did you forget some—" Then her voice dropped off. "I'm sorry. May I help you?"

"Hello," Lillian chirped. "We're here to see Mr. Putnam. Is he in?"

The woman's eyes shuttered. "He's not available. Would you like to leave a message?"

Lisa glowered. "No, we don't want to leave a message. It is imperative that we see Mr. Putnam."

The woman began closing the door.

Lillian elbowed her sister out of the way and stepped forward. "I'm sorry. We don't mean to create problems, but it is critical that we speak with him. It's a family matter."

The door clicked closed in their faces.

The girls turned and looked at each other in surprise.

Retracing their steps to the blue rental car, Lisa fumed. Once they were inside the car, she blurted, "That's the third time we've been treated like that."

Lillian shook her head. "The fourth time."

"The doorman. The desk clerk. And now Ms. Smarty Pants Maid." Lisa waved three fingers at her sister.

"When we first got to the hotel, a woman stepped out of the elevator and stared at us with her mouth hanging open. That's four."

Silence filled the interior of the small luxury car as Lillian maneuvered through traffic.

"They think they know us," Lisa said quietly.

"My thoughts exactly. How weird is that?"

"Weird?" Lisa suddenly laughed aloud. "It's not weird, it's genius! It solves everything!"

"What are you talking about?"

Lisa twisted in her seat to face her sister. "You asked me how we're going to get into Uncle Tommy's party."

"Yes, but—"

"Don't you see? It's perfect."

"Stop right there. Last time you had that look on your face, we ended up in a third world country legal trial trying to explain to a village chieftain through an interpreter why we had relocated a herd of goats without permission."

"It all worked out. The chieftain only scolded us."

"Only scolded us? Apparently you don't remember the two weeks of goat herding we had to do to pay for our crime."

But Lisa didn't answer. The wheels were turning in her head, and that spelled trouble with a capital *T*.

Chapter Nine

The minute their hotel room door closed behind them, Lisa rubbed her hands together. "The first thing we need to do is—"

"How can you have a plan already?" Lillian rolled her eyes before dropping into one of the overstuffed wingback chairs by the window. "We don't even know who people think we are."

Lisa plopped into the other wingback and leaned forward, her elbows on her knees. "I have a theory about that. Maybe they think we're here to spill the beans."

Lillian frowned. "Beans?"

"You know." Lisa winked. "*Beans.*"

"Oh! You think people think we're, like, somebody's illegitimate kids or something?" Lillian sat stunned for several beats.

"Weirder things have happened. How many kids do you think our cousin Clint has around town?"

Lillian shuddered. "I try not to think too much about anything that man does. But there are certainly rumors."

"Right. And if a couple of inquiring strangers showed up with a strong family resemblance . . ."

"I get it. Sad and creepy, but I get it. But if people think we're here to tattle on Thomas—or someone in his family—they'll never let us get near him."

"Maybe, maybe not," Lisa mused. "Actually, if there's a family resemblance, it may do us more good than harm. First, we need to figure out who we look like."

"How do you propose we do that?"

"Oh, a little online research on Uncle Tommy's family should do the trick. But first, let's call Jessica and see if she's discovered anything new."

"If she had, wouldn't she have called us?"

"No. She likes to follow a thread until it comes to an end. *Then* she tells us." Lisa smiled a lazy smile, fished her cell phone out of her front pocket, and speed-dialed their oldest sister.

As soon as Jesse answered, she blurted, "Glad you're calling. I've only got a couple of minutes before the babies wake up, so listen up. Is Lillian with you?"

"Yes."

"I wasn't going to tell you this until I figured out what it meant, but put your phone on speaker and I'll fill you in."

Lisa grinned at Lillian and mouthed the words *Told ya so* before laying her cell on the occasional table. "Okay, Jess, we're on speaker."

"Check your emails. I emailed you both the names of Thomas Putnam's kids—and there are quite a few. Four sons and three daughters. And—get this—he has two sets of twins. One boy-girl set and one set of girls. But that's not the part I'm still trying to figure out."

"What part is that?" Lillian asked.

"I think the twins in our family go even further back. I think Thomas and Grandma Willie are twins. I'm waiting for confirmation on that, though."

Suddenly there was a howling racket in the background. "Oops, the babies are awake, got to go. Love you both." The line disconnected.

Lisa walked over to her bed, picked up her tablet, and started downloading her email. There was indeed an email from Jess with a list of names. Opening a browser, she typed in the first name on the list of Thomas Putnam's children.

The girls divided the list and spent the next hour stalking relatives. They still hadn't found any look-alikes but did find names of the man's grandchildren to add to the search.

When they needed a break, they ordered room service, changed into some comfy clothes, and dropped into some yoga stretches to get some of the kinks out while they waited. Lisa was in downward-facing dog and Lillian was in child pose when the food arrived.

The girls ate quickly, called room service to pick up the dishes, then went back to searching for any newspaper articles or gossip rags that mentioned their great-uncle or his children. It appeared that one of his younger sons was a reckless fellow and appeared regularly in the juicy rumor articles.

As they read, the girls continued culling bits of information—dates, locations, names of other family members—that they added to their list.

At midnight Lillian yawned, then toggled her head back and forth to release the muscles in her neck. "I'm done. I've got to go to sleep."

Lisa shooed her to bed with one hand while keeping her eyes glued to her tablet.

Forty minutes later Lillian was dreaming of basking on warm sand, with an umbrella drink in one hand and a good book in the other, when the insistent voice of her twin came crashing through.

"Lill, wake up. I think I've got it."

"No you don't," Lillian muttered while trying to return to that lovely spot in her mind.

"Wake up, sis." This time Lisa was shaking her shoulder and demanding her attention.

A groan escaped Lillian's lips as she opened her eyes and shoved her hair out of her face. "What are you talking about? What time is it?"

Lisa bounced down on the bed. "Look at this," she said, shoving the glowing tablet in Lillian's face.

Lillian pushed her sister's wrist away. "Cripes, Lisa, I can't read something an inch from my face." She elbowed her way up to half sitting and held out a hand for the tablet to see what had her sister in such an excited frenzy. Once she saw the photo on the screen, she was wide awake. "Who is this? She looks like us!"

A self-satisfied smile tugged at Lisa's lips "Exactly."

Lillian sat up and rubbed at her eyes. "Who is she?"

With a smug smile still plastered on her face, Lisa said, "Our cousin Reiney."

"What did you find out about her?"

"Plenty. She's mentioned in lots of lifestyle pieces in the Sunday papers."

"Quit dragging it out. Spit it out or I'm going back to sleep."

Lisa giggled. "I know where she shops, where she gets her hair done, who her favorite massage therapist is—in other words, lots of details that may help us get into the party this evening."

Lillian frowned. "I don't see how—"

"You will." Lisa glanced at the digital clock on the bedstand. "We can sleep for another three or four hours, but then we'll have to get going. I made a list of things we need to do to get ready. We can't lollygag."

"Ready for *what*?"

"Go back to sleep. You'll see soon enough. I don't think you'll have a single objection to what I've got planned."

"That's not reassuring. Show me the list of things we have to do, or I will never get back to sleep." She thrust out a hand.

Lisa tapped a few times on the tablet and handed it over.

Lillian's eyes widened; then she pursed her lips approvingly. "Wow. I can live with that." She switched off the lamp and snuggled down under the soft covers. She was out in minutes.

"I guess that's that," Lisa said to a quiet room.

Chapter Ten

Four hours later Lisa woke to the sound of the shower running. Lisa stretched in the sheets while reviewing their plan in her mind. Fifteen minutes later Lillian came out of the bathroom dressed in a casual skirt, T-shirt, and sandals.

"My turn." Lisa climbed out of bed and sashayed toward the bathroom.

"I hope whatever you're planning won't get us into trouble today," Lillian mused as they passed each other.

"You worry too much." Lisa grinned. "Order us some breakfast, will you? Fruit and toast for me. I'll fill you in on all the details as we eat."

When breakfast arrived, Lillian put the tray on the occasional table between the wingback chairs. Lisa, joining her, went straight for the coffee.

"So what's up with the spa day?" Lillian buttered a piece of toast.

"First we're going to get our hair done at Cousin Reiney's favorite salon, then shop for little black dresses at her favorite high-end store."

"I know all that, I saw the list last night. But why?"

"Oh, sister, think about it! People already think we look like her

—so let's use that to our advantage. We're not trying to impersonate her—we'll say who we are anytime we're asked—but looking 'familiar' at a distance might come in handy as we scope out the party trying to get to our dear Great-Uncle Thomas."

Lillian frowned. "There's no way we'll get same-day appointments at a posh salon."

Lisa winked. "Watch me."

Lisa picked her cell phone up off the table. A moment later she smiled at her sister as the salon receptionist answered.

"This is Lisa Garrison. I know this is very last minute, but my sister and I just arrived in town for our uncle's event this evening. We've been traveling abroad and didn't have a chance to make appointments but are both in dire need of some attention. Would it be possible to get our hair trimmed and a simple updo? . . . Uh huh, yes, I understand you're booked solid today. Oh, I'm so disappointed. Our cousin, Reiney Putnam, raves about your salon. . . . That's right, Thomas Putnam is our great-uncle . . . Oh, you can. That would be great and so appreciated . . . Yes, we can be there at 4:45. Again, thank you so much."

As Lisa ended the call, Lillian smirked in admiration over the rim of her coffee cup. "I'm impressed. Now what?"

"The fancy-schmancy place where Reiney shops won't be open for"—Lisa looked at her watch—"another hour, so let's snoop around here a bit and see what details we can find out about the event tonight."

Ten minutes later the girls caught the elevator to the main floor. As the doors slid open to the lobby, the girls surveyed a great deal of hustle and bustle. Men and women in business attire multitasking on smartphones on their way to their next meeting. Desk clerks assisting incoming guests. Bellmen carrying luggage. The concierge conferring with an elderly woman wearing a tangerine pantsuit and carrying a straw hat covered with fake fruit.

Lisa grasped Lillian's upper arm and steered her toward a side hallway. "See how easy it is to go anywhere with all the hubbub in there? Now, come with me to the business end of this hotel, and let's see what's what for the shindig."

It took some traveling through the corridors and a few wrong turns before they found the staff working area. As they stood watching, a harried bell captain carrying dry cleaning brushed past them while a member of the culinary staff hurried the other way pushing a room service cart.

A discreet throat clearing behind them made them jump.

"May I be of assistance?" The voice was a nice baritone that rumbled just a bit through the syllables.

Both of them whirled around to find a short, well-dressed older man politely looking back at them with his hands behind his back.

Lillian blurted out, "We sort of took a wrong turn."

The man looked nonplussed at the young women invading his domain.

Lisa smiled. "Hi, I'm Lisa and this is my sister Lillian. This is all so fascinating. How many people does it take to keep a place like this operating with such efficiency?"

Lillian marveled as her efficient, cranky sister turned on the charm. Before long she had the stodgy staffer—who turned out to be the supervisor of special events—eating out of her hand.

With very little wheedling, Lisa asked the right questions and before long knew everything she wanted to know—and then some— about the Putnam event.

Five hundred guests were expected that evening, and they would begin arriving at six. For the first two hours of the party, a staff member would greet people at the door and check their names against the invitation lists. The menu consisted of Greenland prawn cocktail with a lime-and-dill dressing salmon with white wine and lemon butter, followed by lemon cheesecake with vanilla cream.

Lillian didn't breathe easily until they made it outside and the doorman handed them into the cab they had arranged through the concierge.

"Wowzer, Lisa."

"Hey, Lill, what had you so nervous in there? The worst that could have happened is that someone would have escorted us back to the lobby. Instead, we got a nice tour from a surprisingly informative supervisor."

"I think it's the whole thing that has me on edge."

"It was so worth it. Did you hear what he said?"

"I would have been happy with salmon from a can."

"Not *that* part. The part about a staffer only checking names for the first two hours."

"So, we arrive after eight."

"Now you're thinking!"

THE CAB PULLED to the curb on a tree-lined street in front of a stately brick building adjacent to a lush green park.

There was not a quick way to get the dresses they needed. More than once, a store clerk stopped and stared at the pair. Finally, a young woman dressed to the nines approached. She would have been tall in her bare feet, but with four-inch heels with a modified platform, she towered over Lisa and Lillian.

Lillian smiled up at the beautiful amazon. "Yes, we're due at an event tonight for Thomas Putnam, and we *just* got back into the country and our luggage . . . well . . . who knows where it could be. Anyway, we both need cocktail dresses, heels, the works." She flipped her hands up at the wrists and tried very hard to look very proper.

"Of course. How dreadful for you both." Dollar signs danced in the woman's eyes. Please come with me and we will get everything taken care of. I'm Amily, by the way."

Amily marveled at the resemblance between them and Reiney Putnam. She claimed she worked frequently with their cousin selecting her attire and was delighted to help them too. Two hours later they'd spent close to eighteen hundred dollars on two perfect LBDs, turquoise heels, accessories, and accompanying undergarments.

"That was almost painless," Lillian quipped as they exited the store.

"We did great. We stuck to the truth for the most part and picked up interesting gossip regarding our relatives. And neither of us has gotten any new clothes in a long time, and now we have some. Win, win, win."

"Aren't you little Miss Sunshine today, Lisa?"

"Is that a question?"

Lillian laughed as they hailed a cab.

They still had two hours to kill before they had to make it to their hair appointments. After a short nap back at the hotel, they declined a cab and walked to the salon, a short fifteen minutes away.

The two girls entered Salon Alx. Lillian smiled as they approached the sweet-faced, stylish receptionist. Her look was just short of edgy, yet classy. In fact, Lillian thought, the entire look of the salon had the same vibe.

"Hello," the young woman said through a perfect smile.

"Hi. I'm Lisa Garrison. I believe I spoke to you earlier and you were kind enough to fit my sister and me in this afternoon."

"Of course. You're attending the Putnam event. Please have a seat. Alx and Erin will be with you shortly." She quickly lifted the receiver of her phone and tapped two digits on the keypad. "Both Ms. Garrisons are here for their appointments."

A slender young man with bedroom eyes and jet-black hair approached the women. He looked them over approvingly before speaking. "Hello, I'm Alx. So nice to meet additional members of the Putnam family. Please follow me and we'll get started."

The girls exchanged lifted eyebrows. They hadn't expected the owner and premium stylist to take them on himself.

Lisa smiled sweetly. "Thank you so much."

"Was there a particular style you're looking for tonight?"

"A simple updo will be perfect."

"Here we are. I'll leave you in the capable hands of Karen and Dorthia. They'll get you ready."

As Karen and Dorthia led the twins to their changing rooms,

Lillian took in all the shiny black-and-chrome decor and the bright red shampoo bowls. After slipping into crisp red kimono smocks and disposable flip-flops, they were handed glasses of wine and escorted to massage chairs for their pedicures.

Two hours later the girls walked out of the Salon Alx with perfect mani-pedis and their hair coiffured for the evening's festivities. They'd stuck to their story, fending off delicate questions while stylists twisted their hair into updos like those worn by their cousin in many society photos.

"Well, I have to admit, the Putnam name and resemblance certainly opens doors," Lillian mused as they strolled the brief distance back to the hotel. "But will it open doors for us tonight at the party?"

"Have faith, sister mine. Have faith."

Chapter Eleven

The girls ate a light dinner in their room and were dressed and ready to hit the party entrance by seven.

"Okay, Lill, at eight fifteen, you walk into the party like you own it. I arrive twenty minutes later. If possible, we avoid being seen together—and avoid being in the same room as Reiney—until one of us identifies the target. Then we can converge and confront him together."

Lillian laughed. "This isn't some military maneuver. I know what to do when we get there. What I don't know is what happens after we find Grandma Willie's brother."

"No clue. We'll see what unfolds."

"Not reassuring.

"And don't forget to call him Uncle Thomas. We're supposed to be close enough to have landed invites to this shindig, remember?"

"I'm not going to call a perfect stranger uncle anything."

The mulish expression in Lillian's eyes was enough for Lisa to back down on that point. It wouldn't do to get her in a rare snit before they started.

The two looked at themselves in the full-length mirror. "Damn we look good," Lillian murmured. "Too bad there isn't anyone to show off to."

Lisa's mind flashed to a memory of Ian's shocked expression as wine from Meg's glass dripped into his eyebrows. "Yeah, too bad." She shook off the image, but not before Lillian caught it.

"You okay?"

"Yep, so . . . now what do we do for the next hour?"

"Angry Birds?"

Time ticked away with the finger thumps on their respective tablet screens flinging birds and crushing pigs.

At 8:05 Lillian put her tablet to sleep, stood, and smoothed her dress. She checked the little pocket in the side seam of her skirt to verify the envelope and letter in her grandmother's hand was still safely tucked inside. After taking a deep breath, she smiled at her twin and walked bravely to the door. Her fingers trembled imperceptibly as she reached out to turn the knob.

She approached the entrance to the party by 8:15, as planned. When she didn't see anyone vetting incoming guests, she breathed a sigh of relief. She pasted the smile on her face that she and Lisa had practiced and swept into the ballroom.

Her eyes searched the immediate area. No sign of Reiney. A couple of people raised glasses in her direction in greeting. She smiled, waved, and kept pace to a spot she could view the door and disappear all at the same time. Floral arrangements and potted plants served so many purposes, and tonight they would serve her well. She skirted around one rather large palm tree and managed to sink back into a shadow.

Hurry, Lisa, hurry!

Her eyes scoped out the faces she could see and darted back to the entrance with the slightest movement. Still no Lisa. Again her eyes brushed over the crowd. Where was Thomas? Suddenly she spotted him chatting with a well-dressed couple near a stairwell. Lillian's eyes darted frantically back to the ballroom entrance. She gasped in relief.

Lisa had arrived.

Bolting from her hiding place, Lillian stepped directly in front of Reiney Putnam.

Reiney froze, mouth open.

Lillian forced a fat smile, batted her eyelashes, and said, "My oh my, do we look alike or what?"

Then she linked arms with the frozen woman and steered toward Lisa. "We could be twins," she babbled and walked just a little faster.

Shaking off her shock, Reiney tried to yank her arm from Lillian's tight hold. When that failed, she dug in her heels and brought them to a halt. With a false smile to match her captor's, she gritted out, "Who in the hell are you?"

"Believe it or not, I'm your second cousin from Colorado. The granddaughter of your grandfather's twin sister."

"My grandfather doesn't have a sister . . ."

At that moment Lisa strolled up and latched onto her other arm. "Hey, cuz."

Reiney's eyes bugged out of her head as she gasped for breath and swiveled her head back and forth between Lisa and Lillian. She sputtered and then her eyes narrowed. "You have exactly one second to explain, or I will raise the roof with a scream."

"No reason to scream. We just need to talk to your grandfather, and then you never have to see us again," Lisa said to soothe her. "Besides, people are already looking over here. You don't want to attract the attention of the photographers on the other side of the room, do you?"

With a brief shake of her head Reiney relaxed and faked the best friend arm cuddle in the world. "This way. There's an empty conference room down the hall. We can argue about it there."

"Ah, anything to avoid bad publicity . . . right?" Lisa snarked. "Who do you think we are?"

"I have no idea, but a pair of my father's youthful mistakes comes to mind," she retorted.

They navigated the crowded ballroom with ease, despite the startled looks that followed them. When anyone greeted them, Reiney—God bless her image-is-everything heart—took the lead in introducing her cousins. She handled it all without breaking a sweat or missing a beat.

Reiney marched them into a hallway and toward an open door. As soon as they entered the room, they dropped their various grips on each other along with their pretend smiles.

Reiney shut the door behind them and faced the twins, fire in her eyes.

"We'll explain everything to your grandfather," Lisa interjected. "Not you."

The party noise grew louder as the door quietly opened, and then dimmed again as it closed.

"This looks like a hostile takeover," a gruff voice remarked.

The three combatants turned toward the elegant elderly man with graying ginger hair leaning negligently against the door he had just entered. He was accompanied by a young man a few years older than Reiney.

"Grandpa!" Reiney exclaimed. "Thank goodness you're here. And you, too, Thomas," she nodded to her brother.

"Would you care to introduce me to these young women?" the elder Thomas spoke.

"I'm Lillian Garrison, and this is my sister, Lisa. We are Willie's granddaughters and—" Her voice broke off as she went into nurse mode. "Mr. Putnam, are you all right?"

He stared at the girls with a pale, stricken look on his face.

"Grandpa?" Reiney asked. "Grandpa, please come over here and sit down. Thomas, go get Grandma." She took her grandfather's arm with an affectionate squeeze and urged him over to a short sofa.

Young Thomas left immediately to find their grandmother.

He broke the silence. "Tell me again who you are."

The twins looked at each other. Finally, the great-uncle they had plotted and planned to see was in front of them, and they weren't sure what to say.

"It's all right. I'm fine. It was just a shock to hear her name again."

Lisa looked to Lillian to answer. "Mr. Putnam, Willie Garrison is our grandmother, and she's been missing for ten years. We just found out about you, and we've come to see if you've heard from her or have any idea where she might be."

Again, the party noise rose and fell with the opening and closing of the door. Thomas had returned with his grandmother, Dolly Putnam, as well as his father, Mark.

Dolly took one look at the girls and turned on her youngest son. "Mark, not more! You promised me there were only the three!"

"I swear, Mom—" Mark threw up his hands.

"Mrs. Putnam, we are Willie Garrison's granddaughters." Lisa quickly spoke up.

"We're from Colorado," Lillian added.

"I've never been to Colorado," Mark felt it necessary to add.

The short, tastefully dressed woman patted her son on the face and turned to the girls.

"Willie? Oh my," Dolly said. "Why are you here and causing this upset?"

"They were just about to explain when you came in and jumped to conclusions," Thomas said gently to his wife. "Now, unruffle your feathers and come sit down."

The smile they exchanged was a testament to their long marriage and love. She glided over to her husband and sat next to him. They looked at the girls without giving any other emotions away. United and showing it.

Lisa took a deep breath. "Ten years ago our grandfather died, and shortly after that our grandmother disappeared. Until recently, we trusted that the local law enforcement had done their due diligence. We no longer believe that."

Thomas Putnam senior interrupted. "Her disappearing isn't a new thing. She did *that* more than fifty years ago after our parents died."

"We understand she left here a long time ago. We read some of her journals last week, and that is how we found out about you."

"You mean," Mark said, clearly offended, "you didn't know anything about the Putnams until . . . a few days ago?"

"She never talked about her childhood or family at all," Lisa said firmly. "At least not to us. But she did write a great deal about her brother in her journals. I can't say for sure why she never told us about any of you, but I have an idea it had to do with a broken heart." Lisa faced her great-uncle. "She was devastated that she never heard from you."

"How was I supposed to contact her? I never had her address. I didn't even know if she was still alive." Thomas Putnam shook his head. "I don't doubt you're Willowmina's granddaughters, but I don't understand what you're doing here."

Lillian reached into the little pocket in the seam of her skirt and extracted the unmailed Christmas letter from a long-ago time. "Mr. Putnam, our parents were killed the week she wrote this to you. It was never mailed to you. But from what it says, it sounds like she wrote to you at least once a year." She held it out.

He took the envelope with a shaking hand, then simply sat there staring at it. Dolly gently took it from him and extracted the letter. She silently read it before turning to him and placing it back in his hands and whispering for him to read it. She had tears in her eyes.

Thomas reached into his jacket and extracted a pair of silver-rimmed reading glasses. While he read the letter, Dolly turned to the girls again. "Please finish your story."

Lillian asked, "Did she say good-bye when she left all those years ago?"

Thomas finished the letter and looked up at the proof his sister had lived all these years. "Yes, she said she couldn't live under our uncle's roof, asked me to come with her and told me she would let me know where she landed. That was the last I heard from her. We were all of eighteen years old. Did you know that we're twins?"

Silence fell.

"We were hoping she had contacted you at some point," Lisa finally said, clearly at a loss. "I guess that would be a solid no."

"When did you say she disappeared?" Dolly Putnam asked.

"Ten years ago," Lillian whispered.

"Tommy, don't you remember that phone call we got just before we were leaving for Paris?"

"What are you getting on about, Dolly?"

"We were getting ready to leave for the airport. Remember, the phone rang, and everybody was getting our stuff out to the car, so you answered it and it was some hospital. Oh, what was it? Oh yes, the state mental hospital, and they said they had a woman there who was claiming to be your sister. Oh, don't you remember? You said you didn't have a sister, crazy or otherwise, and slammed the phone down." Dolly turned to the girls. "We rushed off and didn't think much more about it. He's been angry at Willowmina our entire married life."

"Longer than that." Thomas shook his head sadly. "I should have taken time with that phone call. Was she . . . losing her mind after her husband died?"

"No!" Lillian and Lisa chorused in horror.

"We were just teenagers when she vanished," Lillian added. "But we spent a great deal of time with her. All of us did."

"All of you?" he asked.

"Um yes, there are four of us. We have an older sister named Jessica and a younger sister named Madison, only we call her Meg," Lisa answered. "What else can you tell us about the phone call?"

"I'd forgotten all about it. Or perhaps put it out of my memory on purpose. I've been very angry at Willowmina all these years."

"Thomas's uncle controlled the world back then," Dolly said, and for some reason he did nothing but demean and belittle his brother's children—and Willowmina in particular. He grumbled that their 'addlepated Bohemian parents' hadn't even given her a decent name —and then had the bad taste to give her a silly nickname like Willow. He criticized everything about the girl. That's why she left." She turned to her husband while reaching for his hand. "Do you think it's possible that he intercepted every letter she sent?"

"It's entirely possible," Thomas conceded, tears in his eyes.

"Ten years ago," Lillian asked, "when you got the call from the mental hospital, what else did the caller say? Anything at all that could help us find her?"

"Something about a Jane Doe claiming she had a brother and that she provided the number they called. I'm sorry, but that's about all I remember other than the woman identifying herself as a staff member of a state mental hospital."

"Did she say what state?" Lisa knelt in front of her great-uncle.

"I don't remember. I'm sorry. You girls look so much like her."

His eyes roamed the contours of her face as he spoke.

Reiney stepped forward. "I think we should try this again." She extended a hand to Lillian. "Hi, I'm your cousin."

Lillian gave a huge smile and pulled her into a hug. "Nice to meet you."

Everyone laughed as the tension eased.

Dolly stood up and brushed her hands down the front of her dress. "Well, now that we know what's what, we should probably go out and rejoin the party. You girls look like triplets, you know."

"We can only stay for a short time. We've got to get reservations on the next flight to Colorado."

"What are you going to do now?" Dolly asked.

"There's only one mental hospital in the state. We can start there," Lisa said.

"So you're not giving up?" Thomas said.

"Not a chance."

"Will you let us know if you find her?" Thomas asked. "Assuming that . . . assuming that my sister will still speak to me?"

Lillian answered for the twins by giving their great-uncle a hug.

Chapter Twelve

The girls checked in at Logan International Airport at four thirty the following morning for their flight home. They were airborne before six.

"Are we going to leave for Pueblo right away?" Lillian asked her sister as they heard a *ding* and the seat-belt sign turned off. Both girls unbuckled their belts.

"We won't get home before three in the afternoon, and it's a four-hour drive to Pueblo. I think we should debrief with Meg and the support group, get a good night's sleep, and head to Pueblo in the morning."

"Meg and the support group? Thank God! I thought you'd want to keep barreling forward without their input—and without thinking any of this through."

"Why would you think that?" Lisa narrowed her eyes at Lillian.

"Um, no reason. We've just been running nonstop since . . . you know, since we left."

"Oh really?" Lisa's blue-green eyes flashed. "You mean since we ran into Ian."

"Look, Lissy, I get it . . ."

"No, you don't get it. I was *not* running from that man."

Lillian eyed her sister coolly.

"Okay, fine!" Lisa snapped. "I needed to get away and I did. I'm fine now." She picked up the inflight magazine. "Are they playing any movies?"

The rest of the flight was spent *not* talking about Ian. By the time they retrieved their car from the Grand Junction Airport parking lot, grabbed a quick lunch, and drove to Elk City, they were very adept at ignoring the elephant in the room.

The Black Chevy Colorado buzzed down Main Street in Elk City just as the businesses were closing up shop for the day. Lillian dug her cell phone out of the backpack at her feet. "Lunch took a little longer than we expected. It's five thirty. Do you think Meg will still be at the condo when we get there?"

"Of course she will. She wants to know everything. Besides, if our earlier conversation with her is any indication, she's still trying to avoid the whole wedding planning thing."

"True."

They both laughed at their baby sister's plight. The least girly girl they knew was being herded by her future mother-in-law into a very froufrou wedding with all the frills, bells, and whistles.

As they pulled into the condo garage, Meg greeted them at the back door. "What took you two so long? I've been waiting for two hours. I thought you were on your way."

"Stop grumbling and take this." Lisa thrust the garment bag full of last evening's attire at her sister. "I need a comfy couch and a snack."

"What's this?" Meg looked at the bag.

Lillian's chuckle rippled across the garage. "Don't ask."

Meg set the bag down on the top of a chest freezer. "Don't bother getting comfy. Grams and the support group are waiting for us at the Golden Bear. So if you don't want to have to repeat your story over and over, I suggest we get into the truck and drive on over."

Lisa drove. As they pulled to the curb in front of the Golden Bear, Lillian thought to herself that the place didn't look as spooky as it did a few days ago. "I must be exhausted," she mused. "This place is starting to grow on me, I think."

A grunt from the driver's seat told her that Lisa didn't share her opinion.

Meg just laughed and said, "Told you."

All three girls walked into the dilapidated building. The front doors had been rehung by Jace—even though he still wasn't allowed inside by the madam, for no man had been allowed inside for over a hundred years.

"At least there isn't that dreadful screech from squeezing through the opening," Lisa whispered.

"Yep, but watch the steps up to the second floor," Meg warned. "They're still a terror."

As soon as they got to the parlor, the twins gaped at the full assembly of the dearly departed. Aunt Ethel and Bridget were sit-floating over the settee, and Grams chatted with a gnome of a mountain man while giving a donkey an apparent scratch behind the ears. In the meantime, an older bewhiskered man stood with Jack by the cobweb-laced fireplace.

The vision of Jack as a shade instead of the vibrant man they had known was hard on both Lillian and Lisa.

Meg tossed a wave at the ghostly forms by the fireplace and sang out, "Hello, William and Julius." In return, William held his moth-eaten fur cap to his chest and bowed, while Julius brayed a joyful "Howwwdeee."

"You two smell fresh like river water." Meg complimented the ethereal mountain man and his companion before turning to her sisters and whispering, "A welcome improvement."

"Did that donkey just talk?" Lillian stared.

"Sisters, meet William and his companion Julius. They're the ones who helped me get down the mountain when . . . after my Jeep slid down the hill on its top. And this"—Meg turned to the whiskered man standing next to Jack—"is Doctor Lindsey, the original one."

The doctor bowed.

"And, of course, you already know Jack." There was a slight catch in Meg's voice.

"A pleasure to meet you all," the twins said in unison.

Julius grinned through his big donkey teeth.

"Meg, this is still so . . . so unusual to us," Lillian said apologetically. "We see a lot of things in our travels that are different. But, well, this is way beyond . . . different."

Meg rolled her eyes.

Eloise clucked. "Meg, be nice."

Ethel drifted over with a devil-may-care grin on her face. "Besides, Meg, you fainted when you came face-to-face with all of this." She twirled her finger around to indicate the assembled company.

Lisa and Lillian relaxed and laughed.

At that moment, Bridget wafted gracefully over. "I am so delighted you could all come for a visit. Please make yourselves comfortable."

The girls took their seats, sending plumes of dust into the room. Lisa's dust cloud was the biggest.

Meg and Lillian coughed and waved their hands in front of their faces.

"Cripes, Lisa," Meg coughed.

"Focus, girls," Grams said firmly. "Boston. What happened in Boston?"

But Lillian seemed distracted. She pursed her lips. "Did Grandma Willie ever have mental problems?"

"Why in the world would you ask that?" Bridget asked.

"Uncle Thomas hadn't heard from Grandma Willie since she left home as a teenager—then ten years ago he got a call from a mental hospital, probably the Colorado State Mental Hospital in Pueblo."

"The state hospital!" Eloise gasped.

"Someone there was claiming to be his sister, but he blew it off."

Eloise began floating back and forth with her hands prayerfully in front of her face, her index fingers bouncing off her lips as she thought. The eerie humming sound she made as she ghost-paced back and forth made the hair stand up on the backs of the necks of the living.

"Grams! Please stop humming," Meg demanded. "It's giving us all the shivers."

Eloise stopped. "Sorry, girls. I used to hum when I was trying to figure something out. I forget it sounds different now. Anyway, this makes sense as I think about it. Willie was very depressed after Frank died. I don't think she would have committed herself without telling anyone, but the day she disappeared she was going to Grand Junction for some kind of gardening class, and she never made it. I suppose she could have had a breakdown and lost her memory or something."

"I know she was sad, but a breakdown? I don't know," Lillian said.

"Well, we mean to find out," Lisa said, standing up and brushing the dust off her jeans. "We're driving to Pueblo first thing in the morning and walking into that hospital and demanding to see Grandma Willie."

"If she's still there," Lillian added.

"I found a good picture of her in one of the boxes of photos from her house—it was taken right before Grandpa Frank died. If she's there, we'll find her."

As the two girls turned to leave, Meg spoke up. "And don't forget to pick one of those fabrics for your dresses! The wedding is coming up fast."

"We'll do it the minute we get back from Pueblo," the twins called in unison over their shoulders.

<hr>

THE EASTERN SKY was just peeking over the mountains as the little black pickup crested Monarch Pass. Traffic was light due to the early hour, and Lisa had cranked up her favorite Miranda Lambert CD.

Lillian refilled their respective travel coffee mugs and passed Lisa's to her before taking a nice slow sip of the fragrant brew.

"When we hit Salida, I will need to stop and drain my radiator after all the coffee I've consumed this morning."

Lillian smiled. "Me too, and I'll be ready for breakfast too. Let's just fast-food it through a drive-through."

"Do you think we'll get any answers in Pueblo?" Lisa asked her question as she geared down to slow their pace down the east side of the mountain.

"I don't know. It's been ten years—plus whoever called Thomas didn't mention Grandma Willie's name, just told him someone there was claiming to be his sister." She gave a small shrug of her shoulder and took another sip. "We may be on a wild goose chase, but we need to try."

"What if she's been locked up all these years because she doesn't know who she is? Do they even do that?"

The questions hung in the cab of the truck without an answer as they wended their way down the mountain pass, each sipping coffee and keeping her own counsel while Miranda Lambert poured from the speakers.

Chapter Thirteen

"Why can't you help us? Just look at this picture." Lisa shoved a photo at the receptionist. "We think she may have been here with memory loss or something else." She glared at the woman behind the counter.

Lillian stepped forward with a conciliatory smile and scooped her long, red-gold hair behind her ears with both hands. "I'm sorry."

The receptionist glared back.

"Really, we're just so"—Lillian looked at the nameplate on the woman's desk—"so anxious, Ms. Temple. We've been desperate to find our grandmother all these years, and this is the first little clue we've had."

Lydia Temple started to thaw a little. "Like I told your sister, I really can't help you, but the registrar will be out of a meeting in about an hour. If you would like to wait or come back, she may be able to help you then. The HIPAA regulations are so strict these days that she may not be able to answer your questions, but you can always ask."

She gave Lillian a small smile and then turned a stern look on Lisa. "If you choose to wait, there are seats right over there." She pointed with a pencil toward a few upholstered chairs in a corner.

The girls looked at each other and shrugged. It wasn't time for lunch yet and they had nowhere else to be. They walked to a waiting area and took seats next to each other with their backs to Lydia.

"Well, at least the magazines aren't too old," Lisa said as she scooped up a year-old copy of *Woman's Day*.

Lillian pulled her smartphone out of her pocket and checked for messages. Finding none, she pulled up a game of Candy Crush and settled in for a few rounds of mindless entertainment. She had just gotten into her first round of level 65 when she heard a loud "Pssst" next to her left ear. She whipped her head toward the sound and caught a whiff of Charlie perfume.

"Aunt Ethel?" she whispered.

"She's not here, is she?" Lisa whispered.

"Can't you smell the Charlie?"

Lisa sniffed the air and shook her head.

"Pssssssttttt!"

Both girls looked up to see 1970s disco personified—by a ghost. Barely out of her teens, the apparition tapped one of her chunky-heeled disco shoes and crossed her arms. The flared sleeves on her paisley blouse were almost as wide as the flared legs of her bell-bottomed pants.

Lisa and Lillian dropped their eyes and quickly looked away.

"Oh, stop pretending you can't see me," the young woman demanded with a flip of her Farrah Fawcett hair.

Lillian looked over her left shoulder to see if Ms. Temple was seeing what the girls were seeing.

"She can't see me. Believe me, I've tried to get her attention since she came to work here back in the '80s—and nothing. But I can tell that you can see me and hear me, so listen up. I think I know where your gramma is."

"Is she . . . is she . . . dead?" Lillian whispered around the lump in her throat.

"Nope, I saw the picture that one was waving around, but if you want to spring her out of this place, we better get moving."

"Where to?" Lisa stood, ready for action.

"I like you. Caution isn't your deal, is it? Go out the doors you came in and turn left toward the grassy area. I'll meet you there. By the way, my name is Felicity Fossette." She popped out of sight.

As the girls passed the reception desk, Lisa said lightly, "We're just going to come back later."

Ms. Temple gave a stingy smile and turned back to her computer screen.

As the twins approached the grassy area, they saw the shimmering disco queen, who led them down a sidewalk between people sitting alone or in small groups on lawn chairs or benches.

Just ahead, the girls spotted a broad straw hat. Beneath the brim, a frail woman wearing a pink floral shirt sat in front of a small easel, working diligently.

Felicity pointed. "That's her. You're going to have to move quick before she has to go back inside the fence." Felicity jerked a thumb over her shoulder at the double-fenced yard adjacent to the hospital building.

"Are you sure?"

Felicity appeared to stamp her platform shoe. "Of course I'm sure. Why does everyone always ask me that? Now, get a move on."

Squeezing each other's hands, the twins stepped forward until they were a pace behind the artist. The woman's red-gold hair was peppered with gray and worn much less fashionably than Grandma Willie had worn hers. Yet the set of her shoulders stirred memories in both Lisa and Lillian. Could this be the woman who had disappeared from their lives ten years ago?

"Oh ho!" the woman murmured gleefully. "Now I've got it."

That simple murmur was all Grandma Willie. The girls moved quickly to either side of the petite woman in the chair.

"Meemaw?"

"Grandma Willie?"

The charcoal pencil clattered against the easel, and the hatted head whipped from right to left. "Lisa . . . Lillian? How . . . when . . . oh my goodness, is it really you? You're so . . . grown up."

Disco Felicity had popped out, and now she reappeared almost before the twins had time to assimilate that the woman between them was definitely their grandmother. "Nice reunion," she said, "but you need to decide now what you're going to do. Her keeper is on the way."

Lillian studied the contours and changes in the beloved face she thought she would never see again. Her grandma didn't seem to see or hear Felicity. "Gramma, we need to get you out of here. Let's go to the office and—"

"No!" Willie stood and frantically scanned the immediate area. "They haven't believed a word I've said since the day I woke up here. Just get me out of this place and we'll worry about paperwork later. Where are you parked?"

"In the visitor parking," Lisa answered.

"Let's get out of here . . . now!"

Felicity slowed their departure for a moment. "Have her leave the hat and pink shirt. I think I can buy you some time."

"Gramma, leave your hat and shirt on the chair."

"What on earth for . . . Oh, never mind . . . here," she said as the hat flopped onto the chair seat and the shirt landed on the back as she turned them all toward the parking area.

Lillian caught a brief glimpse of the shirt and hat floating into place on Felicity as she took Willie's place on the chair. The trio hightailed it out of the area zigging from one sidewalk to another that eventually led to the parking lot. They didn't run, but their breath came in short bursts puffing in and out when they reached the pickup.

"Hurry, girls, hide me and get the heck out of here."

Lisa and Lillian looked at each other. "Hide you?" They said it in unison.

"Yes, hurry, I'll explain all this later," she whispered from her crouched position by the back door. "I'm not crazy."

Lisa yanked open the back door of the little truck. "Get under the backseat. Lill, move our stuff around to cover any part of her that can be seen. Good thing you're so tiny, Gramma."

For a woman in her seventies, she moved like a gymnast and was under the seat in a heartbeat. Lillian arranged their backpacks and her laptop case on the floor in front of the seat. The girls got into the front.

At that moment, activity surged behind them on the sidewalks. Orderlies and nurses were talking on walkie-talkies and looking behind every bush.

Trembling, Lisa started the engine and slammed the gear into reverse.

Lillian touched her arm. "Don't peel out of here and drive wild. No attention at this point is a good thing."

Within a few minutes Lisa had navigated the truck off campus and merged into the traffic on Twenty-Fourth Street. "Where to now?"

They heard the muffled voice of their grandmother. "Don't head home until the hubbub wears down. That's the first place they'll look for me."

Lillian kept looking back, partly in fear that they were being followed. "Why don't we hit I-25 and go to Colorado Springs until we can make a plan. They wouldn't expect that, would they?"

Lisa didn't wait for an answer. She flipped on the GPS. "Well, sister mine, plug it in and we'll head that direction."

Soon, turn-by-turn directions spilled out of the speaker on the little device. Felicity hovered across the front seats examining the device every time the little box spoke. "Won't she tell on us?" the wavering glitter ghost asked.

"Will who tell on us?" Lillian asked.

"You know"—she gestured toward the GPS—"that lady who's giving you directions."

Lisa looked over the sunglasses she had dropped over her eyes the minute they'd hit traffic, and Lillian started laughing until she snorted.

"What's so damned funny, sister mine?"

"Yeah, are you laughing at me?" Felicity hissed.

A few more stifled giggles. Lillian held her arms across her stomach, sucking in a breath between guffaws. "I'm . . . I'm sorry but the look on your face, Lisa, with those aviator shades and . . . and all you need is a . . . a trench coat and one of those earbuds and you could be a secret service agent." Peals of laughter bounced off the interior of the cab for a couple more blocks.

"Is she always like this?" Felicity shook her head side to side to fluff her hair back.

"Yes, she is," Lisa replied.

A very muffled "Is what?" floated up from under the backseat.

That just sent Lillian into another fit of giggles.

Lisa moved them through traffic toward the on-ramp. She merged onto I-25, speeding up to match the traffic.

"Gramma, as soon as we get a couple of miles away we can pull over and get you out from under the seat. Is that okay?"

The muffled voice shouted, "No! I mean, just leave me where I am until we get to the Springs. I'm okay really."

By the end of her outburst she sounded like a weary version of herself.

"It's okay, Grama. I just thought it would be very uncomfortable for you. It's forty miles until we get there." Lillian looked back just in time to see a state patrol light bar come to life. "Are you speeding Lis?"

"No and I've used my signals with every turn and lane change." She used her pinky to flip the right signal on as she decreased her speed to pull over. "Staying right behind us. That officer means to pull us over. Stay calm." Lisa took a deep breath and blew it slowly between pursed lips and the muffled sound of a whimper crept past her ear. "We'll get through this, Gramma."

No sooner had they stopped and the officer was at her window. She buzzed down the glass between them and went on the offensive. "Was I speeding?"

"No, ma'am. Driver's license and registration, please."

Lillian had already gotten the registration out of the glove box, and Lisa was extracting her license from her wallet. "What is the problem, officer?" She asked as nonchalantly as possible as she handed over the requested items.

"Who is Eloise Garrison?" The officer read the name on the registration.

"Our late grandmother. She passed last month, and I don't know when all of the paperwork will be completed to transfer the title to us."

"Keep your hands on the wheel and I'll be right back."

The officer stepped away and went back to his vehicle to do whatever it is they do when they take your license and registration with them. Felicity tagged along and popped into the passenger seat beside the officer. As he talked into his mic, the disco doll watched everything he did.

When he was finished, he walked back to the truck, and the scent of Charlie permeated the truck cab once again. "We have a report that you were at the Colorado mental health facility right before a patient came up missing. I need you both to exit the vehicle and allow me to complete a search."

Lisa spooled up immediately. "What are you talking about? We will not allow you to do a blasted thing. As you can plainly see, there are only two of us in here, and you obviously checked the bed of the truck as you walked up. Was that patient a miniature person like a . . . a . . . leprechaun?"

Lillian's breath hissed in as her nerves took a jolt. What were they going to do? Just as she finished that thought, the officer's patrol car seemed to go nuts. The siren started screaming, the horn was honking, and the mic was being keyed and coming over a loudspeaker. They all turned to look back at the lunatic vehicle. Lisa and Lillian did not look one bit confused as they could see Felicity smiling and waving . . . the officer could not.

Every time the officer turned to say something to them, his vehicle made another noise. Soon the engine was revving. He tried very hard to stay in control of himself and the situation. Lisa and Lillian unhooked their seat belts as if preparing do as he had asked and exit the vehicle.

"You're right. There isn't any place to hide in here." He took a cursory look in the backseat, tossed the license and registration at Lisa, and jogged back to his out-of-control cruiser.

The girls rebuckled their seat belts. Lisa put the blinker on to show her intentions to rejoin traffic. Neither said a word. It wasn't long before the silence was filled with the tinkling laugh of the ghost who had rescued them.

"Boy howdy." Felicity grinned. "He didn't know what to do 'cause I didn't stop fiddling with all the buttons until I couldn't see you anymore. He was asking for a tow truck by the time I popped out. I turned the key off too." Her laughter took on a haunting hilarity that gave the girls the shivers.

Willie spoke somberly from beneath the seat. "Good thing I stayed right where I am."

The rest of the trip to Colorado Springs was spent in silence. For forty miles, even Felicity held her peace and the radio had been silenced, and only a blanket of thought surrounded them.

$\mathcal{A}$cademy Boulevard was buzzing with traffic when they finally began talking again. "Gramma, ready to get out of your hiding spot?" Lillian turned in her seat to look back.

"Are you sure we're not being followed?" came a mumbled question from under the seat.

"I've been watching the mirrors," Lisa said reassuringly. "We can drive to a busy parking lot so it'll be less conspicuous getting you out of the backseat."

"I don't know . . ."

"It will work, Gramma. We'll get you out of this mess somehow."

Felicity whispered into Lisa's ear. "I'll pop back to the hospital and see what I can learn."

"Do it. We'll, um . . . wait for you."

"Please do. I think I want to finish this adventure with you. I haven't been out of that place since 1979." With those parting words she faded out.

Lisa signaled and changed lanes. "Let's go to the Chapel Hills Mall and wait for—"

"Wait for what?" Willie piped up from her hiding place.

"Gramma," Lillian said casually, "we're hoping to figure out where they're searching for you."

"And just how are you going to do that?"

The twins looked at each other before blurting, "Computers."

Lillian added, "Technology has really changed in the last few years. I'll do some research on my tablet as soon as we stop."

"Young lady, you wouldn't be blowing smoke up my skirt, would you?"

"Um, no, Gramma." Lillian bugged her eyes out at her sister. Lisa shrugged as she maneuvered the little truck through traffic toward the mall.

A muted harrumph came from under the backseat.

Felicity, preceded by the scent of Charlie perfume, shimmered into view. "They have some kind of bulletin going out through the cop shops. They are focusing their attention mainly toward Highway 50 through Gunnison and I-70 through Grand Junction."

Lillian opened her tablet and tapped the keyboard a few times for Willie's sake. Then she cleared her throat. "Gramma, looks like they put a bulletin out to all the police departments and state patrol cars between here and Elk city on 70 and 50." Then she winked at the shade who was watching their backs.

Felicity rolled her ghostly eyes. "She really can't hear me, can she?"

Lisa shook her head.

"I always thought she was just pretending. Well, crud." With that she stared thoughtfully out the window, twirling a section of her ghostly blond hair around her transparent finger.

Willie spoke up again from under the backseat. The anxiety in her voice made her next words even more heartbreaking. "I can't go back to that place, I just can't. Whatever am I going to do?"

"Don't worry, Gramma, we'll figure out something." Lisa chewed her bottom lip.

"Ask your Gramma who she knows in the Springs," Felicity said.

"She has friends in the Springs?" Lisa asked.

"I think so. At least she used to ask the nurses to let her call someone in the Springs, but they always told her no."

Lillian's forehead puckered in thought. "Gramma, don't you have some old ranch friends who live near here?"

"Oh my stars! Of course, Bob and Bernie Summit have a little ranch north and east of here. Why didn't I think of them sooner? Lisa, I'll give you directions to their house. Ha! I'm glad you thought of it, Lilly."

Felicity snorted. Lillian mouthed the words, *Sorry about that.*

Forty minutes later Lisa pulled the truck through the open entry gate of the Summit Valley Ranch. Gravel crunched beneath the tires.

Four blue heelers and a large rawboned woman spilled out of the screen door of the mudroom porch. The dogs barked and danced around the small Colorado pickup truck until their six-foot-tall mom called them to sit, eyes on her, stubby tails churning dust off the ground as they swept back and forth. "It's safe to come on out now. My girls are just a little boisterous when greeting new people."

The girls exited the little truck, and Lisa turned to open the back door. Felicity floated out of the truck and faded out.

"Lord, it's good to see you girls!" Bernie's whiskey-smoke voice and bright smile were honest and straightforward. "I can't believe you still had my number! I think you were maybe sixteen the last time I saw you. I bet your gramma would be so proud to look at you." She gave a little sniff. "I sure miss her."

"Well, Bernie, you can quit your missing me now."

Bernie stopped, slack jawed for a few beats. Then, with her single braid flagging behind her, she dashed to where Willie Garrison was stepping down out of the truck. "Oh my, oh my," she said over and over. She picked the tiny Willie up and hugged her like a rag doll. "Where have you been, my friend, where have you been?"

"Put me down, woman, and I'll tell you."

Happy tears accompanied the four women to the mud porch and then into the back door of the white clapboard house. Bernice, known by Bernie, shooed everyone toward the chipped Formica kitchen table surrounded by mismatched chairs. "Sit, sit, everyone.

Do you want iced tea, water, or limeade? Oh, Willie, it is so good to see you again."

The twins opted for water, and Grandma Willie couldn't decide. She hadn't made a lot of choices for herself for the past decade.

"Oh, just get me something cold before I dither myself silly."

Bernie placed a cold beer in front of Willie. "How's that? You used to like a Miller Lite once in a while." She grinned and clinked her bottle against Willie's.

"Oh my! I better sip slowly, I haven't had alcohol in ten years."

Bernie leaned back in her seat and hooked her free elbow over the back of her chair. "Well, well, well. So where have you been?"

Willie squirmed and her cheeks turned pink before she quietly answered, "In the state mental hospital in Pueblo."

Beer spewed across the table before Bernie squawked, "What? No way."

Willie took another small sip of her beer. "Yes way. I don't know to this day how I got there. I just know that I was getting ready to drive to Junction. I took a couple of things to the car and . . . that's it. The next thing I know I'm waking up in a bare room with restraints on my wrists that kept me tied down to a bed."

"That's the first time I saw her," Felicity spoke up, startling Lillian and Lisa who had forgotten she was there. "She was panicked, and they were observing her. Gives me the shivers to think about it. She was considered dangerous, and she was just terrified."

Lillian looked around to see that neither Bernie nor Gramma had heard the fifth person in the room.

Lisa cleared her throat. "Gramma, they found your car in the City Market parking lot in Delta. You don't remember leaving your house?"

Willie looked at the floor. "I didn't leave the house. I'm sure of that." She sighed and took another tiny sip out of her bottle. "I was going to leave for gardening class and that's all I remember."

Bernie reached over and gently squeezed Willie's shoulder in solidarity and understanding. "You don't remember any details?"

Willie's unstylish hair gently swayed with her rocking motion. "No."

Felicity leaned in close between Lisa and Lillian. "I'll be back. I'm going to pop back to the search and see if they've got anything that would lead them here. I sure hope not." With those words she was gone.

Lisa leaned in toward Willie. "Gramma, can you tell me everything you remember about that day? It might jog something loose for you."

"What kind of detail?"

"Just start with when you woke up that morning, and then tell us every detail you remember."

"Okay, I woke up early so I could make the class in Grand Junction. So, I got up at five with the alarm."

"Did you use the snooze button?"

"No. I remember wanting to, but I got up and got into the shower first thing."

"What kind of shampoo did you use?"

"Shampoo?" She thought a moment. "Garnier, in a green bottle. But I don't see how this will help. Can we stop now?"

"Gramma, Lill and I are nurses and . . ."

"Nurses? Both of you? That is so wonderful."

"The thing is, Gramma, I'm a surgical nurse and Lill works with pediatrics, and there are things we've learned over the years about drugs and their effects. I think it's possible you were given some kind of drug."

"But who could have done that? I was at the house alone after Frank died."

"Let's keep jogging your memory to see if we can find some clues, okay?"

"Okay, sort of like those cop shows. We got television there. I liked the cop shows."

Bernie stood up. "I think this is a good plan. While you're working through your questions, does anybody want some lunch?"

Willie's stomach answered for all of them, gurgling loudly.

Bernie grinned. "BLTs for everyone then."

"All right, Gramma," Lisa said, picking up where they left off, "after you got out of the shower, what color of towel did you use?"

"Dark gray . . . one of Frank's." Willie seemed to wilt for a moment.

"Gramma," Lillian said, "we don't have to do this right now. Did you ever get a chance to mourn for Grampa?"

"Oh, I grieved. After waking up at that mental hospital, for two years I fluctuated between sadness, anger, and outrage."

"What were you thinking about during the anger and outrage?"

"I thought about killing Clint for letting me get stuck in there!"

The unfamiliar grit in her voice, especially coming through clenched teeth, was startling. Lisa and Lillian exchanged another look.

Lisa's questions brought to light more and more details of that morning ten years ago. Details like the flavor of tea Willie drank that morning (her morning favorite) and the cup she used (her favorite mug), where her car keys had been, and whether or not she emptied the kitchen bin in the trash can outside.

Lisa asked if Willie had seen anyone around her house that day or the day before, and whether anyone knew she was on her way to a gardening class in Grand Junction.

"Oh, everyone knew I was taking that class. They even encouraged me to do it. You know what people always tell the grieving: 'You'll feel better if you stay busy.'" She rolled her eyes.

Bernie quietly fried bacon, sliced tomatoes, and rinsed lettuce leaves. She assembled the fragrant sandwiches, added home-canned pickle slices and cottage cheese to the plates, and slipped them in front of the lucky recipients.

"Gramma," Lisa said, "do you think someone could have slipped into your house while you were in the shower or blow drying your hair and slipped you some drugs? Maybe in your favorite mug and tea? You never locked your door."

"That could be, but it still doesn't tell us why."

Lillian licked the salty tang of bacon off her thumb and wrinkled her brow. "Not yet anyway."

"Why don't you three gals spend the night here, and tomorrow we'll figure out how to sneak you back home."

"I think that would be prudent," Lillian said.

Bernie smiled ear to ear. "Bob's at a cattle auction in Oklahoma and won't be home tonight, so we can have a regular girls' night and get caught up."

Even though Bernie included the girls, Lisa and Lillian knew that Bernie was relishing the thought of catching up with her dear friend Willie. They also knew their grandmother had hard news coming her way. After all, at some point they'd have to tell her that Grandpa Mike, Aunt Ethel, and Grams Eloise had passed. Too bad Willie couldn't see or hear the dearly departed.

The four women moved into a comfortable, lived-in room with a broken-in couch and two lounge chairs arranged around a flat-screen TV. Lisa and Lillian listened attentively as Bernie and Willie chatted happily about old times, changes on the Summit Valley Ranch, and the aches and pains of turning seventy.

Eventually the conversation came around to Elk City.

"I can't wait to tell Eloise and Ethel where I've been." Willie clapped her hands. "I bet those two will have a fit."

The three women fell silent.

Willie searched the faces of Bernie and the twins.

"Gramma . . . ," Lillian said, then stopped.

"Grandma Willie, Aunt Ethel passed three years ago from a massive stroke." Lisa delivered the news.

Grandma Willie's face fell. "But . . . but she was the youngest one of us."

No one said anything.

"And Eloise?" Willie closed her eyes.

"She . . . she died two months ago from a nasty virus that was—" Lillian stopped and looked to Lisa for help.

Lisa took a deep breath before blurting, "She was basically murdered."

"Murdered? I don't understand." Willie's voice quavered and her face crumbled as she tearfully asked, "How does someone get murdered with a virus?" This would prove to be the only meltdown she allowed herself. Her body shook as the wretched sobs ripped out of her tiny frame.

Bernie, tears running rivers down her own cheeks, tried to console her dear friend. They had been sitting on opposite ends of the sofa, shoes off and legs curled comfortably under them, but now Bernie's feet hit the floor and she practically leaped to the other end of the sofa. She hugged Willie close as the grief poured out of her with Bernie rocking her back and forth like a child.

A decade of grief and fear and despair came undammed at once as she wept for the loss of her husband, her freedom, her friend, and more.

It took the emotional storm almost an hour to subside. They all ended up with red, blotchy skin and puffy eyes and a pile of used tissues on the end table.

Willie took several shallow breaths, seesawing breath into her lungs through her stuffed-up nose. Lillian's sniffs served counterpoint to her sister's low snuffles into the last tissue from the box.

Bernie pulled back and looked down at Willie. "We will get through this, but right now I better fetch us all some more limeade and another box of tissues." At Willie's small nod, she got up and went in search of the things she had spoken about.

"Girls . . . I'm so sorry."

"It's okay, Gramma, none of this was your fault."

"If I hadn't been in such a state . . . if I had paid more attention . . . you girls . . . oh dear." Willie dropped her chin to her chest while she fought back a fresh batch of tears. Lillian dropped to her knees in front of her heartbroken grandmother, and Lisa took the post beside her on the couch.

Bernie bustled into the cozy room with cold glasses of limeade on a tray in her hands and a brightly colored box of tissues under her left arm. A fully loaded cloud of Charlie perfume tagged along behind her. Lisa made eye contact with the wraith known as Felicity

Fossette. The apparition flipped her hair back as she motioned her to follow. Lillian exchanged a look with her sister, and the telepathic twin-speak seemed to work.

Lisa stood up and stretched. "I need to move around a bit. We've been flying and driving for the last few days, and I feel like my knees are permanently bent."

Bernice had deposited the tray of limeade on the little table in the corner. "Well, here, take your drink with you."

Lisa accepted the cold offering and took a long swallow. "Mmm, this is really good."

"I make it from scratch. Tastes better that way and I know what's in it."

Lisa edged out of the room as her sister engaged the older women in light conversation. She followed the scent of Charlie to the mud porch on the back of the house. "Okay, Felicity, what did you find out?"

Felicity shook her mane of ghostly hair away from her face. "I checked in again to see what the scoop was on the search. I don't know for sure why, but the hunt for your grandmother is massive—and you aren't out of the spotlight either."

"What do you mean?"

"I mean, somebody out there is pulling a lot of strings to keep the fire on a missing patient so, well, so . . . *hot.*"

Lisa swirled the ice cubes around in her glass as she contemplated this news.

"Well?"

Lisa looked at Felicity's sparkly top, matching wristlets, high-waisted bell-bottoms, and platform shoes. "I don't know how anyone can *not* see you."

Felicity glowered. "Look, I'm only trying to help. If you don't want me here, just say so."

"We need your help. Please excuse me. I'm just now getting used to seeing people who have . . . transitioned, so to speak."

Another toss of her ethereal mass of hair and she said, "That's better, 'cause I don't *have* to help you, you know. So, what do you want me to do?"

"Please keep an eye on the hunt and try to catch a name or at least find out where this pressure is coming from."

"Far out, I'm on it." With those parting words she dissipated, leaving Lisa to stare out the screened porch by herself.

isa dropped her glass off at the kitchen sink and rejoined the other women in the family room.

"Willie," Bernie was saying, "the first thing you need to do is hire an attorney."

Willie nodded in agreement as Lisa sat next to Lillian on the sofa.

"Of course, you may retain whoever you'd like, but since you've been away, David has made quite a name for himself."

Willie brightened at the name. "Oh, Bernie! How is he? Last I remember, your grandson was working on his law degree."

"Now he works for a highfalutin firm in Denver and does criminal and civil law."

Lillian was listening to the conversation with a smirk on her face. "Highfalutin law firm? Seriously? You're not talking about the David we know, are you?" No one seemed to hear her.

"I don't need to retain anyone else." Willie smiled at her friend. "I would love to have David take care of this mess!"

"Grams," Lillian said hesitantly, "don't you think you need someone . . . knowledgeable? With more experience?"

Lisa chided her sister. "You're still miffed that he knocked you in the river when we were thirteen."

"I'm not miffed at all," Lillian said, defending herself. "Although I should be. He *was* always picking on me."

Lisa smothered a giggle. "If I remember right, you usually started it."

"Girls," Willie said firmly. "Stop it. David isn't a kid anymore. He's all grown up. As are the both of you. You *could* start acting like it." Willie turned to her friend. "Can you invite him over?"

"No need. He always comes out for a meal when his grandpa is gone overnight. He keeps trying to take me to town for dinner, but I miss cooking for all the kids, so I promised him a fried chicken dinner. He'll be here in"—Bernie looked over her shoulder at the clock—"Oh my stars! In a couple of hours."

"What can we do to help?" Willie was already standing up.

"How about we start with some pies?"

The two old friends giggled their way to the kitchen.

An hour later the heavenly smell of fried chicken, mashed potatoes, gravy, and apple pie filled the entire house. The twins had been put to work on the cold dishes, and their bellies were growling at the luscious array of aromas emanating from the kitchen.

A car horn gave two quick beeps as a snazzy red Lexus RX 330 wheeled into the ranch yard. Lillian rolled her eyes. Catching the eye roll, Lisa gave her sister a hip bump.

Bernie snatched up the dish towel, quickly wiped her damp hands, and rushed outside to meet her grandson. Grandma Willie and the girls watched out the kitchen window as Bernie hugged David, all the while talking a mile a minute. David's head jerked up as he looked toward the house.

"Well, I guess he knows you're here now." Lisa hip-bumped her sister again and winked at their grandmother.

David grabbed his briefcase out of the backseat, slammed the Lexus' door, and hurried toward the house, leaving his grandmother to trail behind him.

He let the porch screen door bang shut. Standing in the middle of the kitchen, he stared at the trio for a beat. "Well, I'll be damned."

Bernie was right behind him. "David, watch your mouth," she scolded with a chuckle.

The tall young man plopped his briefcase on a nearby counter and scooped Willie up for a joyous hug. "Aunt Willie, it's so good to see you standing in this kitchen again."

Willie joyfully swatted him on the shoulder. "Put me down, you crazy boy. You still look like Richie Cunningham." They both laughed as he set her back on her feet.

He looked over her shoulder to acknowledge the twins. With a big smile he said, "Hey, Lisa." With a carefully schooled lawyer face he quietly added, "Hey, Lillian."

"A Lexus? Really?" was her only reply.

"Supper's on the table," Willie chirped. "You all go wash up." She made shooing motions with her hands.

Bernie clucked her tongue. "Those two."

Chapter Sixteen

During dinner, there wasn't a lot of talking going on—but there were plenty of "mmms" and compliments over the wonderful comfort food. Willie, in particular, seemed to savor each bite.

After the meal Bernice and the twins volunteered for dish duty so Willie could discuss the business end of this mess with the young man who took on her case without hesitation.

While David and Willie put their heads together over coffee in the family room, Bernice and the twins set the kitchen right. When the last dish was put away, Bernice poured herself a cup of coffee. "Want to go sit on the back porch and enjoy the sunset?"

As the twins began following Bernice toward the back door, David leaned into the kitchen with both hands on either side of the door. "Where are you going? I was hoping you'd be around to meet Kait."

Lillian's eyes widened.

"Are you talking about Kaitlyn?" Bernice asked.

"Yes. I've already called her, and she should be here in the next hour."

His grandmother nodded her head. "Sounds like a good idea to me."

A JAZZY LITTLE MINI Cooper buzzed into the dooryard fifty minutes later. David went out to meet a tall, pleasant-faced woman dressed in a swirly skirt, loose top, and little round glasses. She pulled a messenger bag out of her passenger seat and accompanied him into the house.

As they entered the family room, David had his hand on her back and was saying, "Thank you so much for coming out tonight."

"Of course, of course, what did you think I would say?" Kaitlyn chuckled deeply.

"Kait, this is Lisa and Lillian Garrison. You already know my grandmother, and this is my Auntie Willie Garrison."

The woman hugged Bernie, then greeted Willie. "Hello, Willowmina. I believe David explained to you who I am and how I help people, is that correct?"

"Yes, he did. I'm a little bit nervous considering where I've been for ten years."

Kaitlyn smiled warmly and took Willie's hand in hers. "David has told me a little about your ordeal. I'll be kind, and this may go without saying, but I'm going to say it anyway. Nothing that you tell me here will be used or repeated anywhere without your permission."

"As I explained to Willie, Kaitlyn is a clinical psychiatrist," David added. "Our firm keeps her on retainer. She is qualified in helping people with memory loss. She has a PhD in guided memory recall and is an expert in her field."

"I help a person reach a very relaxed state, sort of like Savasana at the end of a yoga session. I then help them to walk back from a certain point to find little details in the memory that they would normally ignore. The person is fully aware of the present. Willie, do you want to go through this process, and if you do, do you want anyone here or would you rather do this in private?"

Willie took a deep breath and looked at the beloved faces of her granddaughters and her dear friend. "I didn't know if I would ever see these faces again. I want them to stay, but only if they follow your every instruction. I don't think I can do this twice."

"Okay, the next question for you is, may I record this session?"

Willie nodded her assent.

"Thank you for doing this, Willie," David added. "I'm hoping to get in to see a judge in the morning and get the ball rolling on this. Anything you can remember may help me present a stronger case for you."

Kaitlyn pulled a small digital recorder, pen, and pad of paper out of her bag, then addressed the assembly. "Before we start, there are some rules for anyone who stays. One, there can be zero talking, so I will give everyone a pad of paper for you to take notes on. Two, do not distract me while I am working with Willie . . . no matter what. And three, no movement, so get comfortable now. There will be zero deviation from these rules. If you cannot comply, please leave the room now."

No one left. As Kaitlyn passed out paper and pens, everyone shifted into positions they wouldn't mind holding for a while. David sat on the floor with his back to the wall with his own yellow legal pad and mechanical pencil.

Kaitlyn asked Willie to sit in the recliner and tilt back with the footrest deployed. She gave her a pillow to hug and had her close her eyes. Then she began to talk in a lovely timbre until Willie closed her eyes and gently sighed.

Quietly and with professional precision, Kaitlyn took Willie back to the day she woke up in the confusing world of the state hospital. Willie's hands tensed on the pillow. Kaitlyn's melodic voice calmed her again. She scrunched her face in concentration.

"The lights were hurting my eyes and I couldn't move. I could hear voices and they seemed like they were coming from a speaker, but I can't be sure because everything is sort of gauzy."

"That's okay. Just tell me what you notice."

"The bed or table I'm on isn't too hard and my ring finger hurts."

"Which ring finger?"

"My wedding finger."

"Is there anything else in this moment?"

"Mmm, no."

"Very good, Willie, now let's go back to what you remember before that."

"I took some things out to my car for a trip."

"Where were you going?"

"To Grand Junction for a gardening class."

"Tell me about your car."

A small smile crossed Willie's face. "It's the gray ghost."

"What does that mean?"

"My husband called it that because it's silver with dark gray seats."

Kaitlyn learned forward. "What do you smell when you open the door?"

"Wild Country Cologne. It smells just like Frank."

"What do you hear while you are at the car?"

"Calves. They're all around our place today."

Kaitlyn jotted something on her notepad.

"Wait." Willie said. "I'm still outside, and I hear the back screen door squeaking."

Kaitlyn looked up. "What makes you think it's the back door?"

"It makes this weird squeak, and Frank was going to oil it but he didn't get it done before . . ." Her voice trailed off.

"Before what, Willie?"

"He had a massive coronary."

"Let's leave that thought for now. What did you do after you put your things in the car?"

"I listened for a couple of minutes and didn't hear anything else coming from the house, so I closed the car door and went back into the house to finish my tea and get my purse."

"Do you go through the front door or the back?"

"Front door, it's closer."

"What do you see as you walk toward the front door?"

"My flower beds need tending."

"Is the front door open or closed?"

A furrow appeared between Willie's eyebrows. "The screen is closed, and the front door is . . . is partially closed."

"Is that how you left it?"

"I don't think so, but I've been in such a muddle since the funeral that I can't be sure."

"Then what do you do?"

"I open the screen and go inside. I walk over to my roses in the sunroom and check them for moisture."

"Are they moist or dry?"

"They need some water before I leave for a couple of days, so I got my watering can and took it to the kitchen to fill it."

"Did you fill it?"

"I took it to the kitchen sink and started filling it from the faucet . . ."

"Then what?"

"I finished my cup of tea."

"Is the watering can full yet?"

"I-I don't know. I don't remember finishing that chore."

Kaitlyn and David both wrote quickly on their tablets.

"That's okay. What sensation do you feel at the moment you finish your tea?"

"I . . . I don't remember."

"Do you have any impressions between being in the kitchen and waking up at the state hospital?"

Willie was quiet for so long that nobody in the room thought she would find anything in her missing memory.

"I kind of remember panicking because someone was taking my wedding ring off, and then I think I got a drink of water and then everything goes black again."

"When this was happening, do you think you were still in your house?"

"My wedding ring . . . and the drink of water seem far apart."

Kaitlyn tried several more artful questions to help Willie push her memory, to no avail. She waited patiently while Willie stretched and pushed the footrest back into place. She and David continued writing notes for a few minutes; then she put down her pen, took off her glasses, and rubbed her eyes with the index finger and thumb of her left hand. There seemed to be an unspoken conversation between her and David before she leaned back in the couch and smiled at Willie.

"How do you feel?"

"I think a little confused."

"What confuses you?"

"My wedding ring. I've asked over and over in the last ten years for it to be returned to me, but they always insisted that I didn't have any jewelry when I arrived."

"Tell me about your wedding ring. Was it unique?"

"Well, not in design. It was a simple wide gold band, but it was engraved on the inside."

David asked, "What was on the inside of your ring?"

Willie got a misty smile on her face. "On our tenth anniversary Frank had 'I love you X10' engraved on the inside. Then on our twentieth he added X20, our thirtieth X30, and he added X40 on that anniversary. I was looking forward to him adding the next one, but he died shortly before our fiftieth."

Chapter Seventeen

"*I didn't think another conference call between the three of us would be necessary—ever. But here we are, so listen up.*" *The man's slippery voice revealed a thinly veiled edge. He was obviously used to people doing as he said.* "*A young lawyer just got an injunction to stop the pursuit of a certain Jane Doe who disappeared from the state hospital.*"

"*What do you mean?*" *asked a second man, his voice tight with anxiety.* "*Why would an injunction be issued? Who is the lawyer?*"

"*I told you at the start this was a bad idea,*" *said a third man with the gravelly voice of a smoker who'd smoked for decades.*

"*What are we going to do now?*" *growled the anxious man.* "*Do you have a plan?*"

"*Thanks for your time, gentlemen,*" *the slippery voice said, his faux courtesy underscored with disdain.* "*Unfortunately, arresting her at this point would open the whole can of worms. I'll be in touch when I figure a few things out.*"

He hung up the phone leaving the other two still connected.

"*What are we going to do about him?*" *the anxious man asked.*

"*Nothing until we know what he did with the evidence against us.*"

"Look, I've got two back-to-back sessions starting in about fifteen minutes. I'll call you later. This has gone far enough."

THE RED LEXUS pulled into the ranch yard a little after noon. Lillian stood at the sink drinking a glass of cold water and watching as David strode toward the back door holding a couple of folders.

"I hope those folders mean what I think they mean, because I don't know what we are going to do next if he didn't get that judge friend of his to help us."

Lisa stepped up behind her sister and looked over her shoulder. "He sure doesn't give anything away by his expression."

Bernice and Willie sat at the kitchen table sipping iced tea.

"That's what makes my grandson such a crackerjack lawyer. Folks say the opposing attorneys can't read him." Bernie winked at her old friend. "Bob will be back tomorrow, and if we don't have a plan, I'm sure he'll have some thoughts—after he gets over the shock of seeing you again."

The screen door banged as David barged into the kitchen with a big grin. "We've got the injunction for thirty days to prove who you are, Willie."

"Can I go home?"

"Yep, but it was close until I told the judge that I have known you since I was a little kid and could personally vouch for you." He popped a couple of grapes into his mouth from a bowl on the table. "You'll have to check in with the sheriff or state patrol every morning and give them your exact location. I figured that wouldn't be an issue since your nephew happens to be the sheriff in Elk City."

"Thank you so much, David. I finally feel like I'm waking up from a horrible dream."

"Everything should be through the system in the next few hours. I think you'll be able to head home soon without any problem."

Willie beamed a fat smile at him. "You are such a good boy!"

A hearty snort sounded from the direction of the sink. Lisa hip-bumped Lillian as a reminder for her to behave.

Chapter Eighteen

A few minutes later Felicity wafted in and stood next to Lisa. "Things sure have been in flux. First, they upped the search and now they are calling it all off. What's happening?"

Lisa whispered out of the side of her mouth. "See that guy over there?"

"Oh, you mean the one who looks like that kid on *Happy Days*? Oh, what's his name—Richie Cunningham."

Lisa tried to keep from smiling. "Yeah him. Anyway, he's an attorney and he got a court order that gives Gramma Willie thirty days to prove her identity."

"Ah, so that's what put them all in such a tizzy."

"Tizzy?"

"Who're you talking to over there?" Bernie stood and reached across the kitchen table for the empty iced tea pitcher.

When Lisa looked guilty, Bernie laughed and said, "Glad I'm not the only one who talks to themselves. Anyone want more tea?"

Relief washed over Lisa as the denizens at the table declined additional libations.

Willie blew out a worried sigh. "How much longer do you think before I can leave for Elk City? I just want to go home."

"You can leave whenever you'd like, Auntie Willie." He winked at Lillian. "You girls are in the clear too."

A sneer streaked across Lillian's lips, but before she could make a sound, her grandmother jumped into the breach. "Oh, David, thank you so much." She popped up out of her chair and threw her arms around the kind young man and hugged the stuffing out of him.

Bernie's eyes gleamed with happy tears.

"Oh, Bernie, please don't make me cry anymore. I'll be back as soon as this mess is over. I promise."

"Can't you wait until Bob comes home and then go?"

Willie thought about it for a beat. "I'm sorry, Bernie. I've got to get back to my home so I can feel like it's really over."

"I know, my dear friend. I'll be right here waiting for you."

Felicity hovered for a few more minutes before she whispered in Lisa's ear, "I'll catch up with you later." Then she was just . . . gone.

"I CAN HARDLY BELIEVE IT! We will be in Elk City in a little over an hour."

Willie's eyes darted from mountain to mountain. She practically pressed her nose to the side window going over Monarch Pass. She wanted to see everything she'd missed and longed for over the last ten years. Her questions and comments came rapid-fire:

"When did they build that bridge?"

"Lookie how wide the road is now!"

"Is that a new fire station?"

The twins answered every question with big smiles on their faces, so happy were they to have their grandmother back again.

When they were almost within the city limits of Gunnison, Lillian twisted around in her seat. "Gramma, do you want to stop in Gunni and get something to eat?"

"Not really. If you girls don't mind, I just want to go home."

Lillian glanced at Lisa. Lisa winced.

"What is it?" Willie asked.

At Lillian's stricken look, Willie softened her tone. "Girls, it's been ten years. What are you trying so hard to protect me from? I'm a grown woman and I'm not crazy regardless of where I've been."

"About your house, Gramma . . ." Lillian stalled. "The thing is . . . well . . ."

"Oh, for heaven's sake, Lill." Lisa rolled her eyes. "Gramma, Clint took over your house within a few weeks after you went missing. You won't even recognize it anymore. I'm sorry."

The color drained from Willie's cheeks. "What did he do to it?"

"The gardens are gone and he's installed all this security stuff all over."

"What about my things and my greenhouse?"

Lillian sighed. "Gramma, he moved your stuff upstairs, covered the downstairs floor with laminate, and put a giant hot tub in the sunroom. And we have no idea what he did with your rosebushes."

Willie slumped back against the seat for a moment. A calculating look came into her eyes. "Well, I guess I'll fix that after we get my status fixed."

The girls looked at each other in uncertainty. They had never heard quite that tone from their grandmother.

"Well, anyway, I hope The Diner is still open, or Diggers. I want a juicy burger and some yummy fries."

"You and Meg always loved that stuff, and yes, both places are still open and still good. Oh, and speaking of Meg, we haven't told her anything yet." Lillian chewed her bottom lip as she looked over at Lisa.

"Call her now. I can guess her reaction if we don't call her in advance."

Willie leaned as far forward as her seat belt would allow. "I sure have missed you girls. What about Jessica? What is she doing these days?"

"Let me call Meg first, then we'll fill you in on everybody.

Lillian speed-dialed their youngest sister.

"Hey, Meg . . ." She listened for a few moments before breaking into her sister's tirade. "Look, I'm sorry you were so worried, *but* we have Gramma with us."

She had to yank the phone away from her ear at Meg's rebel yell.

They arranged to meet up at The Diner, and when Willie asked if her dear friend Annabel could join them, Meg promised to bring her along.

Lisa ended the call and looked over her shoulder. "Well, Gramma, get ready, because I have a feeling you're going to be surrounded when we get there."

Lillian cut her eyes over to her sister. "Meg's support group?"

Lisa chuckled. "They wouldn't miss it for the world."

"Why is Meg in a support group?"

"She's not, Gramma." Lillian thought fast. "That's just how we refer to her, um, new friends."

"Oh, will I like them?"

"If you ever get to meet them, you will."

<h1 style="text-align:center">Chapter Nineteen</h1>

It was seven thirty when they pulled to a stop in The Diner's parking lot.

"Well, so far so good," Lisa observed. "Jace's truck, Annabel's purple Gremlin, a few miscellaneous rigs, and a couple of out-of-state cars. The place isn't packed, which means the gossip mill hasn't caught the scent of your return." Her snarky tone communicated how she felt about small-town gossip mongers.

"Lisa, you need to think kinder thoughts, young lady. That tone is not becoming on you." The scolding was delivered sweetly but with a core of steel.

Lisa felt a wave of comfort. Every mile closer to Elk City was bringing Grandma Willie a little closer to her old self.

"Yes, ma'am," Lisa said agreeably. "Now, are you ready to meet your adoring public?"

Willie sighed. "In for a penny, in for a pound."

Lisa couldn't contain a big grin.

"Why are you grinning like a Cheshire cat?"

"'In for a penny, in for a pound.' You used to say that all the time. I've just missed it, that's all."

Willie harrumphed. "Get used to it. I'm never leaving Elk City again."

As soon as the three women walked into The Diner, Meg, Annabel, and Jace leaped out of their booth, meeting them just inside the door. As Meg and Jace hugged the stuffin' out of Willie, Alice, the waitress, spotted the commotion and uncustomarily dropped an entire tray of food. Shoving everyone out of the way, she stepped over the broken plates and stood before Willie with elbows akimbo and fists digging into her apron pockets.

"It's about damned time," Alice said approvingly before giving Willie a soft wink and shooing the party back to their booth.

"Alice is usually unflappable," Jace said as he watched Alice efficiently send the order back to be duplicated and cleared up her mess. "Didn't see that one coming."

***

DINNER WAS A CHATTY, loving cacophony of sounds. Lillian watched her Gramma soak in the presence of her dear friend Annabel and three of her four granddaughters. Willie's eyes darted from one face to the next, lingering on Meg's and Jace's first with calculation and then with happiness. It seemed that her grandmother had weighed the relationship and was happy with what she saw.

The scent of sun-dried laundry and Charlie perfume permeated the air around Lisa's head. She cut her eyes toward the scent of laundry and was pleased to see her grandmother Eloise. Lisa closed her eyes before turning toward the scent of Charlie. Would she find Aunt Ethel or Felicity?

She looked.

Whew. Aunt Ethel. Good. She wasn't sure the protocol of introducing one ghost to another. She relaxed and smiled.

"Don't get comfy quite yet," Grams said in her ear. "We need you and Lillian at the Golden Bear as soon as you can get there. There's a small problem."

Great-Aunt Ethel added in the other ear, "Do hurry!" before both ghosts disappeared.

Lisa shot a desperate look at Meg and Lillian. Meg turned immediately to her grandmother and took her hand. "Oh, Gramma Willie, please come and stay with me tonight. The twins got to have you all to themselves for the last two days. I've missed you so much. Please . . ."

Willie smiled at her granddaughter. "Well, I assumed I'd stay at Lillian and Lisa's house tonight, since my few things are already in their truck. But wherever is fine with me—after all, it's not like I can go home." She gave a wistful laugh.

Annabel, who had been unusually quiet for the last few minutes, perked up. "Willie, I agree you should stay with Meg tonight. That way you can get caught up to all the wedding plans. And tomorrow I'll bring breakfast from Diggers, and we can catch up some more. Lisa and Lillian will join us . . . right, girls?"

Lisa pretended to look sad. Lillian gave a fake sigh. "I suppose it's only fair to share you, Gramma. Meg will take good care of you, and we'll see you all for breakfast. And then we can work on a plan to get Gramma's house back."

While Jace kindly paid the check, the women headed to the parking lot to transfer Willie's few belongings from the black Colorado to Jace's truck. Then they spent several minutes hugging and saying good-bye.

As soon as Jace's truck drove off, Lillian looked at her twin. "Small problem, huh?"

"Do they even come in that size?"

"I guess we're about to find out."

Chapter Twenty

The girls sat in dimming light of midsummer with the small truck idling for a few minutes, staring at the menacing hulk of the haunted house. It still took courage just to step onto the eerie property.

"I wish I were as brave as Meg," Lillian said, eyeing the raggedy house. "Who owns this place anyway? How come no one cleans it up?"

"I don't know . . ." Lisa thrust open the driver-side door and hopped out. "Unfortunately, we don't have the luxury to figure that out right now. Are you coming?"

Making their way across the weed-choked lot, the twins approached the creaky front porch. The door swung open with a grating noise without either of them raising a hand to the splintery wood. At least the door wasn't groaning as loudly as it used to.

Stepping inside, they were greeted by the short gnome of a mountain man and his donkey.

William doffed his moth-eaten animal-skin cap and bowed slightly from the waist. He flashed a toothless grin while his companion, Julius, offered a toothy donkey grin and heehawed "Howwwdeee" while dipping a front-leg welcome.

Lillian shivered while Lisa fought an infinitesimal urge to try to scratch the ghostly donkey behind its ear.

"Watch yer step ladies. Thay're waitin' on ya up in the parlor," William said, adding, "Whooowee, they don' know what to do with that gal."

With that scratchy warning the mountain pair faded out of the entryway.

The girls wended their way up the groaning, creaking steps. The dust and cobwebs weren't as evident as they once were, as if a ghost or two were attempting to make the old haunt a little more welcoming. Skipping the bad treads with holes and loose boards, they made their way to the top where they were met by their late grandmother. "Hurry up, you two, that young lady is mad as a hatter and won't let any of us near her."

"What young lady, Grams?" Lillian was confused. "Did a living person stumble in here by mistake?"

"This girl is definitely not a living person, and she swears she knows you two. Just hurry."

Grams floated forward to the parlor with a nervous shimmer. The twins followed.

Everyone in the parlor seemed to be in an uproar. As painful howls filled the room, Doc Lindsey could be seen scowling toward a dark closet while Jack paced back and forth with his hands on his hips.

Aunt Ethel materialized in the middle of the room, threw both hands in the air, and blurted, "Thank God you're here. Do something with her!"

"With who?" Lillian asked. She hoped it wasn't who she thought it was.

"With that disco queen howling and crying in the closet," Jack shouted over the mournful noise.

"Why is she crying?" Lillian asked.

Jack rolled her eyes. "It appears she is afraid of *ghosts*."

Lisa shook off her surprise and stomped over to the closet. "Felicity, what is the matter with you?"

A sparkling silver streak flew out of the closet and wrapped Lisa in a tight hug. Lisa, almost knocked off her feet, flailed and stumbled backward at the force of the sudden chill that had enveloped her. She tried to pry the ghostly arms of the frightened apparition from around her neck without any luck, as her hands slid right through the cold.

"Oh, just knock it off, will ya?" Lisa cut to the chase. "You've been dead since 1979. Nobody here is going to hurt you."

The frightened Felicity cried, "You don't know! You just don't know!"

"Let go of Lisa. We can sit over here on the settee, and you can explain it to us." Lillian spoke in a soothing voice, and it worked. The silver cloud of the terrified late disco queen fell away from Lisa and coalesced into the tube-topped, platform-shoed specter they had come to know and . . . tolerate.

Felicity shimmered over the settee as Lisa followed, rubbing her arms and shivering with every step.

Lillian perched on the edge of one of the wingback chairs. "Felicity, I want to introduce you to our grandmother, Eloise. She's only been deceased since June. She's a very nice grandma."

As Eloise floated closer, Felicity whimpered and shrunk back. Eloise stopped and seemed to squat down in front of her. "Felicity, I won't hurt you."

"I-I don't want to be here. I just got popped in here when I thought about the girls."

"Of course you did. It's because the girls have been here and I'm their gramma. I'm learning many things on this side, and one of them is that this is a place that people like us are drawn to. It's really okay."

Felicity's gaze swung from Lisa to Lillian and back to Lisa. "You're not afraid of these"—her hand swung around to indicate the assembled spirits—"these ghosts?"

"Not really," Lisa said.

"They can turn real mean, you know," Felicity insisted.

"Well, so far we haven't seen any of that."

"But what about . . ."

"That's enough, young lady." Madam Bridget Dougherty floated gracefully into the room. "Not one more word."

Felicity ducked her head, letting her feathered hair drift forward.

The madam drifted to her usual chair and floated slightly above the seat. "Let's try the introductions again, shall we?" Bridget's smooth, cultured tones helped everyone relax.

One by one the others hovered closer. Jack, Doc Lindsey, Ethel, Eloise, even William and Julius introduced themselves and explained how long they'd been in this state of being.

Felicity listened, then in a trembling voice said, "But what about—"

Again Bridget cut her off swiftly but kindly. "There is nothing to worry about."

As Lisa and Lillian exchanged glances, the madam intervened and said, "There are so many things that we aren't allowed to share with the living. I hope you understand."

Felicity pointed at Eloise. "She's really your gramma?"

"She is our mom's mother"—Lillian smiled—"and Grandma Willie is our father's. Didn't you ever have contact with ghosts in the state hospital?"

"They were too scary. I stuck with the residents. Some of them could see me."

"Did you help the residents?" Eloise asked.

Felicity shook her head no and looked sad.

"Then how did you spend your time there?"

"Sometimes I moved wheelchair-bound patients out of direct sunlight if they seemed too hot, or I found things that were lost and put them back where they belonged at night."

"You *did* help people then," Eloise said.

Felicity shrugged a dispirited shoulder.

"Felicity," Lillian said, "if it weren't for you, we would never have found Gramma Willie. You certainly helped us!"

Felicity relaxed into a smile.

Before long, she seemed to feel comfortable with the group, perhaps a little too comfortable.

"My favorite dance song made the top ten just before I died," she said. "'Staying Alive' was the best song to dance to. Does anyone know it? Come on, Doc! I'll teach it to you!"

As she held her hands out to the old doctor, he said gruffly, "Stop attempting to involve me in your bedlam."

Aunt Ethel, fortunately, had no problem with bedlam. Twirling toward Felicity, she began to do the hustle while singing "Staying Alive" a little off-key.

Lisa wanted to groan and throw herself out a window.

As the hours passed, Felicity continued to chatter—and dance. Apparently, Aunt Ethel loved disco dancing and had found a new best friend. The girls wondered if Annabel would make the duo a trio of besties, one living and two from beyond the grave.

Near midnight, Lisa stood and stretched. "I don't mean to be rude, but I'm exhausted and I need to get home and get some shut-eye."

The madam seemed relieved. In fact, all of the ghosts seemed ready to call it a night. Everyone was a looking a little more frail and transparent, as they needed to rest and recharge after the long evening.

"It was so good to see you girls," the madam said fondly. "Tonight we were focused on our guest, but I want you to come back as soon as you can and fill us in on finding your other grandmother. Pleasant dreams, my dears."

"Wait up and I'll catch a ride with you so I'll know where you are." Felicity floated toward the twins.

"Felicity, stay with us here tonight," Eloise said. "The girls need to get some rest."

"And I want to spend some more time with you," Ethel added. "Maybe learn another dance. I can show you later where they are staying."

Felicity looked torn.

"Really, my dear girl," Doc Lindsey added. "Stay here and we can help you get the knack of being a spirit. I can't believe there weren't any ambassadors when you passed."

"I hid from them, if that's what they were."

A collective "aah" rose from each person and wraith in the room.

"Well," Aunt Ethel said warmly, "that settles it. It's a good thing you found us."

Chapter Twenty-One

The next morning, Lillian pulled the Colorado in front of Meg's house and parked behind Annabel's 1979 purple Gremlin and Jace's pickup truck.

As they approached the house, Meg opened the front door. "Hurry up," she said, grinning. "We're starving." Catching the warm scent of The Diner's famous cinnamon rolls, the twins picked up their pace and followed their sister into the house.

Laughter and chatter filled the kitchen. Annabel was serving up plates of cinnamon rolls to Jace and Willie at the table, while Grams, Great-Aunt Ethel, and Felicity added their own spirited energy to the mix. The small space would have felt crowded if half of the guests weren't of the ethereal sort.

"Morning! Grab a chair," Jace said, rubbing his hands together. "The Diner only makes these rolls on Sundays—but Annabel has connections, and they'll make her a batch whenever she wants one!"

"Lucky us!" Lillian said gleefully, claiming a chair and scooting close to the table.

"If you had more pull"—Eloise winked at Annabel—"you could get The Diner to bake pastries that ghosts could eat!"

Ethel quipped, "You could at least have gone to the ghost-ery store and bought us some boo-berries."

Everyone laughed except for Willie, who was getting ready to dive in to her roll, oblivious to the ethereal chatter around her.

Lisa was still chuckling when she heard a reticent knock on the door.

She popped up from her chair. "I'll get it."

Jace checked his watch and stood up quickly. "Um, Lisa, um, let me."

But Lisa was already at the door. She swung it open and froze.

Ian looked just as startled.

Lisa's first instinct was to slam the door in his face. Her second instinct was to run. She did neither. Meg and Lillian were suddenly on either side of her.

"Listen to what he has to say," Meg whispered.

Lillian shot a warning look at Meg, who pretended not to notice.

Ian's eyes darted from face to face. He audibly swallowed and said, "Hey everyone. Just, um, looking for Jace."

Jace eased past the sisters, yanked his hat off the hall tree, and leaned down to buss a quick kiss over Meg's lips. "I was enjoying the company so much I forgot there were cattle to be moved. Come on, Ian, 'daylights burnin'.'" The two men were gone in a flash.

"Would someone tell me what just happened?" Grandma Willie whispered.

Lisa had her eyes narrowed down to mean little slits. "Why. Is. He. Still. Here?"

Lillian and Meg turned around to face not only Grandma Willie and Annabel but Grams, Aunt Ethel, and Felicity.

Meg took the lead. "Well, you see, it's like this—"

"No, it's like *this*." Lisa had fire in eyes. "That man is a snake. He's a liar and a cheat." Stomping into the kitchen, she collapsed into a chair, buried her face in her hands, and started sobbing like she was never going to stop.

Grandma Willie went to her granddaughter and wrapped her arms around her.

Meg stood behind Lisa and began giving her a light massage. She kept her thoughts to herself until she felt some of the tension leave Lisa's back. She waited for her sister to take a few deep breaths before she spoke.

"Lisa, you need to hear what Ian has to say. It's not what you think."

"Stop! Just stop it." Lisa blew her nose into a tissue that seemed to appear out of nowhere. "You keep saying that. I met his wife!"

Lillian, curious what Meg knew, caught her sister's eye. "Meg, let's you and I go into the other room and talk."

"No you won't!" Lisa was getting angrier by the second. "If you have something to say about me, you can say it plainly in front of . . . of *everyone*."

"Fine!" Meg was firing up as well. "You need to hear what Ian has to say! It's not what you think!"

"You've already said that!" Lisa's chair screeched on the floor as she stood up and glowered at Meg. "Try a different verse to that song, baby sister, 'cause that one is getting old!"

The spectral forces were about to intercede when Grandma Willie interrupted. "Okay, you two, that's enough. I don't know the score, but I think Lisa and I are going for a walk. Come on, kid, let's burn off some of those cinnamony calories we just consumed and let the temperature around here cool off some."

Grateful for the escape, Lisa headed for the front door with Grandma Willie close on her heels.

"We'll be back in a while," Willie said over her shoulder, then closed the front door behind them.

Felicity started to speak when Grams' ghostly hand shot up. "We don't know enough about this issue to make any statements yet."

Annabel asked, "What can you tell us, Meg?"

"Um, you guys, it's not my story to tell. I know what Ian's story is. He told me and Jace what happened, and we both believe him. I think if Lisa can hear it from him, the sadness and hurt will just . . . go away."

Eloise studied her youngest granddaughter for a few moments.

"Meg, I think you're right. Now, let's see if your Gramma Willie can bring Lisa around to your way of thinking."

"I don't know if anyone can." Lillian sighed. "I've been begging her to talk to him and get the whole story since the day the blowup happened."

No one wanted to leave until Willie and Lisa returned. The hour they spent waiting for Grandma Willie and Lisa to return was entertaining. Felicity showed them all the "latest" dance moves from 1979. Eloise suddenly perked up. "Wait a sec, I think Lisa and Willie are almost here."

Willie and Lisa were laughing and talking as they came in the front door. The storm seemed to have calmed, and Lisa's blue-green eyes danced at some quiet, silly quip from her grandmother.

No one knew what to say, and an uncomfortable silence blanketed the house.

Eloise floated to Lisa and spoke in her ear. "Break the tension, my darling. Everything will work out fine."

Lisa cleared her throat. "I'm all better, so stop standing around like statues."

Everyone in the room—even the ghosts—breathed sighs of relief.

"Well, girls," Annabel said matter-of-factly, "I'd love to stay and chat all morning, but I should open Soft Comforts reasonably on time today, and I still have dishes to clean up."

The girls jumped into action, helping Annabel clear the table and put the leftover rolls in a Tupperware container.

Once the dishwasher was quietly whooshing away in the kitchen, everyone settled in the living room. Annabel plopped on the couch.

"Don't you have to open the yarn store?" Lillian asked.

Annabel gifted her with a bright smile. "I've changed my mind. Hordes of angry knitters will just have to wait until noon."

"I'm so glad!" Lillian patted Annabel's hand as Meg let out a small cheer.

"So, what's next in the quest to get Willie's identity re-established?" Annabel asked.

"Well," Willie said thoughtfully, "I'd like to figure out how to get my car back."

"But you don't have a driver's license," Lillian pointed out, "and you can't get that until we re-establish your identity."

Willie wrinkled her nose. "*Humph.* I forgot about that."

"We should start by calling Great-Aunt Esther and getting into the house," Lisa said, staring at the ceiling with her head resting on the back of the couch. "Lill, you call her. You're the best at cajoling things out of her."

"Yes, you should do it." Meg giggled. "Aunt Esther still looks at me like I have an extra head or something." Eloise gave a quick pass over Meg's cheek. If Grams had still been among the living, it would have been a quick grandmotherly kiss. Now it felt like a gentle breeze.

"Fine, I'll see what I can do." Lillian pulled her phone out of her hip pocket and began dialing as she left the living room. Ethel followed her.

Annabel watched the ghostly interaction before turning back to the living. "The next question is how do we extricate the sheriff who's taken possession of your house. I know he's your nephew, Willie, but, well . . . truth be told, he's a jackass."

"No argument here." Meg laughed. "In fact, I doubt you'd get an argument from anyone in town."

"He's a well-groomed slime ball," Annabel agreed. "I don't know how he's gotten re-elected so many times. I sometimes wonder . . ."

"Wonder what?" Meg asked.

"I'm sure it's nothing—just thoughts I have in my head."

Lillian returned to the living room. "Well, it seems our sheriff is leaving on a 'much-needed vacation' to Alaska. Aunt Esther said she'll try to get the new keys from him before he goes, so Gramma can get some of her things from the house while he's gone."

"Why does Clint need a new key?" Gramma Willie asked.

Lillian and Lisa grew warm in the face.

"What did you two do?" Willie asked sternly.

Lisa and Lillian looked at each other. Lillian spoke first. "Well, Gramma, we sort of liberated a few of your things from the house without permission, and while we were there we had to mess with some of Clint's security stuff—"

"Basically, he knows someone broke in—even if he doesn't know who or why." Lisa got to the point. "And that's why he's changed the locks."

"You girls broke in?"

"Yes, ma'am, we did. But we wouldn't have found you if we hadn't."

"Oh dear . . . and did you say security?"

Both girls nodded their heads.

Meg jumped in. "Jace says it's rigged so Clint can monitor the house from his phone and send deputies out if anything's amiss."

"How strange. We never even locked the doors when"—Willie fought back the tears—"when Frank and I lived there. Sounds like Clint didn't think I would ever come back. I wonder why he would think such a horrible thing . . ."

Eloise glided to Meg's side. "Chickie, keep her focused. She'll never get her house back if we can't prove her identity, and our best chance of that is getting back into that house."

Meg nodded. "Lill, did Aunt Esther say when she is going to get in touch with him?"

"She said she would call him as soon as we hung up."

Lillian's back pocket started playing the theme to *Bewitched*.

Meg startled. "When did you get that ringtone?"

Lillian held up a finger as she dug her cell out of her hip pocket. "Hello?" She walked away from the others while plugging her right ear with a finger.

"I guess we better pipe down," Lisa said.

Lillian thumbed off the call and turned around. "According to Aunt Esther, Clint has already left town with the keys, so we can't get into the house. She says there should be something in the boxes we already have to help prove Gramma Willie's identity, and she'll meet us at the condo at one o'clock to help us look through everything again."

"She's coming over to help?" Lisa raised an eyebrow.

"She mumbled something about *somebody* needing to oversee this *debacle*."

"Can she come at two instead?" Felicity frowned. "I'm due at the Golden Bear at one for some ghost lessons with Ethel."

When no one answered her, Felicity looked miffed.

Grandma Willie, who had been silent for a while, said, "I don't know what we'll find, but going through those old picture albums will be, well, kinda nice."

Annabel stood up abruptly. "That sounds like a good idea until you can get into the house. I really should open the store." She gathered her Mary Poppins purse and hugged Willie on her way toward the front door. "It'll all work out, I'm sure."

Chapter Twenty-Two

illian, Lisa, Meg, and Grandma Willie had been at the condo for fifteen minutes before the doorbell chimed, sending shivers down their backs.

"That woman was always particularly punctual," Gramma whispered as Lillian opened the front door.

The blustery Esther swept in and took charge. "Lisa, get the boxes open and in order on the floor next to the breakfast bar. Willie and Lillian, get the first box emptied on the kitchen table."

Everyone jumped to Esther's orders. It seemed best that way. Soon the four women were pouring over photo albums and garden journals—many of which Lisa and Lillian had scoured before— looking for any new clues that might help establish Grandma Willie's identity. One silent specter hovered close to Esther. The twins silently acknowledged her presence and continued with their assigned tasks.

Esther wasn't as rounded as her sister Ethel, nor as streamlined as her sister Eloise. She always believed that, between the three girls, she'd gotten the best shape. Then again, she tended to believe that everything about her was the best. After all, she was the oldest sister and had the most experience, wisdom, and common sense.

Esther finished the journal she was going through. She got up and retrieved a photo album this time. Once she was reseated, she plucked her purse off the floor and fumbled in its interior before plopping a large wad of tissues in her lap. She sniffed delicately and muttered something about allergies before lifting the cover of the photo album in front of her.

Lisa noticed that Gramma Willie kept glancing at Esther and wondered why.

Half an hour later, Esther announced, "I think we have our proof."

Willie looked shocked. Lillian squealed. Lisa hopped up and ran around the table to see for herself. As soon as she did, a slow smile slid across her lips. She reached down and hugged her stiff great-aunt.

"Gramma Willie! Come see! She found your passport!"

Joyous bedlam ensued.

Esther placed the passport in Willie's hands with a little squeeze. "Now," she said matter-of-factly, "you have what you need, and I need to go." With those words, she gathered her purse and strode to the front door.

She only paused when Willie spoke up in her sweet tones. "Thank you, Esther, thank you so much."

Esther responded with a decisive nod and left.

"You need to call David right now," Lisa blurted, handing her cell phone to her grandmother.

Willie, who had been staring at the closed front door, startled. "I imagine I do!" She pulled David's business card out of her pants pocket and looked blankly at the phone. "Um, could someone dial this contraption for me? I'm not sure how it works."

Lisa laughed and took the phone. As soon as David was on the line, she returned it to her grandmother.

"Oh, David, we did it!" Willie blurted. "We found my passport . . . uh, huh . . . yes, yes . . . okay, we will. I'll tell the girls you're on your way. And, David, thank you."

She handed the little phone back to Lisa. "David said that this information should do the trick because it's a government-recognized photo ID. He's on his way as soon as he clears his calendar, and he asked if we could book a room at a good hotel for him tonight."

Lillian's eyes twinkled mischievously.

"Oh, no you don't," Lisa intervened. "*You* might think booking him in a flea-bitten motel would be funny, but he won't, trust me! Let's find out from Meg which is the best hotel in town and book him there."

Willie hugged the little piece of freedom to her chest. She then laughed joyously and brought it close to her lips to feign a little kiss for luck. "It smells like"—she took another little sniff—"like vanilla and cinnamon. Smell for yourself." She held it out.

Lisa plucked it from her grandmother's fingers and held it to her nose. "It smells like a spice cupboard." She handed it to her sister.

Lillian sniffed. "You're right! It smells like cookies."

"I wonder why? I never kept it in the kitchen." Willie put it in her pocket."

Lillian noticed a thoughtful look on her grandmother's face, and a few telltale worry wrinkles between her brows.

———

At 5:15, the doorbell chimed, announcing David's arrival.

"Figures he'd show up in time to eat," Lillian said. A look passed over her face that reminded her grandmother of a thirteen-year-old girl plotting David's doom.

"Lillian, act your age and answer the door," Willie chided gently.

The bell chimed two more times. As Lillian swung the door wide, she said snarkily, "Wake the dead, why don't you."

David ignored her and dropped his attaché on the dining room table. "Well, Willie, we're going to get you established sooner than I thought. We have a few things to go over tonight, and tomorrow we can start at the sheriff's office."

"Nice to see you too, David." Willie's eyes twinkled.

He stopped moving and smiled. "Sorry about that. I get focused and the niceties get lost. Wonderful to see you, Willie. Where would you like to begin?"

"Let's make a little something for dinner and then we can dive in."

"Sounds good to me. How about takeout?"

Willie conceded with a smile. David definitely had a one-track mind.

Meg made a quick run to Diggers; then she and the twins ate at the breakfast bar while David and Willie took over the dining room table, eating their burgers and talking while surrounded by files and papers.

A little after eight, Meg said quietly to her sisters, "They should wrap up. David has to check in at the B and B before eight thirty."

Lillian started to get up, and Lisa waved her back down. "Oh no, sister of mine, you're spoiling for a fight and now isn't the time."

Lisa turned around. "Hey, Gramma, David, it's eight and David's supposed to check in by eight thirty. After that, the doors are locked."

David looked at his watch. "Thanks Lisa. I think we've got everything we need for tomorrow." He gave Willie a gentle smile. "It's going to be fine. You know that, don't you?"

Willie smiled back. "David, I don't know where we would be if you hadn't jumped in to help."

David put everything neatly into his attaché, stood up, and plucked his suit coat off the back of his chair. By the time he got to the front door, Lillian was holding it open. "You know, if it had been up to me, I wouldn't have reminded you of the time—and then you could have spent the night in your car."

"You know, sometimes your eyes really light up," he said sweetly before adding, "you know, like a demon's."

He grinned as he strode down the front steps toward his car. Lillian slammed the door shut behind him, which only made his grin bigger.

A gentle breeze floated by Lillian's cheek as she stood with her back pressed to the door.

"Sweet Lilly," Eloise said.

Lillian couldn't respond—at least not without Gramma Willie hearing her and wondering who she was talking to. Not that she would know what to say anyway. Why was she always sticking her foot in her mouth around David?

When Lillian rejoined Willie and Lisa in the family room, Willie said, "By the way, David is still working on a few loose ends where you two are concerned."

"Loose ends?" the twins responded in unison.

"Yes, loose ends. It seems there is still a bit of consternation concerning my rather unceremonious exit from the state hospital. As you can imagine, mental institutions frown on that sort of thing."

"Are we in serious trouble?" Lillian asked nervously.

"Is jail time involved?" Lisa asked.

Willie stood between her beautiful granddaughters with an arm around each one. "David's trying to sooth a few ruffled feathers. If he succeeds, I won't have to bake any cakes with files in them for either of you."

Chapter Twenty-Three

*L*illian got up before sunrise and padded barefoot out to the back patio of the condo. She was surprised to find her ethereal grandmother waiting for her. They sat in companionable silence for a moment. Eloise gave her time to drink in the clear, sweet air of their Colorado high mountain valley before she asked, "Do you want to talk about it?"

"Talk about what?"

"David."

Lillian hung her head. Her grandmothers knew her so well.

"Gramma, what is wrong with me. I'm the mature, stable twin, right? So why do I always turn into an awkward teenager when he shows up? I become very childish, and I can't seem to help it."

Eloise looked at her for a few more beats before a gentle grin played across her ghostly face. "Sweetie, I'm glad you see it. But don't beat yourself up. Love makes us do silly things."

Lillian opened her mouth to object, but Eloise kept talking.

"Did I ever tell you I used to want to kick your granddaddy in the teeth?"

Lillian felt a shock down to her toes and it must've showed. She had always known her grandparents as the best of friends and very close.

Eloise gave a rattling rendition of her once-heartwarming laugh. Lillian shivered. Some things certainly took getting used to.

"Back in high school, your granddad was considered quite the catch and he knew it. Every time I saw Mike, he had his arm draped around a different girl and she'd be gazing up at him like he'd hung the moon. Whenever he said hi to me, I'd ignore him and stick my nose in the air, which made him laugh—and made me feel like smacking him upside the head. This went on for a few months and his antics got worse. He'd wait till I looked in his direction and give me a big old wink and grin as if that was going to make me like him. I'd be at a dance with my friends, and when it was over, there he'd be kissing some girl and leaning on the car we'd come in. Lord, he was a pill."

"How did you two end up together then?"

"You know the Elk City Fourth of July picnic?"

Lillian's long red-gold hair shimmied as she shook her head yes.

"Well, used to be, there was an annual lunch box raffle to raise money for Thanksgiving and Christmas meals for the poor. Boys and men would bid to eat lunch with whoever made that box. That morning, Momma helped Ethel, Esther, and me prepare three identical lunches. Two ham sandwiches, home-canned pickles, and two slices of homemade apple pie went into each box. Esther had her heart set on eating lunch with Frank's brother, Big John, and wanted to decorate her box differently so he'd know which one was hers, but Momma said no. She told us the purpose of the auction was to raise money for the poor, *not* to catch a husband."

Eloise wiggled her eyebrows at her granddaughter and they both laughed.

"Go on," Lillian prompted.

"At eleven thirty, the word goes out that the auction is about to begin. Esther had indeed made her box a little different by letting a napkin corner poke out from under the lid, and she beat feet to get a spot close enough to the stage so she could try to signal to Big John which box was hers. A few minutes into the auction a ripple went through the crowd. Ethel, most of our friends, and I stopped our giggling conversation and turned, trying to figure out what was going on. Well, Charlotte jumped up to investigate. A few minutes later she hurried back to us, her eyes open wide. She ran up to me and said, 'It's your box.'"

"What happened to your box?" Lillian asked.

"Let me get to that part of the story," Eloise clucked. "All around, people turned to stare at me. I figured the worst had happened, that someone awful, like an escaped prisoner or something, had bought my box."

"Well, Gramma, what *did* happen to your box?" Lillian shifted in her chair.

Again, the eerie chuckle.

"Well, it turned out that your grandpa was making a spectacle of himself, and at the time I felt like it was at my expense. You see, those lunch boxes usually brought in around three dollars, and a 'special' box fetched around five to six dollars. My box was being bid at eighteen dollars, *and* your grandpa was collecting money from all his friends to pay for it. He had been in a bidding war with Big John, and he won and now he had to pay up."

"He knew it was your box?"

Grams nodded. "He'd figured it out somehow."

"But why did Big John bid it up?"

"Because he hated Mike. He lost by a quarter, by the way."

"Ewww, you almost had to eat lunch with Big John. That sure would have made Aunt Esther angry."

"Well, Big John told Esther he thought the box was hers. Calmed her right down when he paid four bucks for her lunch box and donated another fourteen dollars to the charity."

"What happened with your lunch and Gramps?"

"I reluctantly sat down for the picnic lunch . . . surrounded by my friends. While I was stuffing my sandwich down as fast as I could, he kept a leisurely pace and an audacious crooked smile on his face. He'd ask me questions and I'd grunt and he would chuckle."

Lillian laughed. "Sounds so romantic."

"Then suddenly, he jumped up and ran as fast as he could toward the swimming hole in the middle of the park. None of us knew why at first. He just kept running and then jumped into the one place in the swimming hole everyone avoided because it was a place so deep that several kids had drowned in it over the years."

"Obviously he survived the plunge, but why'd he do it?"

Eloise's eyes had a faraway look. She gave a little shake of her head and went on with her tale. "He surfaced after what seemed like a very long time, but he wasn't alone. He had a little boy under his right arm, and he didn't waste a second getting back to dry land. He plopped that kid on the ground and began pumping his arms and pushing on his midsection until the kid spewed water and started coughing. By then the sheriff had located his parents and they were standing next to him clinging to each other in abject terror as your grandpa saved their little boy's life. After the drama was over, Mike swaggered up to our picnic blanket, picked up his hat, gave me that silly grin and said, 'I think our picnic is going to have to wait.' I watched him squish away with soaked clothes and boots that would never survive the dunking."

"So that's when you stopped wanting to kick him in the teeth," Lillian teased.

"Maybe I never really wanted to kick him in the teeth. Sometimes, when we are young, we don't know how to recognize our true feelings. When we're older, it's as plain as the nose on our face. Or should be. Unless we get stuck and stubborn and refuse to see the truth. So, yes, sweetie, that was the moment I knew I was in love. And I think you are too.

Lillian sputtered. "I. Am. Not. In. Love. With. David." She jumped up from her seat, feet slapping against the patio, and ran into the condo.

Gramma Willie was eating breakfast at the table. "Lilly?"

But Lillian didn't stop. She didn't want to talk to anyone right now, especially another gramma who probably had wrong ideas too.

Chapter Twenty-Four

he phone rang three times. Someone answered, groggy and perturbed. "Who the hell is waking me up at this hour?"

"It's me, your honor," snarled the angry man. "We've got more problems and we better act before it gets worse."

"Act? We're done acting." The man with the smoker's voice let out a long sigh. "What we did twenty years ago isn't nearly as bad as what's going on now. That jackass has had us by the shorthairs for too long. This has to stop. I'm thinking about turning myself in."

"Like hell you are!" The nervous man exploded. "You may not care about your cushy career, but I've got too much to lose. You hear me? I've already put a plan into play, and everything will be taken care of by the end of the day."

"What are you talking about?"

"Never mind. The less you know the better. And as for the jackass who got us into this mess, I'm going to deal with him too."

LILLIAN PEERED out the second-story bedroom window as Lisa and Gramma Willie climbed into David's car.

Jace needed to see Willie at the sheriff's office, and Lillian had convinced Lisa and David to take Gramma and go without her. There were protests, of course, but Lillian needed time to think, and she needed time to herself. The trio relented when she insinuated that she had cramps, although David looked doubtful as he walked out the door. The band of ghosts had also chosen to leave her in solitary peace to sort through her tangled emotional state.

On the way to the sheriff's office, Lisa settled into the luxurious leather backseat of David's red Lexus. In the front seat Gramma Willie was chattering. Listening to the nonstop nervous talking, Lisa's eyebrows knit together. Grandma Willie had, in fact, been chattering since they found her. She had once been so calm and collected. Is this who she'd become in the last ten years? What happened to her? This nervousness wasn't in character for Willie, at least not how Lisa remembered her.

As they pulled into the parking lot of the sheriff's office, Lisa set aside her thoughts for another time. She would take them out and examine them after they got Gramma's identity straightened out.

In the parking lot Willie was greeted by a large contingent of deputies. Some of them had been friends with her late son and had spent many nights camping in Willie and Frank's backyard. Other deputies knew Willie from the times she had volunteered in her granddaughters' classrooms. There were many hugs as well as introductions to the officers who had not met her.

After fifteen minutes David interjected. "We'll have a barbeque in the next couple of weeks so you all can catch up. Right now we need to find Deputy Taggerty so we can help Willie get established as herself." He put his hand on Willie's elbow and guided her gently through the well-wishers and into the building.

Inside the office, Jace was leaning against the booking counter. "Good morning, Willie, Jace said with a wink. "Sorry we have to start with your fingerprints in this area, but it's expedient. I'll need to take a scan of your fingers plus your right thumb. Don't worry, I'll help." He reached out and took her right hand and began the process of scanning her prints.

"I've done this before . . . at that . . . place."

He finished getting her prints uploaded. "At least we don't have to ink you up to do it nowadays."

Jace led Willie and Lisa toward two chairs facing a desk in the middle of a room full of desks. When the women were seated, Jace sat on the other side of the desk in front of a computer, with David standing behind him.

The relaxed posture of both men made Willie sigh and lean back in her chair. Maybe everything was going to be okay after all.

The mouse clicked and moved smoothly under Jace's hand as he brought up the information downloading with Willie's prints. Then he rotated the monitor toward the two women. "Willie," he said gently, "I want you to know what we're dealing with."

Lisa looked confused. Willie looked confused, then embarrassed.

There was a rap sheet on the screen for a Millicent Garron. According to the description, fifty-five-year-old Millicent was five feet tall, 140 pounds, with short red hair and green eyes.

"I don't understand." Lisa looked at Jace and then David. "Who is this Millicent, and what does she have to do with Gramma?"

David cleared his throat. "This is the name and identity attached to Willie's fingerprints and social security number. This is who the hospital claims she is."

"But . . . but . . . ," Lisa sputtered. "It's not even her description! This woman is twenty years younger than my grandmother!"

"And she's fatter," Willie huffed. "Except when I was pregnant, I've never weighed more than a hundred pounds."

"Oh my gawd!" Lisa exclaimed, reading the screen again. "*And* she was arrested for stalking, assault, attempted murder, and kidnapping!" She turned to Willie. "Did you know anything about this?"

Willie's eyes filled with tears. "I know they called me Millie. They didn't listen when I said that wasn't my name at all. They just patted me and gave me more pills. Like I was a child. Like I was . . . crazy."

"Gramma, why didn't you tell us?"

Willie shrugged. "I don't know. When everyone around you believes you're crazy, you start to believe it a little bit too. I didn't know I had a rap sheet, though."

Lisa looked horrified. "Gramma, you don't have a rap sheet. This isn't you. You do know that, don't you?"

Willie patted her granddaughter's hand. "Of course I do, sweetheart."

David knelt in front of Willie and touched her on the shoulder. "We know what we're dealing with and there's an FBI cyber specialist flying into Gunnison as we speak. We'll figure out how this happened. We'll get this all straightened out."

Willie looked into his earnest face and nodded.

Lisa took her grandmother's hand in hers. "Gramma, let's go back to the condo and let the FBI specialist work their magic."

"We *will* get this right," David promised again. "Now, let's get you two home and I'll head to Gunnison and pick Veronica up from the airport. When are you backcountry people going to get an airport here?"

Jace chuckled. "When we can move mountains out of the way, I suppose."

LILLIAN WAS surprised at the early return of her sister and grandmother. She had been thinking about a lot of things over the last hour.

"That didn't take long," she said as she looked up from the book she was holding.

"Well, we got a nasty surprise when they ran my fingerprints." Willie kept moving until she was ensconced in the recliner next to the couch.

"What do you mean?"

Lisa leaned against the door frame. "Here, feast your eyes on this." She held out the copies of Millicent Garron's rap sheet. "This is the identity of the woman they admitted to the mental ward. This is who they think Gramma is."

Lillian scanned the papers. Her eyes felt like they were popping out of her head by the time she got to the end. "You're not kidding about a nasty surprise! Where's David?"

"That dear boy is on his way to pick up a computer specialist from the FBI at the airport. Someone in cyber crimes or something to figure out how this mess got started."

"How'd he get an FBI specialist to come here?" Lillian asked.

"Sounds like somebody owned somebody a favor," Lisa explained.

"I don't think I want to know about favors," Lillian replied.

"Anyway, we've got the rest of the day," Lisa said. "What do you two want to do?"

Grandma Willie sighed. "I think I just want to sit here. You two can do whatever you want to do."

LISA DROPPED her sister off downtown to get stamps and pick up a package waiting for her at the post office. The plan was for Lisa to pick up a few things at the supermarket and meet Lillian later at Annabel's Soft Comforts yarn store.

The usual hustle and bustle of a small-town grocery store hummed around Lisa as she pushed her cart down the produce aisle. What should have taken fifteen minutes to grab a few things ended up taking half an hour as Lisa was approached by people determined to get firsthand news about Willie's return to Elk City. Lisa left the market with a silly smile on her lips at the crazy things she'd heard from the gossips at the store about Gramma's return.

While juggling a grocery bag on her left arm, she fished her keys out of her pocket and unlocked the doors of the truck. She stowed the grocery bags in the backseat, then hopped behind the wheel. She slid the keys into the ignition and buzzed the window down. The fresh mountain air felt good today brushing across her face, and she intended to enjoy every second of it.

The ignition caught, and she dropped the gear lever into reverse as she reached for the seat belt.

Suddenly a swift pressure on the back of her head slammed her face into the steering wheel. She felt a sickening crunch as her nose met the top of the steering wheel. Just as suddenly, the pressure shifted and she felt a hand grab a fistful of her hair and try to repeat the process. A graveled voice snarled, "That'll teach you to screw around in other people's business."

Lisa slammed her foot on the gas pedal as she cranked the wheel around to the right. The little truck shot out of the parking slot, running over her assailant's feet. She didn't care. She heard the voice cussing a blue streak as she shot out of the parking lot.

What had just happened? Her nose was pouring blood down the front of her white tank top. She didn't care. All she knew was that she needed to find her sister. Every instinct in her body told her that she wasn't the only target.

The little pickup shot down side streets and careened around corners as Lisa desperately tried to stem the blood pouring from her nose. She could feel her eyes swelling. She skidded around a corner just in time to see someone with hair the color of her sister's being pulled into the alley behind Soft Comforts.

She slammed her foot on the brake, causing the Colorado to go into a sideways slide that left dark skid marks on the pavement. She righted the slide, and when the truck halted, she slammed it into park and bailed out, running full tilt toward the ally.

Lillian was cradling her left arm and sitting on the warm pavement with her face pressed against the bricks.

Both women could hear Annabel's staccato steps approaching as fast as her short legs could carry her.

"I've called 911 and help is on the way," Annabel blurted, then took one look at Lisa's face and exclaimed, "Oh my God! What happened to you?"

"Did you see the person who hurt Lill?" Lisa said, kneeling at her sister's side.

The dear little woman shook her head. "I heard a scream and tires squealing and called 911 and ran out the door. I had no idea who had been attacked!"

Sirens screamed and tires screeched at the end of the ally opening. Suddenly the girls were surrounded by deputies and EMTs. When Jace arrived, he knelt beside the girls, wincing at their appearance. He asked a few questions as EMTs checked blood pressures and oxygen saturation levels.

"Okay, girls, I want you to go to the hospital with the ambulance crew, and I'll get your statements there."

Lisa shook her head. Through a nasally tone she pleaded, "No, no, no, we can't. The person who did this to me . . . I think I ran over at least one of his feet. He might be there."

Jace keyed his mic. "Bentley, go to the ER and check for any new admits with possible tire tracks on one or more feet and possible broken bones. Let me know ASAP."

The radio squawked. "Roger that."

The EMTs were ready to transport the girls. Jace had them hold up for another few minutes. The lead tech looked like he wanted to argue but held his tongue.

The com on Jace's belt came to life. "There is a guy at the ER with two broken feet. Swears some witch ran him over on purpose. They are admitting him and taking him to surgery in five minutes."

"Thanks, Bentley."

"Do you need anything else here?"

"Yes, quietly tell the staff that we'll be transporting the girls there as soon as they take him to surgery. You stick to him like glue, because he's going to jail as soon as I can manage it."

A moment later Jace's radio crackled to life again. "They're taking him up now and he's had the 'I don't care' drugs. All clear to transport the girls."

That was all the ambulance crew needed to hear. The girls were strapped onto gurneys and rolled into waiting ambulances. Lisa could no longer see through her bruised and battered eyes, and breathing through her nose was impossible, but the bleeding had slowed to a trickle. The right side of Lillian's face looked raw and swollen from being scrubbed against the rough bricks, and her left arm was immobilized with the possible dislocation of her shoulder from having her arm wrenched up and behind her.

"I'll call Meg and meet you there. Annabel, can you go to the condo, pick Willie up, and take her to the hospital?"

Annabel nodded, then turned on her heel and rushed toward the alley entrance of her store. Jace saw that she was muttering to someone.

He hoped she was getting a full description of the guy who attacked Lillian.

Chapter Twenty-Five

Annabel pulled her purple Gremlin into the driveway of the condo. A frantic Felicity popped in front of her as she got out of the little car and hefted her hot pink bag onto her shoulder.

Annabel's swiftly drawn breath sent Felicity into a tizzy. The disco queen waved her hand up and down in front of Annabel's nose. "Oh dear, oh dear, please be one of the ones who can see me. I can't remember who's who."

"Of course I can see you! What's wrong?"

"Willie is huddled down in the kitchen scared out of her mind."

Annabel's short legs moved efficiently as she hurried to the front door. "Fill me in."

"She was in the kitchen and dropped her passport, and when she bent down to get it, a bullet lodged in the side of the fridge. If she hadn't bent over . . . ." Felicity shivered and became even messier.

Annabel fished a wad of keys with key chains out of her purse, selected the right key, unlocked the door, and shoved her way inside. Felicity was flying about the room ahead of her, doubling back every second of every step until the small woman walked around the kitchen peninsula to see her friend cowering in the junction of the cupboards with a cast iron griddle held in front of her like a shield.

Annabel leaned into her friend's space and shouted, "It's okay now." She wondered if she was going to have to slap the quivering woman to bring her to her senses. People did that in movies, you know.

Willie flung the griddle to the side. "Get down here!" she hissed. "There might be more." She grabbed Annabel's arm and yanked her behind the cupboards.

Annabel hugged her friend. "Tell me what's happened."

"I really don't know, except someone shot that into the house." Willie's shaking finger pointed to a rather large hunk of metal embedded in the side of the fridge. "Lord, we've got to call all three of the girls and warn them. Why didn't I think of that sooner? Do you know how to make those fancy phones work?"

Annabel pulled her trusty little flip phone out of the depths of her Mary Poppins bag. She thumbed in 911. "Yes, I need officers at 2011A Deer View Drive. Someone shot into the condo and I don't think it was an accident . . . Yes, this is Annabel Banks. Oh hello! . . . Thanks, we'll stay in place until someone gets here . . . Um no, no injuries, at least not this time. Let them know the door is unlocked." She closed the little phone and tucked it back into her purse before turning to her friend.

"The deputies are on their way. It's going to be okay. They said not to discuss the incident too much but to keep it fresh in our minds. Since I wasn't here, I guess they meant you."

"But . . . but I don't know anything," Willie sniffed.

"I know some stuff," Felicity threw out as she ghost-paced the kitchen. "I tried to follow the bullet's path, and I know some stuff."

Annabel mouthed the word *Later*, and Felicity rolled her eyes.

Sirens approached, tires screeched, and three deputies stormed into the condo. One of them was the acting undersheriff, Jace.

"Don't give me that look Annabel," Jace said, defending himself. "All three of the girls insisted I come here." He knelt in front of Willie, taking the griddle from her clutch and lowering it to the floor. In the meantime, Deputy Max Young walked toward the back window—and right through Felicity. They both shivered.

Felicity suddenly appeared on the ceiling fan, the perfect place to stay out of the way and still watch all the activity. She had been assigned this watch for her first official training assignment, and hoped one of the others would show up soon.

Jace spoke quietly with Willie, jotting notes into his tablet as Deputy Max and another deputy calculated angles and trajectory possibilities to determine the direction the bullet had traveled before lodging into the side of the fridge.

Jace stood with hands on hips, looking from the refrigerator to the windowpane with a single hole in it. "I think we're going to need help. I'll put a call into the CBI. Willie, let's go sit at the dining table. I've got a few more questions and some things to tell you."

At the table, Jace filled Willie in on the attacks on the twins. As soon as he finished, she jumped up from the table, grabbed her purse off the peninsula, and looked over her shoulder at him. "Well, get a move on. I need to be at the hospital."

"I've got to stay here until we get the bureau involvement settled. I'll have one of the other deputies take you to the hospital, and you *will* stay with him until I tell you otherwise. Do you understand me?" He raised his left eyebrow and stared at her until she relented and promised him she would do as she was told.

As soon as Willie had gone, Annabel turned to Jace and quietly asked, "Do you see our extra guest?"

Jace nodded.

Felicity floated down next to Annabel. "He sees me?"

Annabel smiled. "Yes dear, he does. You can talk to him and tell him what you know. When Jace answers you, let's hope that Deputy Max assumes he's talking to me."

Felicity stood a little taller.

"What can you tell me?" Jace asked.

Felicity turned to look at Annabel. "I'm not used to so many people being able to see me."

"Just tell us what you know about this whole situation," Annabel said softly.

"Okay. I tried hard to track the bullet that came through here, but I'm not sure I did it correctly. It's a new thing for me. Anyway, I tried to follow the air disturbance back to the place it started." Felicity twirled her ghostly hair around her finger. "Did you know that when stuff moves, it disturbs the air and leaves a trail for a few secs?"

Jace shook his head no. "When you tried to track it, what happened?"

"I ended up on that little hill, right up there." She pointed out the back window.

Jace and Annabel walked to the window with the bullet hole in it. Felicity floated behind them. "See that hill way over there? That's where I ended up. There was an older guy up there, but he had already packed stuff into the back of his Jeep and was zipping up the cover down."

"Define older," Jace said.

"Kind of like fifties, I think."

"Could you describe him or be able to identify him if you saw him again?"

The ethereal disco doll nodded her head up and down. "He was actually very handsome if you don't think about how old he was. He had really short, almost military, hair, and he was dressed in hunting clothes. In fact, his Jeep was painted to match his clothes."

"An orange Jeep?" Annabel asked.

"No, not that kind of hunting clothes."

"Are you talking about camo?"

"Camo?"

"Camouflage. Splotches of browns and greens that might help a person hide in a forest," Jace explained.

"Yes, it looked just like that. Anyway, he drove down the back side of that hill, and I popped back in here to check on Willie. She's under my watch, you know. Oh, I need to go and keep watch."

She started to shimmer out when Anabel stopped her. "Stay here for a couple of minutes in case there are more questions. I'm pretty sure that Eloise and Ethel are with the girls, and Willie is on her way there too."

Felicity stayed put. Annabel turned to Jace. "What's going on in your head?

He started to shake his head, but the little woman in front of him narrowed her eyes. "I've known you since you were a little bitty kid. Spit it out."

"I'm not going to speculate. As soon as I know what the CBI is going to do, I've got something to check out."

"Don't do anything foolish or alone. I watch all those crime dramas on TV and it never turns out good."

"Don't worry, I'm not foolish—nor am I on a crime drama."

The little round woman scrunched her eyes at him.

"Okay, fine, I promise."

"All right then. See that you're careful. Come on, Felicity, you can ride with me. I could use the company about now."

Chapter Twenty-Six

isa lay still on the narrow gurney in the ER, listening to the humming, blipping, and buzzing. The sounds were familiar, and the IV solution dripping into her veins was warming. She wasn't scared, but she was frustrated at not being able to open her eyes. The nurse had placed ice packs on her eyes to help reduce the swelling, while the ER doc and radiologist looked over the digital X-rays and cat scan.

A nurse told her that an orthopedist was examining Lillian and deciding if her injuries would require surgery to repair.

How much longer would they be?

A warm hand wrapped around her cool fingers.

"Hello?" Lisa turned her head toward the presence. "Who's holding my hand?"

"Hello." The greeting in the husky, honey-slow Georgian accent was accompanied by a tender squeeze on her hand.

Lisa tried to twitch her fingers out of his grasp. He tightened his hold just a little.

"You know, I'm not goin' anywhere and this time you aren't either, and yellin' in here isn't yer style. So I'm goin to tell you some things and then I'll leave you to think it over."

"Ian," she huffed through swollen lips, "this is not a good time."

"I disagree."

The *grrrr* that rumbled in her throat said it all. She wished she could jump off the gurney and leave. But as a captive audience, a growl was the best she could muster. His quiet chuckle would have set her teeth grinding if it hadn't hurt so much.

"I know you think I fell in love with you while cheating on a wife—"

Lisa growled again.

"But nothing could be further from the truth. Years ago I married a young woman, but she was never my wife, and I was never her husband."

Lisa stopped trying to twitch her fingers out of his grasp. "That doesn't even make sense."

"Ah, now I got your attention." Again, that smooth chuckle. "I'll tell you the whole of it if you let me."

Crud, she thought. *It's not like I can throw him out of the room.* She conveniently forgot that she had a call button by her left hand.

He took her silence as permission.

"Lisa, I rushed here as soon as Jace told me what happened. I'm so thankful you're gonna be all right. I wish I could have been there to protect you from that attacker, but the truth is, I couldn't even protect you from a misunderstandin' that brought you great pain. I tried, but I know now that not tellin' you the whole story from the start was the worst thing I could have done. And you've suffered greatly because of it."

Instead of inciting her anger, his voice calmed her. She found herself wanting to hear what he had to say.

"Remember when I told you about my best friend, the one whose family owned a logging company? The one who died with most of his family in a nasty boat accident?"

She mumbled agreement behind the ice packs.

"He had a younger sister who wasn't with 'em that day. Her name is Brina and she was barely seventeen when it happened. Now, their momma was in that accident, and she fought for her life in the hospital for several weeks. But while doctors were trying to save Brina's momma's life, an uncle was trying to get guardianship of Brina. Not because he wanted to make sure his niece was taken care of, but so he could get access to the family business as soon as his sister passed, which she was expected to do. So Brina, her mom, and I spiked his guns. I married Brina, at her mom's deathbed, with the understanding between the three of us that once Brina reached her majority, either one of us could quietly get a divorce."

"How long ago?"

"Eight years now."

"How old is she now?"

"She's twenty-four. *And* before you think anything else, get your mind out of the gutter. We were married in name only. And it worked. Her uncle left Brina—and her family's estate—alone. Then, a couple months ago, Brina met someone special, and I knew she would be all right. And I met someone special too. Special and feisty and beautiful."

Lisa pursed her lips.

"So there was no reason to keep up the charade. I did what I had to do to help my best friend's family. Maybe there were better ways to do it, but it's what her mother and I came up with at the time, and it worked. I have no regrets. I just always figured the woman I would fall in love with for real one day would understand."

"Hmm," was all Lisa said.

<hr>

GREAT-AUNT ETHEL and Grams hovered in the upper corner of the ER cubicle. "Do you think he could see us if we turned up the juice?" Ethel asked her sister.

"No, he isn't sensitive to us. And even if he could see us, I don't know if he would understand the whole spirit deal."

The two shades kept their conversation behind the veil so Lisa wouldn't hear them and react. They watched and listened to his explanation.

"Now, before you ask, *you* are the reason I was ready to finally go through the trouble to get a divorce."

Lisa lay motionless processing what he had just said. "Are you sure it's me?"

"Of course I'm sure. I had an offer to return to Africa. Why do ya think I took the job with Kai?"

Again, Lisa said, "Hmm."

"Well, she isn't telling him off," Ethel said.

"No she isn't. That's something, isn't it? Let's let her know we're here. Then you keep watch over her and I'll go check in with Lillian. She may need her gramma."

Lisa felt the cool brush of her late grandmother's touch on her cheek.

"Lisa, I'm going to check on Lillian, and Aunt Ethel is going to stay here, just in case."

She gave a small nod so that Ian wouldn't notice. She wondered how much her two ghostly relatives had overheard.

Not being able to see anything happening around her made her appreciate the strong, warm hand holding hers—at least for the time being. And knowing that the dearly departed were watching over her —along with the familiar sounds of the hospital—gave her the sense of safety. Lisa drifted off into the stillness of sleep.

SOMETHING TICKLED her mind from the sweet oblivion of sleep. Lisa realized that the hand holding hers wasn't Ian's anymore. It was petite in size but had the surety and conviction of belonging.

"Ah, there you are. Ian was kind enough to relinquish your hand —I am your grandmother after all."

Lisa recognized Grandma Willie's voice immediately. Ah, now *this* was the voice she remembered from childhood. It was no longer the hesitant voice of the nervous woman they had rescued from the state hospital, but the voice of the strong, whimsical woman who made silly snowmen, planted flowers all over her yard, and laughed with her granddaughters over the mundane as much as the marvelous.

Lisa wasn't sure what had brought about this change in her grandmother, but she felt safer for it.

Chapter Twenty-Seven

ithin the hour, Lisa and Lillian had been transferred to a secure space within the hospital, and deputies had been assigned to guard the entrance to their room and the hall.

Their private room was filled beyond capacity. Meg, Jace, Ian, and Grandma Willie—as well as the otherworldly crowd including William and Julius—surrounded the girls' beds.

Lillian, reclining in the hospital bed and drugged on happy juice, kept giggling. People were talking around her, but nothing made much sense and she couldn't care less. Suddenly she burst out laughing.

Then she blurted, "Who would have thought a talking donkey would be standing in a . . . a . . . ha-ha-ha-ha-ha . . . a hospital room!"

The room silenced immediately as everyone turned to stare at her.

She couldn't help it. Even that cracked her up.

Lisa scowled.

Lillian took one look at her sister's black eyes and burst into a fresh round of hoots. "Oh my, Lissy, you look, you look . . . oh my goodness. You look like a raccoon!"

"Oh, shut up," Lisa gritted out.

This only served to push Lillian into louder merriment.

Grandma Willie, who had parked her chair between the girls' beds, jumped into the fray. "Now, girls, hush now. Lisa, darling girl, you know they gave Lillian medication for pain and she's not quite herself. And Lillian, try to calm down, sweetheart. You know Lisa is in pain and isn't on the strong medication that you're on."

Meg watched her grandmother take charge and realized that she seemed more like herself. Jace quietly held Meg's hand. The ghost support group collectively waited to see if there was going to be any fallout from the "donkey" comment. Ian just looked confused.

Willie kept talking to each girl in a soothing voice. Lillian finally stopped giggling, Lisa stopped growling, and Willie smiled into the peace that ensued.

"Now, we need to decide where we're all going to stay when the girls are released."

Jace spoke to the entire ensemble. "I think we can reasonably be assured that the girls will be safe here tonight. Ms. Willie, do you want to stay here? The nurses will be glad to bring another bed in for you. If you would be more comfortable in a real bed, you can go home with Meg, or I can take you out to the ranch to stay with my folks."

"I think the three of us should stay together. I can watch over the twins. Besides, there are deputies here to protect us, and until we know if the bullet in the fridge was an accident or not, I don't want to endanger anyone else."

There was a sudden verbal outburst on the other side of the closed door.

"What do you mean I'm not going in there? You need to step aside. Now!"

Lillian burst into laughter again and stuttered, "It, it's D-D-David. He can't come in here and I-I-I think he's ticked off." Peals of laughter hit her again.

Jace kissed the back of Meg's fingers before he left the room to speak to the deputy on guard as well as the angry attorney.

When Jace returned, David was on his heels. His eyes went immediately to the twin with her arm in a sling. "I wasn't gone three hours and someone shot at Willie? And the girls were assaulted? Is there any idea who is behind these attacks?"

Nobody had ever seen him lose his cool in regard to anything since Grandma Willie had been found. Yet there he stood with hands on his hips and fire in his eyes.

"David, just calm down." Willie spoke in a grandmotherly voice, but her tone was all business. "We're all fine—well, mostly fine— and we are fresh into this predicament and haven't found anything that points to anyone. So, you can join in and help."

"Forgive me. No one gave me any details and I was very concerned—and I hadn't expected to be locked out of the room."

"That's my fault," Jace said. "I forgot to put you on the list of allowed personnel. Things have been happening too fast. We can catch you up now."

Again, Lillian started cracking up. "I haven't seen you this angry since we played cow patty baseball in the p-p-p-pasture."

Hilarity rolled out of her as she lay trying to catch her breath. Meg covered her mouth with both hands to keep the laughter inside. Jace was working hard to maintain a serious demeanor, and poor Ian was more confused than ever.

"Cow patty baseball?" Ian repeated.

Lisa pulled the ice pack lower on her face, but not before Ian caught the twitch of a smile. "Jace or Gramma," she said, "would you tell Ian what is so dang funny?"

Jace grinned. "Well, Ian, one summer all the families had been working together to gather herds, sort them, and then push them into different pastures. After working all day, we kids couldn't wait to fish or play games while we waited for supper. David here was particularly fond of baseball. We got a game going in an empty pasture, and the score was tied until someone hit the ball too far. Like into-the-next-pasture too far. That pasture was for the bulls, and we weren't allowed to go in there unless we were on horseback."

"So . . . the ball was gone?" Ian asked.

"Yep, so Meg says we can still get in some batting practice, all we need are some dry cow chips. Pitchers could toss a chip and batters could try to hit it. As you can imagine, every chip exploded on impact. When it was Lilly's turn to pitch and David's turn to bat, she scoured around for a dry cow chip, but she was taking a long time. We all complained until she seemed to find just the right one."

Peals of laughter burst out of Lillian's mouth before she added to the story. "Oh, it was perfect. Perfectly dry on top and squishy on the bottom."

"And when I hit the dang thing," David joined in, "it exploded cow crap all over me, and Lillian took off running and laughing like a loon."

The room burst into gleeful hoots of laughter. Even David was laughing at the memory.

Lillian gasped. "I've never seen a donkey laugh before!" Then she grabbed her stomach with her good arm and laughed some more.

Grandma Willie was trying to get Lillian to calm down when Felicity shimmered into the room. She whispered something to the collection of ghosts, and they all vanished except for Eloise. She floated over to Meg and spoke something in a quiet voice.

Meg looked surprised.

And then Eloise was gone.

Chapter Twenty-Eight

Felicity was the first to rematerialize at the dilapidated Golden Bear. She ghost-paced back and forth while the madam hovered calmly above her favorite chair and waited for the others to arrive.

"Felicity, please stop stomping back and forth in those ridiculous shoes."

The young disco queen started to argue, then thought better of it.

Jack, Old Doc Lindsey, Ethel, and William had appeared by then, followed in short order by Julius.

They all turned to the madam with anticipation.

She got straight to the point. "I believe we may know where the shooter is hiding."

"The man who shot at Willowmina?" Jack asked. "How did you find him?"

Felicity blurted, "'Cause I have an ability to follow stuff and people, and I found his trail and tracked him over there."

The expressions on the faces of the other ghosts changed from surprise to annoyance.

"Uh-oh, I better get Eloise. We'll be back in a flash." Ethel popped out of the room.

"Why are you all staring at me?" Felicity defended herself, clearly angry. "I figured out how to do some stuff with a . . . a . . ."

Bridget gave Felicity a stern look that caused the young ghost to finish her statement vaguely.

"With some help."

"Tracking is a very specialized skill," Old Doc Lindsey said firmly.

"I *know*!" Felicity squawked.

"Now, now, dear girl, no one is doubting the possibility that you have it, we're just saying that it is rare." Doc spoke a little too loudly, then added with growing agitation, "And it can take years to master."

By then Ethel had returned with her sister, and Eloise floated into the fray with both hands extended, palms out. "Felicity, you are very new to this group, and no one knows you well yet, so calm down. Doc, you are very knowledgeable and have much wisdom to share, but you can be intimidating, so keep that in mind."

Both apparitions nodded and went silent.

"Good. Now, where are we?"

Felicity looked to Eloise for approval before speaking. Then, in as calm a voice as she could manage, she announced, "I was able to track the shooter to a cabin."

THE HOSPITAL ROOM finally calmed down. Meg made her excuses to her gramma, whispered something to Jace, and quietly left the room.

Jace resumed the aborted conversation regarding where Willie and the twins should stay once they left the hospital, when they should leave the hospital, and where the investigation stood at this moment.

"I think it best they stay in Denver," David suggested. "I have a big house—"

"No!" Ian blurted, then turned a bit red around the ears. "I mean, don't we need to keep Ms. Willie"—his eyes inadvertently darted toward Lisa—"nearby in case the FBI figures out the identity conundrum?"

David shook his head. "We should take them where they will be the safest. And that's in Denver."

"Ian's got a point," Jace said. "Plus, they're under court order to stay in this county until we get the identity crisis cleaned up. So the question remains, where do we stash them until we find the two assailants who are still missing?"

Lisa had been listening closely. She pulled the ice pack off her eyes and said, "What about Jack's cabin?"

Silence followed that hospital bed announcement for a few beats. Suddenly, they were all talking over the top of each other.

"That sounds . . ."

" Maybe it would . . ."

"Is it far . . ."

Ian put two fingers to his lips and whistled loudly. The room fell silent . . . again.

"Can any of you even hear what you're sayin'? There are at least three conversations happenin' all at the same time."

Lisa actually gave him a lopsided smile around the swelling in her face.

"David, what do you think?" Jace asked the attorney.

"I need to think about it for a moment. Now, all I can think about is getting Willie and the girls out of here and hiding them."

"If we do it right, Jack's cabin would be a good hiding place."

"What do you have in mind?"

Jace looked at the two men, Willie, and the twins, but the wheels behind his eyes were spinning.

"I have an idea. First, we need to make sure the girls' doctor is willing to work with us on a little trickery—nothing illegal, of course. Second, when we take them out of here, it will need to be without being seen. And third, we need to have a vehicle that no one recognizes."

David shook his head. "Won't work. Sneaking around in this small town is next to impossible."

"I'll work out the details. In the meantime, we've got round-the-clock protection on this room, and one suspect is handcuffed to a hospital bed and well guarded. Things are stable for the moment."

David looked around the room and announced, "I think I'll stay here tonight. I just think an extra person on guard will let Willie get some sleep."

"Ya know," Ian said, "I think that's a real good idea. I'm stayin' too."

Lisa looked surprised but not displeased.

Willie smothered a laugh with her hand, but Lillian wasn't so discreet. Still loopy, she began laughing aloud and singing, "First comes love, then comes marriage . . ."

"Lill, knock it off," Lisa barked, which of course only made her sister laugh harder. A moment later Lillian grew calm and, with a faint smile, closed her eyes to rest.

"Thank goodness!" Lisa said, still annoyed. "Maybe those ridiculous drugs are finally wearing off."

Grandma Willie saw what everyone else missed. David had taken Lillian's uninjured hand in his and was quietly stroking her fingers with his thumb.

Chapter Twenty-Nine

*J*ace pulled his personal vehicle in behind the Golden Bear and turned off the engine before dialing Meg's number. It rang several times before she answered.

"I'm parked out back," he said. "Can you come outside and talk?" He listened for a moment with a surprised look on his face. "Are you sure? Great. I'll be right in."

He thumbed the phone off and sat for a second. He had been invited "in." No living man had been allowed to enter the inner sanctum. Any man stupid enough to try in the past had been promptly scared out of his wits.

As soon as he stepped inside the dilapidated structure, Jace stood still and allowed his eyes to adjust to the dim interior.

"We're up here," Meg called down from the banister on the second floor. "Be careful on the stairs. There are some treads missing and a couple of them might not hold your weight."

As he began the ascent, cobwebs drifted in and out of the beams of late-afternoon light filtering through the broken walls. His long legs stepped over missing and weak treads. It didn't take him long to get to Meg.

She took his hand and led him down a stretch of ratty carpet to a parlor that seemed cleaner than anything he had seen so far. At first the room appeared empty to him. Then Eloise appeared suddenly.

"Hey, Jace. Don't be scared of anything. You're welcome here and everyone knows to turn up the juice so you can see them."

She floated over to her sister Ethel, who was smiling a huge smile.

Meg tugged him over to meet all of the "people." She stopped and introduced him to William and Julius. Meg felt him start to pull his hand from hers to shake hands and tightened her grip. When Julius let out a huge donkey "Howwwdeee," it about sent Jace out the door.

Everyone chuckled. Meg said, "Julius knows five words. William and Julius have been wandering around for over a hundred years."

Next came an older man in a suit that was reminiscent of the Waltons. "This is Doc Lindsey, and yes, he is related to the living Dr. Lindsey."

Doc Lindsey tipped his head to Jace.

"You already know Jack."

They moved to the next person. "This is Felicity Fossette. She's new to the group. She came back with Gramma Willie."

Felicity upped the wattage in her smile as well as the wattage in her shimmery attire.

"Shimmer down, Felicity." Meg hooked her arm possessively through Jace's. "He's taken."

Then Meg guided Jace over to a lovely woman who stood to meet him. She looked so much like Meg that his head swiveled several times between the two women.

"This is Bridget Dougherty. She's the one who owns this property."

Jace snatched the cap from his head. "Ma'am, it's a pleasure."

The madam smiled serenely up at Meg's young man. "It's a pleasure to meet you. Please have a seat and excuse the dust, as it has been many years since I've been able to give the place a proper cleaning."

Her tone was polite with a touch of steel.

Jace replied with the respect she deserved. "Yes, ma'am, and thank you for inviting me in."

Eloise smiled at Jace, putting him at ease. "Thank you for joining us, Jace. We want to do our part in protecting the girls and Willowmina from whoever is trying to do them in. We know you have your own plans, and we don't want either one of us to muck anything up for each other. Can you tell us what you have planned?"

Jace stood up, hat in hand. "I think better on my feet."

Ghostly heads nodded in understanding.

"We want to have the doctor say they are being discharged a day later than when the real discharge will happen."

"Who is the doctor, young man?" Doc Lindsey twitched his ghostly mutton-chop whiskers.

"Right now they are still under the care of the ER doc. Your, um, grandson is their doctor of record, but thanks to the deadly flu mist situation, he's currently under a suspension hearing protocol. We all know he'll be cleared, but it won't be in time."

"Do you think the ER doc will go along with this ruse, or do you have another doctor in mind?"

"Well, sir, we don't know the ER doc all that well. He's new. I've been wondering about Olivia Meeker. I know that she's applied for hospital privileges and is now engaged as an osteopathic doctor at Kai's clinic. If she has her privileges established at the hospital, I think she will help us. Along with your grandson, she was instrumental in solving the contaminated virus case that killed so many in Elk City. Thanks to her work, Meg and I got to know her pretty well."

Eloise smiled a very smart smile. "I can check out the computer system in the hospital director's office and find out if her privileges have been established. *And* don't worry about getting the girls out of the hospital unseen."

"What do you mean?"

The other ghosts had crafty smiles on their faces too.

"Jace," Meg said, "do you remember wondering how I got into the hospital without being detected?"

"I sure do."

"Well, you're looking at the folks who made that possible."

"So you're telling me that Grams and friends have been playing fast and loose with the law?"

Eloise looked offended at first. "Not exactly, young man."

"Then tell me what legal means you would use to check on Dr. Meeker's credentials—or get us out without detection."

Grams narrowed her eyes at Jace like she did when he would misbehave as a kid and she was about to tell him to "go pick a switch."

Jack chuckled. "Simmer down, everyone. Jace, yes, what we can do would be considered illegal if a 'living' person did it. But I don't think ghosts are in anyone's jurisdiction—and who would believe it anyway?"

Jace pulled his right hand down his face before muttering, "Me."

"Honey, stop worrying," Meg said. "It's not like you're dealing with bad people—I mean, bad ghosts."

"Walking a mighty fine line here." He drew in a deep breath. "Alrighty then. Eloise, how soon can you find out about Dr. Meeker's hospital privileges?"

"Give me a few minutes," she said before disappearing.

The madam said, "Jace, while we wait for Eloise to return, let's get to know each other a little better."

Jace and Meg sat on the settee while the otherworldly crowd gathered around in a comfortable conversation tableau.

Fifteen minutes later Jace was in the middle of a funny story: "So Meg ended up grabbing the rafters in the apple shed to get off that Shetland pony. I had to stop laughing before I could go over and snatch up the clothesline rope around its neck and pull him out of the doorway so she could drop down and escape."

Everyone chuckled at the image of two six-year-olds trying to catch a pony with a clothesline rope.

At that moment, Eloise reappeared flashing a Cheshire-cat grin. "Olivia was approved today. Her privileges begin in the morning."

The small group cheered.

Meg turned to Jace. "Do you want to contact her, or do you want me to?"

"I'll do it. This is going to be a little off the books, and I don't want to jeopardize anyone else at this point. How do you want me to contact you when I get the plans finalized with Dr. Meeker?"

Ethel piped up. "We're keeping tabs on the girls twenty-four-seven, so you can always find one of us in their room."

"That sounds good. I need to get back to the office and work on a few things. I don't know when the sheriff is coming back from Alaska, but when he does return, the plan needs to be in place."

"Jace, I'm going to stay here for a little longer. Meet me at seven? I'll fix us some dinner."

Jace gave Meg a quick kiss. "Sounds like a good deal to me."

He turned to the others and said, "It was nice meeting you all." He put his cap back on his head and headed out of the room. Meg turned back to the phantom crowd with a silly smile on her face.

Bridget smiled at her great-great-great-granddaughter or something before saying, "Meg, I really like your young man."

"Me too." Felicity chimed in.

Meg gave Felicity a look that might have killed her if she weren't already dead.

Eloise chuckled. "Now, girls."

Chapter Thirty

*B*y three the following afternoon, Olivia Meeker was established as Lisa and Lillian's primary care doctor. The biggest delay was waiting for Lillian's drugs to wear off enough for her to be considered "in her right mind" to sign the documents.

A few hours later, in their hospital room, Lillian and Lisa were trading war stories.

"Wowzers," Lillian said. "Now that the drugs have worn off, my shoulder is a seven-point-five on the pain scale."

"Quit complaining," Lisa barked. "If you want more pain meds, call the nurse. At least you can have some. Thanks to my concussion, I don't get any. I'm just glad the swelling in my face is down enough I don't talk funny anymore."

"I don't think I want any more of the serious pain meds."

"Well, the rest of us will be grateful for *that*. You should have heard yourself."

Gramma Willie listened to her granddaughters as they bickered. "For all of your medical experiences as nurses, you two make horrible patients," she smiled. "Dr. Meeker should be by to see you both soon. Then we can figure out when we'll get to leave here."

Lisa frowned. "I don't like lying around with nothing to do but complain."

"Hopefully the ibuprofen they finally gave you will kick in soon," Lillian said pointedly at her sister.

Meg and Kai walked through the door, creating a welcome distraction.

"Hey, you two." Gramma perked up.

"Hey back, Gramma," Meg said as she walked over and gave her grandmother a hug.

"You know, I don't think I ever considered what a pregnant pixie would look like, but now I know just looking at you, Kai." There was a smile in Grandma Willie's voice as she hugged Kai, all of five two and six months pregnant. She looked like she had a volleyball stuffed up her shirt.

"Ha-ha," she said, patting her belly. "Don't give Little Jack any ideas that his mom isn't a giant in his world."

"You're having a boy?" Meg asked, delighted. "When did you find out? I thought you wanted to be surprised," Meg said.

Kai shrugged. "I did, but when they did the last ultrasound, it was, um, pretty obvious. I happened to look at the screen at the same time he turned his bottom up and—voila!"

"And you're naming him *Jack*? Meg asked. She would have said more, but it was hard to talk around the lump in her throat. She gave Kai a hug. It was still hard to think of Jack being dead. At least he wasn't gone. Kai could still see him, but what about the baby? Would his son be able to see him too? Meg shook her head. Too many questions without answers.

"Kai," Willie said tenderly, "thank you for letting me and the girls bunk at Jack's cabin for a few days."

"Ms. Willie, think nothing of it. When Jace asked me, I agreed with him that it's the perfect place for the three of you to hide out until they catch those imbeciles who attacked you all. I'm so glad they already nabbed the guy who pounced on Lisa."

Lillian chuckled. "I hear he's got a broken foot and fractures up his tibia. After what Lisa did to him, he's probably happy to be safe behind bars."

"Good morning, ladies!" Jace walked into the room. He raised his hands before being peppered with questions. "Yes, you're getting out of here soon. Everything's in place. I'll fill you all in after Dr. Meeker gives us the go-ahead."

Willie and the twins grinned at each other. They couldn't wait.

Jace crossed the room to give Meg a quick kiss. "How're the wedding arrangements coming along with Mom?"

"We're in the final countdown. A few details, like getting my sisters to finalize the color of their bridesmaid dresses"—she stared pointedly but good naturedly at her sisters—"got lost in the shuffle, but we're making do."

"Well," Willie pointed out, "if the girls had been dutiful with the wedding plans, they might not have found me."

"Very true, and so I've forgiven them." Meg smiled lovingly at her grandmother. "So, no custom-made dresses, but there are some ready-made options." Meg sighed dramatically. "They just won't get much voice in what I choose for them."

The two bedridden sisters groaned aloud at the threat.

"Oh, girls, I'm sure it won't be a problem at all. Meg wants a beautiful wedding. She won't put you in something unbecoming, will you, dear?" Grandma Willie raised an eyebrow at Meg.

"No, Gramma, I won't, but it is fun to scare them about it."

The grin on Meg's face didn't leave Lisa feeling reassured at all.

Chapter Thirty-One

*S*hortly after Jace left, Olivia Meeker arrived to examine her new patients.

"Lisa, have you developed a worsening headache or slipped into any nasty migraine symptoms?"

"No, the head pain seems to be centralized to the impact area."

"How about sensitivity to light or sound?"

"No."

"Difficulty concentrating, memory loss, or loss of coordination?"

"No."

"Nausea, slurred speech?"

"Nausea has dissipated, and I think my speech has improved as the swelling has gone down in my nose."

Everyone in the room nodded an affirmative to that statement.

Dr. Meeker took her pen light out of her lab coat pocket and examined Lisa's eyes. "How blurred is your vision?"

"It's getting better as the swelling reduces, but I still have trouble seeing distance clearly."

Olivia put her pen light back in her pocket and held out two fingers on each hand. "All right, squeeze my fingers."

Lisa complied, and the next moments passed with Olivia performing a neurological examination.

"I've looked at the CT scans as well as the X-rays and you're one lucky woman. There is a hairline fracture to your nose that should heal nicely without intervention."

She turned to Lillian, asked a series of questions before she examined the injured shoulder. "How much pain are you in, Lillian?"

"About a seven point five. The nurse was going to check my chart and bring me some ibuprofen. That's been a while ago."

"That's my fault. I asked her to hold off until I saw you. I needed a clear assessment before you got anything."

"Huh, she could've at least told me."

"I'm sure she would have, except they're short staffed and they were all called to attend to a violent patient who was trying to destroy his bed."

A collective "aah" came from everyone in the room.

"Let me get the orders in for some heavy-duty Motrin for you and acetaminophen for Lisa. I'm keeping you here one more night for observation, and we can work on getting you outta here. I'll give Jace a call to work out the details."

Lisa started to speak. "I think the plan . . ."

"No." Olivia held up her hand good-naturedly. "I don't need to know any more than I already do. The less I know, the less chance I have of accidentally spilling the beans."

As soon as the doctor left the room, Gramma said, "Looks like we're here for another night. And she's right, you know. The fewer people who know the whats and the whens of our departure, the better."

"I wonder what's up with the 'violent patient'?" Meg asked.

"Probably the idiot who attacked Lisa," Lillian snarked. "I hope they knocked him out with a club instead of a syringe."

Lisa grinned. "A little bloodthirsty, are we?"

Chapter Thirty-Two

The next morning, Lisa awoke to see Gramma Willie sitting up on her cot. She was staring peacefully out the window, watching as the sun peaked over the mountains.

"Good morning, Gramma. Did you sleep well?"

"I did actually," Willie whispered back. "I just like watching the sun top the Colorado mountains in the morning,"

"You don't have to whisper. Lilly can sleep through anything."

"I'm not asleep," Lillian said as she pushed herself up with her one good arm. "I've been awake for an hour."

"Why didn't you say something?" Willie asked her grand-daughter.

"I enjoy watching you watch the morning."

The two smiled at each other. When the twins were little and spent the night at Gramma Willie and Grandpa Frank's, mornings were always special. Lillian, blankie in tow, often crept down the stairs at dawn to find Gramma on a bench, watching the sunrise from the sunroom. Snuggling together, they would watch the day wake up.

It was so good to be together again.

At nine a.m., Jace got a call from Olivia Meeker to finalize the twins' discharge plans.

By ten, he'd gotten a briefing from the FBI cyber specialist on the investigation into Willie's identity theft.

Shortly after that, he got a call from Meg telling him he'd been summoned to a meeting at the Golden Bear. She would meet him there.

Things were certainly happening quickly.

Driving over to the dusty old bordello, Jace pondered what he'd learned from the FBI that morning. The digital manipulations that had changed Willowmina Garrison into Millicent Garron—and kept her incarcerated in a mental hospital for ten years—was deep and complicated. Furthermore, they all appeared to originate from the same IP address. Whether they were looking for a hacker or someone in power with access to government records clearance wasn't clear at this point. The FBI was subpoenaing the internet service provider to get additional information. With any luck, they should know soon enough who had stolen a decade of Willie's life —and why.

Jace pulled the truck to the curb. He pulled his sheriff-issued ball cap down a touch, left the marginal security of his truck, and entered the haunted bordello.

When he passed into the inner sanctum of the madam's parlor, he spotted Meg and flashed her a smile. Then, snatching his cap off his head, he greeted the haunting specters of six souls.

"Hello, Jace," Eloise said. "What news do you have for us?" The crafty look on her face would have been funny if it weren't so fitting.

"Dr. Meeker has cleared the twins to be released tomorrow evening, but she's going to wait to upload the orders until we've got Willie, Lisa, and Lillian out of there. Anyone who has access to hospital files won't know what's happening until they're gone."

"Excellent," Bridget said approvingly.

"Is everyone good with their assignments?" Jace looked around the room. "You know what to do?"

Everyone nodded.

"I'll need everyone in place no later than one a.m. Go-time is one fifteen."

Again, nods all around.

"Good. I'll be on my way and see you all at one."

The madam held up a dainty hand. "Before you leave, I want you to know that you are always welcome here."

"Thank you. I feel privileged that you have welcomed me."

A ghostly smile crossed her lips. "Just take good care of my girls and you will always be welcome."

"Yes, ma'am."

The implied threat that something unpleasant would happen if he didn't, hovered unspoken in the space between them.

That evening at seven, Jace relieved the deputy on guard outside the twins' hospital room. When he checked in with Willie and the twins, he was peppered with questions. He held up a hand to slow them down. He smiled. "One at a time, please."

"What about the cameras in the hallways and security?" Willie twisted her hands nervously. "Won't they see everything? What if they don't let us leave?"

The fear she had lived with for ten years was showing up in her speech and body language. Lisa and Lillian left their beds and closed ranks around her.

"Ms. Willie, it's all under control," Jace said. "Do you trust me?"

She nodded.

"Good. I won't let anyone stop you from leaving here—or follow us once we leave. It's going to be okay." He smiled gently at her, and the girls hugged her back to the present.

"Oh, go on with you," Willie said, recovering some of her familiar moxie. "We'll be ready and I'm sure you know exactly what you're doing."

"Remember, be ready by midnight."

Grandma Willie gave him a thumbs-up sign, and he slipped out into the hall to resume his place on guard duty. At ten a nurse entered the room to check on the monitors and deliver paper cups of medication. Other than that, the hours passed quietly.

At 12:55, Eloise appeared in front of Jace. "We're in place."

"All right, at 1:15, start the show and I'll get the girls to the elevator."

Eloise popped out. Jace signaled Willie and the twins with a quick rap on their closed door. Then he shifted his position so he could see the call-light board at the nurse's station.

At exactly 1:15, four different room call lights lit up the board at one time. The night nurse and the CNA on duty left the desk to check those patients.

Jace stood and opened the hospital room door quietly. Lisa, Lillian, and Grandma Willie quickly followed him past the empty nurse's station and down the hall to the bank of elevators.

The spectral form of Doc Lindsey stood by the elevator that went down to the loading dock area. The silver doors slid open. Jace hurried the women inside, looked down the hall, stepped in himself, and pushed the button for the basement. The doors rapidly closed as the elevator seemed to descend at light speed.

"What about the cameras?" Willie blurted.

"I've got friends working on that. Hospital security won't see a thing."

"Friends? Not deputies? Will you get in trouble?"

"It's okay, Gramma." Lillian patted Willie's arm. "They're the same ones who helped Meg when she needed to move about the hospital without detection."

The doors swished open. Doc shimmered out. When he reappeared, he gave Jace a thumbs-up.

Jace ushered the women down the hall to a set of double doors leading to the loading dock. Before entering the loading dock, he waited for another thumbs-up from Doc Lindsey, meaning the online cameras had been disabled. As soon as the group was on the dock, a silver SUV pulled into sight with Meg behind the wheel and Ian next to her.

Jace retraced his steps until he was back at his post.

At the nurse's station, three nurses and the CNA were trying to figure out what had just happened.

"The patient I checked on wasn't even awake. He certainly didn't push the button."

"Two of the rooms that alerted didn't even have patients assigned to them."

"I turned off the alert in room 405, but it immediately came back on."

The head nurse shook her head. "I'll make a notation and call maintenance first thing in the morning."

"It was like they were possessed," the CNA added.

A small smile crossed Jace's face.

The CNA left the nurse's station. "It's a little early for rounds, but I'll check on some of the patients in the other rooms since I'm already on the move."

As the young woman approached, Jace arranged his face to portray night duty boredom.

"Hi," she said, "I'm just here to do rounds."

"Sure. I just checked on them and they're sleeping soundly."

She checked her watch. "Well, they're not scheduled to have vitals recorded for another few hours. I'll let them rest for now."

"Sounds like a plan. I'm sure if they need anything, they'll push their call light or let me know to get you."

As she walked away, Jace relaxed back into his chair. Eloise or Jack would let him know when Willie and the twins were safe and Dr. Meeker's discharge orders had been uploaded into the computer system.

Forty-five minutes later, Jack wavered into visual range. "They got safely to my cabin—and discharge papers are in the system."

"Good. Anything else I need to know right now?"

Jack grinned. "Just that there are no video images anywhere of the girls leaving, and the security people are still scratching their heads as to why all of the video equipment in one sector completely malfunctioned."

Jace chuckled. "If they only knew."

As Jack faded out, Jace stood up, stretched, and walked to the nurse's station. Both the nurse and the CNA were busy with paper-work. He cleared his throat.

"Yes, sir, what can we do for you?"

He smiled an official smile before saying, "Lisa, Lillian, and Willowmina Garrison have been transported to a new location."

"But . . . but they haven't been discharged!"

"I believe the records have been updated recently. I'm sorry it had to be this way, but for safety reasons, we couldn't let anyone know the specifics of the move. I'm sorry to have left you out of the loop."

The nurse said, "Stay right there." She turned to the computer and punched a few keys before reading the discharge orders that hadn't been there a few minutes earlier.

She turned to face Jace squarely. "I understand the need for secrecy, but let me tell you, for the sake of clarity, that this is not an acceptable way for the sheriff's office to treat this hospital."

"Yes, ma'am. In the normal course of things this would never have happened. There are many circumstances pertaining to their safety that led us to proceed in this manner."

"See that we don't have a repeat performance on my shift again."

"Yes, ma'am. Now, if you'll excuse me?"

She nodded her head and Deputy Taggerty left the nurse's station to check in with the deputy guarding the man who had attacked Lisa.

Chapter Thirty-Three

"*What's with another conference call in the middle of the night?*" the bold and angry man snarled.

"*You'll be on any conference call I say is necessary,*" the man with the slippery voice said, an unspoken threat hanging in his words. "*Now, which one of you decided it was a good idea to attack the Garrison women?*"

"*I did,*" the emboldened man said. "*And I don't care what you think. You've been in charge for too many years and look where it's landed us. You weren't doing anything to stop the threat, so I stepped up.*"

"*This is getting out of control,*" the man with the smoker's voice interjected. "*Both of you are out of control. I'm not sure I want anything else to do with this mess.*"

"*Oh, so you're ready to kiss the State Supreme Court appointment good-bye?*" the angry man shot back.

"*I'm ready to let the chips fall where they may. I knew nothing good would come out of allowing ourselves to be blackmailed. I'm surprised you want to continue this farce. Not just continue but dig an even deeper hole for yourself!*"

"*I have a new book coming out and a juvenile center opening next month, and I don't need the past making a mess of things. What choice do I have?"*

The man with the slippery voice hadn't said much during this exchange, merely listening to the bickering of the desperate men. But now he chuckled. "You made your choice years ago when you were caught partying with underage girls."

The stark reminder hushed any further objections from the other men on the line.

"If you think you were helping matters, you're a moron. As we speak, one of your hired idiots is handcuffed to a hospital bed, and the other one will undoubtedly be caught soon. Tell me where your second hired idiot is hiding out, and I'll see if I can't clean this mess up."

The angry man was silent.

"I don't have all night."

"Fine." His anger was giving way to anxiety again. "He's holed up at the Econo Lodge in Gunnison."

"A little word of advice to both of you. Stay the hell out of this and I'll take care of it."

The line went dead.

The judge slowly replaced the handset in its cradle. Lord, he was tired of this mess.

OVER THE NEXT THREE DAYS, Lisa, Lillian, and Grandma Willie settled into a quiet routine at Jack's cabin. Each morning, Ian returned to Elk City to work at the clinic—he was swamped with a full caseload of clients Jack had been seeing before he died—while the women spent the day playing cards and board games. Before dinner, Ian would return to the cabin, sometimes bringing items from Meg that she thought Willie or the twins might need. Evenings would find Lisa and Ian with their heads together talking softly while Gramma Willie and Lillian tried to best each other at poker.

They had round-the-clock protection of the supernatural sort.

Felicity, Jack, William and Julius, Eloise, Ethel, and Doc all took turns watching the grounds.

Lisa and Lillian were aware of their guardian angels, but Ian and Grandma Willie seemed blissfully unaware. Ian only questioned Meg once about how she knew exactly what Willie and the twins needed from home. She said it was a "sister thing."

And he believed it.

THE CONVERSATION and hum of the sheriff's office suddenly went silent. Jace looked up from the report of Willie's identity mess prepared by the FBI specialist. There stood Sheriff Clint Garrison, back from vacation, all spit and polish.

"Deputy Taggerty, would you mind stepping into my office and filling me in on the past two weeks?"

Jace nodded his head and reached to replace the report in his desk drawer.

"Bring that with you."

As the two retreated to Sheriff Garrison's private office, the conversational buzz in the bull pen picked up again.

The two men entered the well-appointed, tastefully decorated office. More the office of an executive than a man of the law. "Sit down."

Jace gulped. It sounded like Sheriff Garrison already knew what had taken place during his absence and for some reason wasn't happy with the way it was handled.

Once seated, the sheriff leaned back in his own chair and said, "Well, what the hell happened while I was gone? I hadn't been back for more than an hour last night and the old biddy network was calling me with what was in the rumor mill."

Jace relaxed a little before filling him in on the attacks on the twins, the capture of one of the perps, and the bullet into the condo.

"I understand that the women were hospitalized and now they're not."

"Yes, sir. Once they were cleared to leave, I arranged to have them taken to a safe house until all guilty parties are apprehended."

"In the middle of the night?"

"Yes, sir."

"Why?"

"To mask their leaving and to transport them to a safe location."

"Hmm." Sheriff Garrison leaned forward. "And what about that FBI report?"

Glad to have a shift in subject, Jace said, "We don't know yet who entered the false information into the DMV, state systems, and our own systems, but we've identified an IP address and it appears all the cyber hacking originated here in Elk City. The FBI is going to keep working on it, but some of the holes may never be recovered. They've subpoenaed records from the ISP, so hopefully we'll have a lead soon."

Clint shifted his position, making a steeple of his fingers. Back and forth he brushed his fingers across his lips grooming his perfect Burt Reynolds mustache. Jace didn't know if the conversation was finished or if there was more to come.

"I'll go get the daily reports for you." Jace stood up. "If you have more questions after that—"

"Where are they?"

"Who?"

"My nieces and aunt."

Jace hesitated. His every instinct was screaming to keep that information to himself. "Sir, I haven't told anyone where they're located, and I'd like to keep it that way."

"I understand that it's your duty to keep them safe. However, I am the duly elected sheriff and I need to know."

He took a deep breath. "Yes, sir. They're . . . at Jack's cabin."

"Very good."

Jace felt icy tendrils running down his spine. He gave an involuntary shudder. "Anything else?"

"Keep me abreast of investigations regarding these attacks. And, Deputy Taggerty, you're responsible for their welfare."

"Yes, sir. Anything else?"

"Get the daily reports for me."

Jace left the office to get the dailies and felt a heavy weight pressing into his chest. Something was off.

THAT NIGHT, under a full moon, a gentle breeze danced through the pines, carrying earthy scents into the open windows of Jack's cabin. Lillian breathed deeply and snuggled into the soft sheets next to her grandmother. The silence of the forest permeated and consoled the sequestered inhabitants of the little cabin. It had been three days without incident, and all three women felt optimistic that they would escape more craziness and that life would eventually get back to normal.

Outside the cozy cabin, William and Julius patrolled the grounds, listening to the night sounds and staying alert for unnatural movement.

Felicity suddenly popped in next to the duo. "Hi, guys. I'm here to take my turn."

William flinched just a bit. "Gal! You need to warn a body!"

"I'm sorry. Has anything been happening?"

"Nothin' fer as we can tell, but the night seems too quiet for a full moon. We've been a listenin' fer a spell and the critters ain't actin' right. Jist can't put a finger on it."

Felicity's disco shimmer wavered like a shudder. "I'll be especially watchful. Do you think you could check in with me once in a while? I've never had night duty before."

The donkey's head bounced up and down in a yes. William added, "Yep, just like Julius said. We can check in wunst in a while. We'll go a piece and check out the woods further 'round the cabin."

"Thanks, guys. Where do you think is a good spot to be to keep watch?"

William patiently pointed out a high peak on the cabin roof. "Jist perch yersef up there and keep a good watch. We'll check back in after while."

The two watched while the disco doll perched herself up on the roof. She had her right hand above her eyes as if it would help her see better. William, with Julius by his side, floated away shaking his head under his animal skin cap.

Felicity was determined. Nobody was going to hurt her friends on her watch. By the beginning of the second hour, she was sit floating on the roof looking at the sky in between looking around the grounds. It really was a pleasant night. The moon was full, the sky was clear, and the trees were playing peekaboo with the moonlight. Enjoying her "Rocky Mountain High," she was soon humming that very song and swinging her legs in time to the music.

Suddenly, twigs snapped under the heavy tread of someone approaching the clearing. The humming disco vision was back on full alert, scanning the terrain for the intruder. It only took two passes before she caught sight of a shadow inching its way down the north side of the property. At first she thought it might be an animal sneaking through the denser part of the forest until the prowler stood up from its bent position. That's when she caught sight of the gas can in his hand. Felicity couldn't see all of his features, but she could make out the outline of a small beard protruding outside the hood he had pulled up over his head.

Not on my watch! she thought, disappearing from the roof and reappearing behind the prowler. Now she could see the wet trail of gasoline he was laying around the trees.

Panic rose up in her mind, threatening to overtake reason. She stomped her platform shoe. No, by golly, this wasn't going to happen.

She popped over to the shed and found a shovel propped against the side of the building. Then, returning to the intruder, she found a pine tree with low branches in his path. Using as much energy as she dared, she heaved a limb back and, as soon as he passed by, let it fly.

Wham! The limb connected with his butt. He dropped the gas can and straightened up. Felicity closed her eyes and concentrated. Levitating the shovel, she connected the flat side with his face as hard and fast as she could.

He went down like a ton of bricks.

Surveying her work, she dusted off her hands and prayed that she had done enough to keep him out of commission until she could rouse someone from the cabin.

Back at the cabin, Felicity whispered in Lillian's ear. Lillian kept snoring. Quickly, Felicity went in search of Lisa and found her snuggled in Ian's arms on the couch, sleeping peacefully.

"Lisa! Wake up!"

Lisa bolted upright, away from Ian, and fully aware. "What's wrong?"

"We've got trouble. I think I have it, well, contained for now. But, oh dear, hurry, please."

Lisa eased off the couch, crept to the front door, and found her shoes. "What did you see?"

"A man . . . out there . . . was putting gas all over the forest. I knocked him out . . . I think. Grief, I hope I didn't kill him." Felicity worried her lower lip before continuing. "Just *hurry!*"

Suddenly Lisa shrieked. Ian was right behind her.

"Babe. What's going on?"

"I-I thought I, um, heard something outside," she stammered.

"I thought I heard you talkin' in your sleep. Are you sure?"

"Yes."

"Then I'll go out and check on it. No need in you gettin' a chill."

"No! I mean, no, I'm sure it's okay, I just need to check for myself."

"Well, then, I'll come with you and see for myself too."

Ian gave her a sexy grin and a Southern-boy wink. In a flash, he'd put on his boots and grabbed his pistol off a shelf by the door. "Now, you stay behind me. Understand?'

Lisa squeaked out an affirmative.

He opened the door and looked out. He stepped onto the back porch. Ian looked to the right first and then scanned to his left. Had he been able to see ghosts, he would have seen Felicity standing at the edge of the clearing, pointing with exaggerated motion at a large dark lump at her feet.

Lisa tapped Ian on the shoulder and pointed to the edge of the clearing to the dark shape.

"Stay here," he ordered.

Of course, she didn't listen to him at all, and he gave her a black look as they approached whatever was lying on the ground.

The closer they got, the stronger the odor of gasoline became and the dark form took on the shape of a man.

Ian looked at Lisa. "Go back to the house and call 911. When you're done with the call, get Lillian and Willie awake and dressed. Looks like this is goin' to be a long night."

Lisa didn't argue. She turned on her heel and ran for Jack's cabin and did exactly what Ian had told her to do.

Chapter Thirty-Four

Before long the peaceful night was splintered by screaming sirens and a kaleidoscope of red and blue lights. The flashing lights illuminated the forest and reflected off the cabin's windows.

Jace had been the first on scene followed by three other deputies, EMS, two fire trucks, hazmat, and Sheriff Clint himself.

While Lisa and Ian were being questioned in one of the department's SUVs, Lillian and Grandma Willie huddled together in the backseat of another vehicle. Felicity hovered in the front seat, contemplating playing with some of the gadgets on the dashboard.

Jace guarded the wounded man as the EMS team placed a collar around his neck and started an initial assessment of his condition. The shovel had been bagged and tagged as evidence even though the man kept saying it had come out of nowhere and hit him in the face by itself. The gas container was also bagged and tagged into evidence.

Paramedics brought a gurney and were preparing to load the man onto it when he looked past Jace's right shoulder and froze. If possible, his face paled even more.

Jace whipped around to see what this joker had seen. He saw the same people who had been there all along. So, what was different? He turned to question him further, and the guy had gone silent and still. No more chatter. Not even to the paramedic who was asking him questions.

Sheriff Clint Garrison appeared at Jace's left shoulder. "Everything okay over here?"

"I was just about to get a statement from this guy."

"What's his name?"

"He won't tell us."

"Not even the EMT crew?"

"Nope."

The sheriff looked the guy over before saying, "Deputy, you seem to have everything in hand. I'll wait for you at the office." With that statement, he returned to his vehicle and left the area.

ONE BY ONE the emergency responders finished up and left, except the hazmat team and Deputy Jace Taggerty. The gasoline cleanup was going to take the rest of the night and long into the upcoming day.

Sitting in his SUV, Jace was studying something on his Toughbook laptop. The glow from the screen lit up his face. Looking up, he spotted Ian leaning on the rails of the front porch of the cabin. He got out of his rig and headed over.

"How are they doing?" he asked, still holding the tablet as he rested his forearms on the rail next to Ian.

"Still shaken, as you can imagine."

"We'll move the women tonight. We're going to plan B. There isn't any other option until we unwind this mess to keep them safe."

"Are you gettin' anywhere with the unwindin'?"

"I've got some suspicions. I'll need to talk to Willie and the girls before we move them. I've got a picture for Lillian to look at and see if the face looks familiar."

"Where did you get the picture?" Ian asked.

"I just ran the would-be arsonist's prints and got a hit. I downloaded his rap sheet and mug shots."

"You need to come clean with me, Jace. I'm worried. It didn't take long for someone to figure out where we were and hatch a plot. If Lisa hadn't heard somethin' outside, there would have been one hell of a forest fire, and I don't know that we woulda gotten out of here alive." Ian spoke calmly, but his eyes shot sparks of anger. "I'm not comfortable sending them anywhere without someone to watch over them. I'm going with them."

"Ian, you've got a full load at the clinic. You've taken on Jack's patients as well as some of Kai's. If I thought they'd be in danger where we're taking them, I'd let you cancel your life and go with them in a heartbeat. But we're taking them someplace so secluded, I don't know why I didn't think of it in the first place. I'm confident they'll be safe." He didn't add that there would be some ghostly guardians helping to keep them that way.

Ian didn't look convinced.

"C'mon, let's go inside. I need to ask Lillian something."

Ian opened the front door and swept his forearm across his body like a doorman. As Jace walked into the cabin, the three women pinned him with frightened stares.

"Evening, ladies. You'll be glad to know we're moving you to a safer place."

Ian stood behind Lisa and rested a hand on her shoulder. She rested her hand over his.

"But first . . ." Jace set the Toughbook on the coffee table. He flipped it open, brought the mug shot up on the screen, and turned the laptop to Lillian.

She sucked in a quick breath of recognition. "That's the man who attacked me in the alley."

"Are you sure?"

Lillian kept her gaze glued to the picture on the small computer screen and nodded her head slowly. "I'm very sure," she whispered.

"That's all I need for now." Jace closed the Toughbook and looked at the three women and Ian. "It's time for plan B."

"We've got our go-bags packed and ready." Grandma Willie had obviously picked up some of the lingo from the twins.

"What about food?" Ian asked.

"Stop worrying. I've made arrangements, and everything they need has been stocked."

"You're sure?"

"Yes, Ian, I'm sure."

As Lillian and Grandma Willie retrieved their bags, Lisa lingered for a moment under Ian's hand.

"I've got to go, don't I?" It was more of a statement than a question.

Ian kissed the top of her head. "Yes, darlin', I'm afraid so."

"Well, then." She heaved a sigh. "Let's go. As the Duke would say, 'We're burnin' daylight." Grabbing up her own bag, she kissed Ian soundly on the lips. "See you soon."

JACE GOT them into his patrol SUV before pressing a number into his cell. When someone answered, he simply said, "Rendezvous point two." Then he started the engine and eased the vehicle around the hazmat vehicle parked behind him. When he reached the road, Jace turned right toward the mountains instead of left toward town.

Willie was the first to break the silence. "Where are we headed?"

Jace shook his head. "I'll tell you as soon as we get to the first stop."

He turned onto a dirt service road designated for Forest Service Employees Only. They bumped and bounced over the rutted, washed-out parts of the road, and each time someone asked where they were headed, Jace refused to give an answer. After an hour of bumping, bouncing, and jouncing, they pulled over into a wide spot and stopped. Still he wouldn't tell them anything. It was as if he was afraid someone would overhear them.

It wasn't long before a pair of headlights bounced off the trees in front of them. Jace told the women to stay put. He got out of his vehicle and walked toward the Jeep until he saw that the man behind the headlights was exactly who Jace was expecting: his younger brother Jed. Only then did Jace motion for the women to get out of the SUV.

Once the women were seat-belted into the Jeep, Jace's brother punched the accelerator and they took off through another section of the forest.

The smell of dust and pine permeated their senses for the next twenty minutes until they arrived at a juncture in the road with another road coming up from the south. They were at the edge of the protected-wilderness part of the forest. An old brown Ford pickup with a horse trailer was parked off to the side with two saddled, dun-colored horses and yet another of Jace's brothers waiting for them.

As Jackson helped the women out of the Jeep, Jed gathered the go-bags and packed them into the saddlebags of both horses. The guys were quite chatty under normal circumstances, but not now. The safety of Lisa, Lillian, and Willie depended on it.

"Lisa and Ms. Willie, come over here and I'll get you settled on Shadow. Lillian, you'll ride with me on Sparky here," Jed said in his serene way.

Jackson finished checking the cinches on Shadow and held the bridle and reins while Jed lent a hand to the two women, settling them into position. He handed Lisa the reins as the rider in front; then the two men turned to Lillian.

"Lillian, you're going to ride behind Jed and we'll both help you up. We don't want to mess your shoulder up any worse than it is," Jackson stated.

Once Jed and the women were situated on horseback, Jackson left in the Jeep down the southbound road.

The creak of saddle leather and the soft thud of horse hooves were the only sounds coming from the foursome as Jed headed up the mountain and into the thick of the forest. It was eerily bright inside the tree line as the full moon ventured across the night sky to the west.

After twenty minutes, the silence within the trees had become deafening.

"All right, I can't stand another minute of not knowing where we're going," Willie stated emphatically.

Two of the other three riders seemed to let out a sigh of relief. Jed, the quietest brother of all the Taggerty brothers, said, "We're going to the honeymoon cabin."

"The one Eloise and Mike used to go to every now and then? The one above tree line?" Willie asked.

"Uh-huh."

"See, that wasn't so hard to tell us, was it?"

"Not once we got away from the vehicles," Jed answered.

"What?"

Jed sucked in a breath and said, "Ms. Willie, Jace isn't sure who is trying to kill you, and he didn't want to take any chances with people overhearing anything. We made an agreement to stay quiet until we were away from everything."

"Kill me?"

"Gramma, what do you think all of this caution and hiding has been about?" Lillian asked.

"I thought it was because you two were attacked."

"That's part of it, but you *were* the one with a bullet whizzing past you."

"Oh, for crying out loud! I thought that was some sort of accident."

"Nope," Jed said.

The saddle leather creaked in time to the thud of horse hooves moving up the moonlit trail. For over an hour, each was lost in their own thoughts while listening to the sounds of the living forest. Soon they rode out of the dense trees into the clearing of the mountaintop. The moon was giant as it slid a little farther west.

"Frank used to call this the 'hush' time of the morning. As if the world hushed for a few minutes before the sun sent light into the dark," Gramma Willie said.

For those few moments, they sat silent and still, waiting for the sun to burst onto the scene as it would this high up in the mountains. The air was bright and sharp in their lungs, but oh so sweet and fresh.

Chapter Thirty-Five

"There's bottled water stacked over there and plenty of freeze-dried stuff in that cabinet," Jed said as the three women stood next to him and surveyed the one-room cabin. "There are a few tin dishes and forks in the same cabinet. There's just the one bed, but there are sleeping bags and camping pads for everyone. Most important is the satellite phone here." Jed pulled it out of his inside jacket pocket. "You can't use it in here, but if you go down the hill about twenty feet, you can hit service. But unless there's an emergency, stay indoors. And no fires."

"No fires," Lisa grumbled.

"Yes, fires make smoke and you don't want to get the Forest Service sending someone up here to check it out."

"Thank you. Do you know how long we're supposed to be here?" Lillian asked.

"Not sure, but the hope is to have you back before the wedding."

"That's a week and a half away! Do they have any idea who's behind all of this?" Lisa demanded.

"Jace has an inkling, but no facts yet. One of us will always be at the other end of the sat phone. Any other questions?"

All three women shook their heads in the negative as they looked around the new "safe house."

"Well then, I better get out of here." Jed left, and the women looked around them with disappointment etched into their expressions.

Willie dusted her hands together and announced, "It's not too bad. We have all we need here, and I for one believe we will be back to civilization long before the wedding."

The twins stood still for a moment more digesting their grandmother's pronouncement and decided that if she could tolerate the crazy stuff, so could they.

"You're right, Gramma, this will be our first Colorado campout in years," Lillian said.

Lisa was already taking inventory of the food supplies, first aid kit, and dishes when she hooted and held up her prize. "I think we can thank our baby sister for these."

In her hands were the makings for s'mores, with a note attached to the front of the marshmallow bag. The note said, "Hey, Gramma and Legs, I knew you would love some s'mores. Sorry you can't make a fire in the stove or outdoors, but the little propane stove should toast the 'mallows good enough for now. Sticks are to the right of the cabinet. Love, Meg."

"Great, no fire *and* she called us Legs again." Lisa frowned.

Grandma Willie laughed.

Lillian walked the short distance to the lovely wood burning stove that they wouldn't get to use and opened the top of the little propane camp stove. "We will have to open the door and use this close to it so it vents. No use in taking a chance with asphyxiation, and I for one could use a s'more . . . for breakfast." She laughed and proceeded to move the table next to the open door and place the little stove on top of it.

It wasn't long before melted chocolate and marshmallow oozed between graham crackers and trickled down Lillian's arm.

"Careful there, Lilly. I don't see a means for a bath here and we don't want to waste water to clean you up!" Lisa said before she licked melted marshmallows off her own hand and arm.

"Well, now that we've had dessert for breakfast, what shall we do next?" Gramma Willie asked.

Soon the three got serious about laying out their freeze-dried meals and arranging their meager entertainment choices.

"Gramma, you lay out your sleeping pad and bag on the bunk. Lilly and I will be fine on the floor over there."

"I don't mind taking a turn on the floor," Willie stated.

"We know, but Lisa and I are used to sleeping in all kinds of places. It won't be any different for us to take the floor. In fact, having a pad under us is a treat," Lillian said as she hugged her grandmother.

The three women each took their rolled-up sleeping bags, which had their names printed in their sister's quick hand on little tags.

"She's kind of bossy deciding who gets which sleeping bag," Lisa said.

"We could swap them around if it's a problem for you," Lillian responded.

"Now, girls, be nice," Gramma Willie said. "There might be a reason she did that."

They each unfurled their assigned sleeping bags.

"Look," hooted Lillian, "cotton yarn and a crochet hook."

Lisa was already hugging her sudoku puzzle book to her chest. "Thank you, Meg, wherever you are!"

Gramma Willie had a sweet smile lighting her face. On her sleeping bag lay an artist's journal and a box of colored pencils with another note. "Gramma, I loved all the drawings the twins found in your journals. I'm looking forward to seeing more of what you see. Love, Meg."

The rest of the day was spent enjoying the gifts Meg had tucked into each sleeping bag. Lillian crocheted two pairs of booties for Jessica's babies, Lisa mumbled to herself as she worked her way through ten of her puzzles, and Gramma Willie sat in the doorway of the little cabin and sketched the hawk flying above the trees. Soon they broke out of their singular worlds for a midday meal.

"Well, the macaroni and cheese was okay for what it is," Lillian said.

"It's better than some of the stuff we've had overseas," Lisa answered.

Gramma Willie grinned. "I don't think I've ever had anything like this. It's handy, but I don't think your grampa would've eaten it. I used to cook for days before we went to hunting camp. He always said, 'Willie, I'd starve to death up there if it weren't for you,' and I made sure it stayed that way."

They all laughed and cleaned up after themselves, chatting the entire time about insignificant things. Once they had tidied everything they could and stowed the trash in a bear-proof container, they weren't sure what to do next. They all stood looking at each other for a few beats.

"I've got it," Lillian said. "Let's break out the pinochle deck and the rule book over there and learn how to play."

Gramma Willie shrugged her shoulders and said, "What the heck. I like learning new things. Set 'em up girl and let's give it a try."

The three of them sat on the camp stools around the little table, rolled up their sleeves, and proceeded to become pinochle champs until the sun sank low enough they would need their headlamps and flashlights to make supper.

Great-Aunt Ethel had night watch over them the first night. Lisa and Lillian found comfort in the care.

Day two was much the same as the day before; only, Eloise popped in to keep watch the second night. The girls would've loved to talk with her, but they didn't think Gramma Willie would understand and she would think they were nuts.

Day three proved to be another repeat.

"How much longer are we going to be cooped up in this cabin?" Lisa was mumbling as she worked on the last puzzle in her book.

"Quit griping!" Lillian had finished the last of her yarn making a pot holder yesterday, and she was not in a kindly frame of mind.

Even Gramma Willie was tired of the inactivity and had stopped sketching.

"Is it bedtime yet?" Lillian asked.

"Not yet. If we went to bed now, we would be up long before sunrise," Willie replied.

Lisa sighed. Lillian huffed out a breath, and Willie wanted to groan. So they all did nothing until supper.

Finally, night came, and the women prepared for bed. They had snuggled down into their bags, knit caps on their heads.

"This high in altitude sure is nippy once the sun goes down," Willie said. "Who would ever think August would be so cold?"

Felicity had been assigned the night watch. She popped in around ten and saluted the two girls in sleeping bags on the floor. The night was quiet—and boring—and before long Felicity felt the need to entertain herself. Soon she was doing her best disco dance steps and singing the chorus to "Staying Alive."

The twins grimaced at the off-key singing, but since they weren't sleeping anyway, they figured they might as well let her do her thing.

Felicity's sparkly tube top and flowing pants were moving to more of the Bee Gees when suddenly Gramma Willie sprang into a sitting position.

"Would you just *shut up!*" she shouted.

Lillian and Lisa shot straight up and stared.

Willie had both hands over her mouth.

For a few seconds nobody moved or made a sound.

And then Felicity popped to the foot of Willie's bed and shouted, "I knew she could see me!"

The twins extricated themselves from their sleeping bags and rushed to their grandmother.

"Gramma, can you see her?" Lillian blurted.

Willie dropped her hands and stared at the twins for a moment. "Can *you?*"

Chapter Thirty-Six

"Gramma, can you see and hear Felicity?" Lillian repeated the question.

"You can see her too?" Willie was trying to process the idea.

"Yes."

"Both of you?"

"Yes," Lisa said.

"So, none of us are crazy?" Willie asked, eyes wide.

"No, Gramma," Lillian said.

"See, I knew she could see me all these years," Felicity said and floated closer to Willie, who retreated from the specter.

"Back up! Good grief! No need to get in her face," Lisa told her.

Felicity floated back, but just a bit. Her eyes seemed to flash in anger.

Lillian gently took her grandmother's hand. "Gramma, Meg can see them too."

"Them?"

"Um, yes, there's a . . . a . . . support group of ghosts, and they hang out at the Golden Bear," Lillian answered.

"And we're not loco?"

"Nope."

"Huh, how 'bout that."

"Do you want to talk about it?" Lisa asked.

"No, not right now. I need . . . time to digest this. Um, is she dangerous?"

"*Dangerous?*" Felicity stomped her foot. "I'll have you know—"

Lisa interrupted the young ghost. "We know! You've been watching over her for years. Calm down."

Felicity popped over to the corner, arms crossed over her chest and a narrow-eyed, mean look on her face. She glowered at the three women.

"Let's go back to bed and try to get some sleep," Lillian said wearily. "Felicity, you're a very good lookout. Go back to your job, and please stop singing so we can go to sleep. Okay?"

Felicity grudgingly capitulated.

As the women finally fell into a light sleep, Felicity drifted outside the cabin and began patrolling the grounds.

An hour later Felicity was back in the cabin in a fluttery panic.

"WAKE UP, WAKE UP NOW!" she shouted.

Lisa bolted upright and started to speak, but Felicity's terrified countenance and finger across her lips stopped whatever she was about to say.

"Thank God you're awake!" Felicity blurted. "I left for five minutes to report in with the gang at the Bear, and when I got back, the man—the one who shot at your gramma—was on his way here!"

"What?" Lisa whispered as she got up.

"He's right outside. What do we do?"

"How far away is he?"

A sharp *thunk* sounded at the door.

"He's here!"

Lisa shouted shrilly at the door. "Who's there? Who are you and what do you want?"

No one answered, but the thudding continued.

"Go out and see what he's doing," Lisa hissed. "I'll wake up Gramma and Lillian."

Felicity popped out and Lisa shook her sister awake.

"Lillian! Wake up! The guy who shot at Gramma is outside!"

Then she woke Gramma Willie from a sound sleep. "Gramma, the guy who shot at you is outside the cabin!"

Felicity popped in again. "He's gone back down to the edge of the trees and is getting things out of his saddlebags."

"What kinds of things?" Lillian asked, sitting up and shoving her sleeping bag off her legs.

"He has several cans of charcoal lighter fluid and some old rags."

The three women looked at each other before they all said, "Fire!"

A sharp metal-on-wood sound reverberated inside the little cabin.

Gramma Willie had had enough. Through gritted teeth she hollered, "Who in the hell is out there?"

A familiar voice responded, "Aunt Willie, it's just me."

The women fell silent in shock.

"Clint," Lillian said.

"Smart girl," he responded.

"Why are you here?" Willie asked. "I thought nobody knew where we were."

A muffled laugh came through the wooden door. "Well, they think they have you secreted away, but since we're family, I figured it out. Remember all the stories Eloise and Mike told about the 'honeymoon cabin'? Wasn't hard to figure out."

Clank.

Felicity stuck her head through the wall to see what was making the noise. Then she pulled her head back in and faced the women. "He's soaking the side of the cabin with that charcoal fluid. He just emptied the first can and tossed it on some rocks."

"How many cans does he have?" Lisa asked breathlessly.

"At least a half dozen."

The girls jumped to the door to open it.

It wouldn't budge. They yanked and tried to muscle the door open. Nothing.

Another muffled laugh came from outside the cabin.

Another *clank*.

"What do you want, Clint?" Willie shouted.

"Funny you should ask. I know you have documentation for the legacy, and I need those papers to show the attorney. He thinks he can break the trust so Dad and I can have what rightfully belongs to us."

"What are you talking about? I've never heard about any legacy." Willie lied.

Clank.

"Now, Aunt Willie, we both know you're lying. Those documents are passed down through the wives of our family. It appears Grandmother didn't trust my mom to keep them safe, and she gave it to you. Rumor has it that only females of the line can inherit the fortune, but I beg to differ."

"Gramma, what's this about?" Lisa whispered. "Is this about the haunted bordello?"

"If it is, just let him have the scary old thing!" Lillian pleaded.

Clank.

Willie waved her granddaughters' words aside. "Good grief, Clint, let us out of here and I'll try to figure out what you mean."

"Oh please. Don't take me for an idiot. I've been through every inch of your doily- and potting-soil-infested house, and I can't find it. But you're going to tell me where it is. When I have the legacy documents in hand, we can talk about letting you out of there."

They all knew he had no intention of letting them out of the cabin . . . ever.

"Felicity," Lisa whispered, "go to the Bear and get help. We're in trouble."

The young ghost nodded once and was gone.

"Listen to me, Clint Garrison," Willie spoke to her nephew harshly. "You're not going to get away with this and I'm not going to tell you a blasted thing."

Clank.

"Now, Aunt Willie, I've already gotten away with quite a lot. You don't think the last ten years happened by accident, did you?"

Willie blinked as his words sank in. "It was you? *You* locked me up?"

"Who else would be able to tuck you away so neatly?"

The shock in her voice gave way to fury. "You locked me up for *ten years* so you could live in *my* house and search for some imaginary legacy documents? Documents you think I'm somehow keeping from you? Documents you're willing to *kill* for?"

Clank.

Felicity popped back in and said, "The gang is on the way. Get ready to leave and then help me move the bed. Quick."

"Move the bed? Where?" Lisa asked.

"Over there by the door," the young ghost ordered.

All three got their shoes on, and Lisa and Lillian, sore shoulder and all, began shoving the surprisingly heavy bed from its position.

"What are you ladies doing in there?" Clint shouted from outside the cabin.

"None of your business, Clint," Lisa snarked.

Another muffled laugh came from outside.

The smell from the lighter fluid was starting to infiltrate the interior of the cabin.

"Well, Aunt Willie, I'm waiting."

"You can wait until the cows come home!"

Smoke began drifting into the small vents at the top of the walls and curling down into the interior.

"What now, Felicity? What do we do now?" Lillian begged.

"Just wait. I told you they said help would be here in a minute."

The smoke was curling into the room at a fast pace.

Willie had grabbed washcloths and water bottles. She doused three of them and showed the twins to put them over their mouths and noses. The heat radiated into the small room. The looks jumping between the three of them turned to deadly fear.

The crackling flames were already making their way through the door. Clint had set the whole cabin ablaze.

Suddenly the floorboards groaned as several planks popped up to reveal a dark hole with a grinning donkey peeking over the top.

"Quick, grab your backpacks and flashlights," Felicity said.

The top of an old wooden ladder appeared in the hole, and William said, "Get a move on, gals. This here place is old timber and it won't hold much longer."

Lisa donned a headlamp, switched it on, and rapidly descended down the rickety ladder. Lillian followed suit without her sling, and Gramma Willie quickly repeated the process.

The tunnel widened marginally.

"Okay, gals, you need to follow me and be quick. Don't want no smoke or flames to foller us."

Lisa turned to look at where they had come from.

"Doncha worry none. Thet Felicity gal will get the floor shut up. You jus' keep your eyes peeled on me an' ole Julius here and we'll getcha outta here."

They heard a loud thud followed by the scraping of a heavy object above them. The darkness would have been complete if not for the small light shining from Lisa's forehead.

"Um, how far does this tunnel go?" Lillian asked.

"We'll have a fair piece to travel, but there's sort of a place that we kin rest ya a spell in a little while," William said. "Now, you'll need to get them packs off'n yerbacks 'cause there's a skinny spot coming up."

"Do we leave them here?" Willie asked.

"Nope, you're goin' to need 'em. Jist hold 'em in one hand or the tuther."

Lillian knew her left shoulder was no good after climbing down the ladder. She turned on her headlamp before dropping her backpack off her right shoulder and catching the strap with her hand. Willie and Lisa did the same.

"Alrighty. We're goin' about ten paces and then turn sideways 'cause the gap we're goin' through is plenty tall but it ain't very wide. But you'uns are skinny enough to make it through."

Crushing silence accompanied them as they moved warily forward. Julius, the donkey, was the last to follow into the blackness. The passage narrowed by increments until the three had to turn sideways to sidle a step at a time. Their backs scraped against the stone wall behind them, and the small light from their headlamps reflected onto their faces. One step, another, and another. For twenty-five feet, they inched their way through the narrow passage.

Reaching the widening portion of the tunnel seemed to take forever.

"I think I don't like tight places," Willie said as she ended her time in the passage. "The donkey is no longer behind me . . . right?"

Lillian looked behind them as far as her light would shine, squinting into the blackness. "I don't think so, Gramma."

"But there *was* a donkey?"

"Yes, and his name is Julius," Lillian said.

"Okay."

"Enough jibber-jabbering ladies. We got a ways to go," the funny little mountain man ordered. "Julius is up here with me now. You jist keep yer eyes on me. I'll tell you when things change."

"Are we walking on a downward slope?" Lisa asked.

"Yep, and we'll get purty deep into this here mountain before we git to the end."

Willie, Lisa, and Lillian each took a deep breath, fortifying their courage, before hefting their backpacks into place. There was only one way to go, and that was forward.

Chapter Thirty-Seven

Clint stuffed the cans into his saddlebags and stood smirking while he watched the flames consume the old timber.

Felicity popped into the tree line and watched the sweet little cabin burn. That horrible man thought he had gotten rid of her friends. Felicity narrowed her eyes and was ready to hurt him when the madam appeared.

Bridget stood there with her fists clenched at her sides, tapping her foot. Angry energy poured out of her. Clint didn't see her, but he kept stopping to rub the back of his neck.

He slapped the saddlebags filled with empty cans over the back of his horse, causing the hapless animal to sidestep. Clint growled a command at the horse before strapping the bags into place. Then, stepping into the stirrup, he swung his leg over the saddle. But when he tried to put his foot in the other stirrup, it wasn't there.

He leaned over to take a look.

The wayward stirrup was, in fact, lying on the ground.

He let out a curse, then shifted his weight to swing back down off the horse. But before he could do that, Bridget let out a screech that echoed off the mountain peaks. At the same time, she stood in front of the unlucky horse and waved her arms. The horse reared up, eyes rolling, hoofs pawing the air. Flinching, he pitched forward, then reared back again so far he almost toppled over.

Clint couldn't keep his seat with only one foot in a stirrup and one swinging free. He flew off backward, landing flat on his back.

Felicity soared over to look down to see if he was still living. He was, but he didn't look conscious. She looked back to see the madam soothing the horse with sweet words, and as soon as the animal calmed, she swung up on its back with ghostly grace and took off down the hill and through the forest. The image of full skirts and petticoats seemed to stream behind the horse as it raced through the trees.

After a sorrowful glance back at the cabin, Felicity followed. Felicity found the madam, Eloise, and Jack at the base of the hill.

"Hey everyone," she called out, but no one turned or even acknowledged her. They were concentrating in unison on a horse trailer hitched to the camo-painted Jeep that belonged to Sheriff Clint.

The trailer unhitched itself from the Jeep and rolled several feet.

Then the trio began focusing on the Jeep. There was a sudden spark of energy, and the Jeep slammed onto its side.

Eloise dusted her hands together in a blur of motion. "That should finish that off. Jack and I will finish discombobulating the electrical systems, and I'll make sure Clint's cell phone will *never* work again."

She wiped the vengeful look from her face and turned her attention to Felicity. "I know you got the girls out of the cabin. Thank you for saving them." She smiled kindly. "I will go and check on that jackass and make sure he doesn't have any other phones on him." She popped out of sight.

Bridget glided next to Felicity. "It's too bad about the cabin. I know it held beautiful memories for Eloise, but she loves those girls and Willowmina, too, so I guess it was a small price to pay to catch the man who wanted to hurt them." Silence filled the early morning for a couple of beats. "Run along, dear. I know Willowmina and the girls will be glad to see you and have your help."

"Yes, ma'am."

"And Felicity . . ."

"Yes?"

"You know we all cherish you. Keep them safe."

Felicity beamed her happiness at Bridget before she faded out to join her charges.

"Hey everyone," Felicity announced when she popped in behind Grandma Willie.

Willie jumped like she'd been shot. Her headlamp clattered to the hard rock under her feet, and her heart began beating in her ears. "Oh, oh, wh-what . . . ?"

William glared at Felicity. "Gal, you gotta find ya a better way to enter a place!"

"Oops. I'm sorry."

Grandma Willie regained her composure and her headlamp. "Now, now. It's okay. I'm just . . . unnerved with everything that's happened and it is so dark and close in here."

"It'll be okay in a bit. We's jist about to the restin' spot," William said and took his place in front of Julius. "Now then, we need to go about twenty paces, then you'uns will need to stop and one atta time you will have to go through the hole and drop down into the big room where we can take a rest."

Lillian gulped. Her shoulder felt like it was on fire.

"Felicity, you git up here, 'cause I'll need hep getting them back bags outta the way."

She did as she was told.

"Now, you girls keep those little lights shining high until ya git to the place whar yer looking at a rock wall. Then ya look down and you'll see the hole you's gonna skinny through. Now, don't pile too close tagather 'cause the best way down is to git on your belly and slide down till your toes touch."

"How far down to . . . toe touch?" Lisa asked.

"Well, back in my livin' days, my toes touched at about the time my underarms were on the edge there."

"How did Julius get through?" Gramma Willie wanted to know.

"Ah shucks, he didn't never come through here until we was dead."

All three women gulped.

"Exactly how did you, um, pass away?" Willie asked.

"Oh, we was a wanderin' around in the wintertime and a big snowslide took us over a cliff and buried us deep."

"Oh," Willie murmured. She was reminded of how her son and daughter-in-law were killed by an avalanche when the girls were small.

Lillian read her grandmother's distress so easily, since she felt a pang of loss for her parents at odd moments herself. "It's okay, Gramma. We all miss them, don't we?"

The silence blanketed them, and the darkness pressed in from every side. Their only reprieve from the inky blackness came from the small circles of light shining from their headlamps. The glow emanating from William, Julius, and Felicity helped too.

The little mountain man, sweet donkey, and the disco doll all popped out, leaving the three women in the dark with their thoughts.

"Well, we better get moving before William decides we need scolding," Willie said.

The three walked carefully forward, extending the space between them carefully. The light from one still touched the person in front, and Lisa's light touched the darkness until a rock wall took shape in front of her. They all stopped for a couple of breaths.

William called up to Lisa. "It's all right. Drop yer pack through the hole down here and turn around, then drop to yer hands and knees and back up. I'll guide yer feet."

Lisa took a deep breath. She slid her backpack off her shoulder and slowly drug her gaze down the rock surface until she found a black hole at the bottom. It didn't look very large. She dropped the bag into the hole and turned to face her sister. "Here goes," she said and swallowed her fear as she slowly got on her hands and knees.

The floor was dry, hard rock. Using small increments, at a snail's pace, Lisa backed toward the hole. Suddenly her right knee had nowhere to land and she fell to her belly. "Oof!" The breath left her body for a moment, and she scraped the side of her face and nose on the rock surface under her.

"I think I found the hole."

"Don'cha worry none. I'll guide yer feet once ya get the second one through the hole and start scooching back," William called up.

Lisa slowly pushed her left leg through the hole and scooched backward until her hips were going into the hole. A soft pressure took her ankles and guided her until her toes felt solid ground.

She called up to Lillian, "Your turn. The hole is closer than you think, so go slow. And we must be taller than William because I didn't have to go very far to touch the bottom."

Julius guided Lisa forward into a large cave.

"Felicity, you go on up with Miz Willie whilst I get Miz Lillian guided down," William instructed. "That way she won't be alone up there."

Lillian wanted to groan when she dropped her backpack through the hole. She knew she needed to protect her left shoulder and wasn't sure how to do that. She turned and looked at her gramma and saw Felicity already behind her.

"Gramma, Felicity is right behind you, so you'll have company while I get down to the next level." She thought she was being comforting, but her grandmother heard the tightness in her voice and saw the pain radiating out of her eyes.

Lillian warily got down to her knees using the cave wall with her right hand as support. She took a deep breath before placing her right hand on the ground. She kept the left against her belly as she began the slow crawl backward. Instead of stepping her knees back, she slid them. First one, then the other. Once her left foot started sliding through the air, she placed her left hand down for balance until she could lay on her stomach and inchworm her way until the gentle pressure on her legs steadied her to the next solid level.

Once Lillian hit solid footing, Julius escorted her to the cave where Lisa was waiting. He stayed with the twins as William and Felicity got Grandma Willie through the hole and brought her into the place where they could all rest.

Absolute darkness surrounded them except for light from their headlamps, now fainter than when they started.

"This is a good spot to rest," William told them. "Felicity and Julius and me can turn up the juice for a few minutes so's ya kin look about if you want us to. It's kind of perty in here."

"Right now I just need some water," Lillian said.

"I've got you covered," Felicity said. "I was able to get three bottles of water in each of your backpacks, and, Lillian, I got your prescription pills into yours."

At that moment Lillian wanted to hug the ghost. "Thank God and thank you!"

The women dug into their backpacks. Through the sense of touch, they found bottled water and Lillian found her pills. It took a moment for her to figure out which bottle held which pills. She didn't dare go for the stronger prescription drugs. Instead, she shook out four of the ibuprofen tablets. "Eight hundred milligrams should take the edge off until we get finished with this odyssey."

"We're about halfway done. Julius and me are going to rest for a spell. Felicity, how are ya doin'?"

"I've got plenty of juice for now."

"We've got a fer piece ta go yet, but me an' Julius needs to recharge a tad. Otherwise, you won't be able to see us no more," William said. "You'uns rest up a bit, and we'll be back quick as we kin. Missy there will keep you company."

With those parting words the little man and his donkey faded from sight and Felicity began telling the girls everything that had been happening on the mountain since they fled the burning cabin.

$\mathcal{E}$loise floated over the sleeping form of her future grandson-in-law. "Come on, Jace!" she shouted. "Wake up now!"

The young deputy shot up out of a dead sleep. "What?"

"Sorry, Jace, you need to focus now." She waited a few beats until the sleep left his gaze. "Clint set the cabin on fire with Willie and the girls in it. We got them out of there, and several of us took care of him for the time being, but you need to get a move on."

Eloise's urgent words penetrated Jace's foggy brain. Jumping out of bed, he grabbed his uniform. "Details, Grams, details," he ordered as he yanked his boots on.

Eloise filled him in on how they had slowed the sheriff down, how Willie and the twins had escaped, and where they were now. The whole time she was talking, Jace was building a mental list of things he needed to do. By the time he climbed into his official SUV, he had dialed dispatch to find out who was on duty and if anyone had called in to report black smoke on the mountain.

The next call he made was to his brother Jackson. "Do you see smoke on the mountain?"

"Jed is saddling the horses now."

"Tell him to be careful." Jace paused for a minute before adding,

"Jackson, it's Sheriff Garrison. The girls are safe, I think, and I need you to pick them up at the Lady Bird Mine."

"What? How . . . ?"

"Jed can head up to make sure the fire is contained. Have him take Dad with him. He also needs to take a rifle with him—and Jackson, tell them they need to act ignorant if they run into the sheriff. They need to stay safe. I'll take care of Clint when I get there."

"Understood. Uh, Jace, how did those women get away from the cabin?"

"Not sure. All I know is they're going through the mountain."

"Through it?"

"Yes, I don't have many details yet. Bring them to the sheriff's office after you get them."

Jace focused on sorting the rest of the list in his head as he drove to the station. Dispatch had already sent a patrol car to coordinate with the Forest Service on the fire. Next, he called Meg.

When she answered, she skipped any sort of greeting and simply said, "Aunt Ethel is here, and I know what's happening. Please stay safe."

A smile played at the corners of his mouth before he responded, "I will. And Meg, I love you."

"I love you too. Now, *be safe!*"

She hung up the phone before he could answer her.

He swung the SUV into the parking lot and took a deep breath. Damn that greedy SOB. If Clint had killed those girls and Grandma Willie, he wouldn't have lived to tell his lies. Jace and his brothers would have seen to that.

Jace shoved those thoughts away and entered the building.

"Jace, what are you coming in so early for?" The clerk at the front desk was surprised to see him before his shift began.

"My brother called me about some black smoke. Figured it would be all hands on deck."

"You're right about that. You don't happen to know where the sheriff is, do you?"

"Um, no, haven't you been able to get him on his phone?"

"He isn't picking up or calling back."

Suddenly the doors burst open and one unshaven, bleary-eyed, angry attorney barged through. David Summit marched up to the desk waving a file folder over his head. "Where is Sheriff Clint Garrison?"

Jace said to the clerk, "I'll take care of this."

She shot him a grateful look.

"This way, David." Jace turned to the first open room he saw. "I'm glad you're here."

Deputy and attorney went into an empty interview room. Both had angry strides. Both had information regarding the same man. Both had blood in their eyes.

Jace closed the door, then went to each window and closed the blinds. One more stop and he made sure all recording and listening devices were off, including the one Clint didn't think anyone knew about. "Sit down, David. We have a great deal to discuss and I'm guessing a short time to do it."

David cocked his left eyebrow and said, "Indeed," before slapping the hefty folder on the table and taking his seat.

Jace filled him in on what was happening to the girls and Willie, as well as his suspicions about the sheriff. When he finished, David let out a long, low whistle through his teeth.

"You're sure the girls are okay?" David's eyes were shooting angry lasers.

"Wait until you see what I've got." One by one, David laid out letters and documents signed by his friend the judge. "Sheriff Garrison has been blackmailing my friend to go along with whatever he wanted to do to get Willie out of his way. And not just the judge. He's also been blackmailing a psychotherapist. That's how he was able to get Willowmina Garrison incarcerated in the state hospital for ten years. He monkeyed with her identity and got those two to sign off on her institutionalization."

Jace tapped on the photo of the psychotherapist. "Isn't this the guy who started all those juvenile offender camps?"

"Yes. Apparently Clint caught him and the judge with underage girls about twenty years ago. They've been under his thumb ever since.

Jace whistled through his teeth. "Isn't your judge friend in line to be a Colorado Supreme Court justice?"

"Not anymore. He had me meet him at his house and told me everything. He gave me all this documentation and said he would take whatever punishment the state decided to hand out. He also apologized over and over for everything. I may forgive him . . . someday," David said.

Then Jace asked bluntly, "Are you ready for everything that comes next?"

"Damn straight," David answered.

"Then we better get moving. And, David, I'm playing it close to the vest until all the pieces are in place."

"Understood."

Jace opened all the blinds in the small room before the two men left.

"Deputy Taggerty, I still can't raise the sheriff," the clerk said as he and David walked past her station.

"Keep trying. And, Cathy, call Max and the coroner to come into the office."

"On it."

Even though he didn't feel like it, he smiled for her benefit.

THE "RESTIN' spot" William had picked for Willie and the twins was dry, but black as pitch. The pools of light from the women's head-lamps were dimmer than ever.

"Felicity, how much longer do you think William and Julius will be?" Grandma Willie asked. "I don't know how long the batteries on these lights are going to last."

"Don't worry. William and Julius are recharging now. They'll be able to light your way, plus you have me, and if we need more of us to come and light the way, they will come."

Lisa gave a smidgeon of a laugh. "So, 'if we build it, they'll come.'"

"Huh?" Felicity tilted her head.

"Nothing." Lillian grinned. "Lisa was just quoting a line from the movie *Field of Dreams*. Loosely, I might add."

"Oh."

The foursome sat in silence for another half an hour. Felicity got too bored and once again began practicing her disco dance steps and singing loudly. Now her song of choice was "I Will Survive."

After a few beats, Grandma Willie joined in. In the dim light, the girls couldn't see much of their grandmother's dancing, but they both couldn't help but tap their toes and giggle.

When their rendition of Gloria Gaynor's famous song ended, Felicity upped the wattage of her glow so Willie could safely make her way back to the twins and sit down.

"Whew! Your Grandpa Frank and I used to 'Boogie Oogie' the nights away back in the day. That was fun! Thank you, Miss Felicity!" Willie's smile outshined their fading headlamps.

Wille and Felicity found another seventies tune to sing together; the living one sounded good, the other, not so much, but they entertained themselves and the twins for a few minutes until William and Julius shimmered into view.

"Well, gals, let's get ta movin'. Did you get enough to drink and such?" William asked.

"We each drank a full bottle of water and had a protein bar." Lisa said. "If you would help light up the area, we will make sure we've got everything packed up before we go."

With their energy restored, the light emanating from William and Julius illuminated a large area of the room-sized cave.

"Wow, this is a really clean cave," Willie said.

"Yeeesss, maa'aam," Julius brayed.

The cave was solid granite and smooth. It looked like water had hollowed out a gigantic fishbowl deep inside the mountain.

William and Julius dimmed their shine to the size of a good

flashlight while the three women stood and slipped their backpacks into place.

"Now, listen up good, 'cause there's still a couple skinny spots to go."

The rest of the trek through the mountain was dark and cold, just like the previous path they had followed. There was one area the women had to slither through sideways and another place that required them to crawl through on their hands and knees.

"What time is it?" Lillian asked.

William nodded at Julius, and the donkey faded out for a few moments and popped back in. The two conferred for about a minute, and William turned to the girls. "According to Julius, the sun is just about above the east mountains."

Lillian sighed. "How high is the sun going to be when we get to, well, wherever it is we're going?"

"We're almost there, gal. Just a bit more and we'll be in the spot they call the mouse hole. When we stop there, you're goin' to have to get the attention of the folks down below."

"Down below?" Lisa asked.

"You'll see. It'll be fine." William and Julius continued trudging forward. There wasn't any choice for the women but to follow.

Another hour passed before the little mountain man and his donkey friend stopped. Light shone brightly at the end of the tunnel.

"We're here," William said matter-of-factly. "It's a far piece down to the ground, so don't go too close to the edge. You'll have to get their attention down thar. The men are jist now comin' to work and they're loud."

Lisa, Lillian, and Willie cautiously inched their way to the opening.

Willie gulped. "Shall we all yell, 'Hey!' down to them?"

"Sure," Lisa said.

"Okay. On three?"

The twins nodded.

Willie began the count. "One, two, three . . ."

All three yelled, "Hey!"

Not one person turned or even heard the yell.

"Okay, girls, cover your ears," Willie ordered.

Once the twins had complied, Willie made a circle with her middle finger and thumb, placed it just so in her mouth, took a deep breath, and let a shrill, sharp whistle fly. That did the trick. All activity below stopped, and several machines immediately shut down. Willie didn't know it, but a sharp whistle in a mining operation means something is wrong and everything grinds to a halt.

The supervisor turned his head in several directions before he looked up toward the mouse hole. When he did, his first reaction was shock. His second reaction was to start giving orders.

A scissor lift was positioned below the mouse hole where the women stood. It was only a fifty-foot separation between them and safety below. All three of them were brought down at one time. The man who rode the lift up to them joked it was a good thing they were all so skinny.

As the lift slowly lowered them down, Willie looked back and mouthed, *Thank you*, to William, Julius, and Felicity, who stood watching until all three women were safely on the ground.

Chapter Thirty-Nine

"How in the hell did you get up there?" the foreman demanded.

"We came through the mountain," Lisa replied.

"What?"

"Maybe I can help," Jackson said, approaching the group of miners clustered around the three women.

"Who the hell are you?"

"Jackson Taggerty."

"Well, Taggerty, what makes you think you can shine any light on how these three got inside the mouse hole?" The foreman was angry and just a little unnerved by the sudden appearance of three women in an area that nobody was allowed to go.

"They've been lost for days, and Deputy Taggerty suspected they fell through an opening we found on the mountain. I was in the search party that found the hole. The deputy sent me here to ask if you know anything about where the mouse hole comes out, but I see you've already found them. Thank you so much. I'll take them back to town and have the police report forwarded to you so you can safety-check where they entered."

"See that you do." The foreman turned to the gawking miners. "And the rest of you, get back to work . . . *now!*"

When Jackson had the women safely ensconced in his truck, he asked, "Do any of you need medical attention?"

Everyone looked at Lillian. She shook her head no. "I hurt like the devil, but I know what's wrong. Right now I just want to do some serious damage to Clinton Garrison!"

Shock crossed everyone's faces. Lillian was the nice one.

Then Gramma Willie said, "I'm as bloodthirsty as you are. But getting a medical opinion on that shoulder is first on the list."

"Sorry, Gramma. I think surgery will be the only fix for my shoulder, and it won't be an emergent type of surgery. I'll take care of it until then. Right now let's just get that man," she said through gritted teeth.

By the time the foursome got to the sheriff's office, it was full daylight and the activity level was in full swing. Deputy Max, the coroner, and David were sequestered behind closed doors with Jace. The dispatcher was talking on the radio to a deputy who reported that Sheriff Garrison's Jeep had been overturned. A fire command team was debriefing in one of the larger conference rooms.

The clerk looked up and saw Jackson and the girls. "Holy Moses! You three look like you crawled out of a ditch. Are you all right?" she asked.

"Yes, we're okay. I think Jace may be looking for us," Lisa said.

"He's not the only one. Ian Connors is in the little interview room, and he is pacing and coming out here every couple of minutes —" She was interrupted at that very moment by an angry Southern drawl.

"Have they located them yet?"

"I'm right here," Lisa called out.

Those three words stopped the angry tirade. The man practically flew down the short hall to grab Lisa and look her over from top to bottom before squeezing the breath out of her. "You're nevah going to go one otha place without me. Do you hear me?" Now he was shaking her and pressing her to his heart in turns.

An office door opened. Jace, Max, David, and Ben Davis, the coroner, joined the group. Jace addressed Willie first.

"We've got him. He won't be causing you any more trouble." He turned and faced everyone else in the sheriff's office. "You are not to say one word about these women to *anyone*, including the sheriff. I promise to explain everything to you, but for now this is a regular day with a fire situation. Is that clear?"

Everyone, including the Forest Service people, nodded in acknowledgment. Max took the three women and Ian to another office that had no windows. "You three stay in here until Jace, David, or I come to get you. Don't speak to anyone outside this room. I'll bring you some water. Do you want anything else?"

"If this is going to be more than an hour or two, we're going to need food. It wasn't light out yet when this all started," Willie said.

"Not a problem. I'll see what I can get for you without raising any more suspicion. I'll also see what I can do to help you clean up a bit." Max left the four people sequestered in the little office.

"Do we really look so bad that people want to get us cleaned up?" Lisa asked.

"Darlin', you're beautiful to me, but, um, you're smoke smudged, scraped, and bruised," Ian said in his honey drawl.

Lillian asked, "All of us?"

"'Fraid so."

The three women finally took a good look at each other. Gramma had one sleeve of her jacket hanging by a few threads, her hair looked like a bird's nest after a windstorm, and her face was smudged with dirt and soot.

Lillian's face was in various stages of healing from old scrapes, plus new ones. Dirt and soot decorated her clothing, hair, and face. The knees of her jeans were ripped, and her right leg had specs of blood from the tear halfway down her shin.

Lisa not only had two black eyes, scrapes down the left side of her face, and a dried-blood trickle on the corner of her mouth, but she also had soot and dirt streaking her face and hands.

"Lord, we're a mess," Willie said.

Max brought bottled water and paper towels as well as chips, popcorn, and one granola bar.

"Thank you, Max. What's happening out there?" Willie asked.

"Nothing yet, but it's the calm before the storm. Sheriff Clint is on his way here. He's about half an hour away. But you'll be safe. Just stay out of sight for now until Jace needs you."

Lisa and Lillian thanked the deputy again and he left, closing the door softly behind him.

WITHIN THE HOUR, the front doors banged open. Sheriff Clinton Garrison stomped into the front office. "Who in the hell locked the back entrance and *why* doesn't my passcode work?"

The disheveled, dusty intruder with torn clothing didn't look anything like the spit and polished man they knew as the sheriff. He almost looked homeless, and except for the expensive haircut and perfectly groomed mustache, he could have been any rodeo bum.

"Someone give me some answers," he barked. "And what are all of these people doing in *my* offices?"

Jace stepped forward.

Clint Garrison's gaze landed on the coroner. "What is *he* doing here?" Clint's eyes naturally narrowed, but they were glaring at Jace now.

"Sir," Jace said firmly, "if you'll come with me into your office—"

"That won't be necessary. Is there anything else you need to report to me?"

"No, but I need to speak with you in—"

Clint cut him off again. "Then that'll be all, Taggerty. I'm going into my office now to clean up, and I'll speak to you later when you have something to report."

Jace stepped in front of him. "I've been as polite about this as I want to be. You know why the county coroner is here. He's the only one who can arrest a sitting sheriff."

Clint narrowed his eyes to slits. Beads of sweat started popping out across his forehead. "What is it you want to say to me, Jace, before I fire you?"

"It isn't me who will tell you anything. Mr. Davis will do the telling."

Ben Davis stepped in front of the sheriff. "Clinton Garrison, you are under arrest . . ."

Clint backed away from the coroner fast and stumbled against a wall of state patrol officers. He turned his head left and right looking for a way out.

Ben stepped closer and began again. "Clinton Garrison, you are under arrest for kidnapping, false imprisonment, extortion, and attempted murder." He then pulled a card out of his shirt pocket and read, "You have the right to remain silent and to refuse to answer questions. Anything you do say may be used against you in a court of law. You have the right to consult an attorney before speaking to the police and to have an attorney present during questioning now or in the future. If you cannot afford an attorney, one will be appointed for you before any questioning if you wish. If you decide to answer questions now without an attorney present, you will still have the right to stop answering at any time until you talk to an attorney. Do you understand these rights that I have read to you?"

Clint's vision skittered from face to face. "What a bunch of bull," he blustered. "Just who did I kidnap or imprison or try to kill?"

The door to the small office swung open, and out stepped Lillian, Lisa, and their grandmother Willie. The look on their faces coupled with their soot-smudged, bedraggled appearance spoke volumes.

David stepped up from behind Jace. "I've got enough proof, just on the extortion charges, to lock you up for a very long time."

The two state patrol officers grasped both of Clint's arms. One stepped behind him and calmly said, "You can either put your hands behind your back thumbs up and turn into that wall to your left, lean into it, and spread your legs, or I can do it for you."

Clinton Garrison knew he was caught. He complied with the orders of the state patrol officers.

As he was being handcuffed, he yelled, "Call my daddy! Now!"

No one lifted a finger. Nope, they all knew he would get his one phone call just as soon as he was booked into the Gunnison County Jail.

<h1 style="text-align:center">Chapter Forty</h1>

*W*illy stood on a stepstool, paintbrush in hand. She was painting the walls in her own living room, and her otherworldly cohorts were helping best they could.

Clint's furniture had been removed two days after he was admitted into the Gunnison County Jail. In the meantime, David and his entire law firm had been working around the clock to restore Willie's rightful identity.

"Boy, that David moved fast to quash any claim Clint thought he had to this house and your share of the ranch," Eloise said admiringly as she waved her finger and made a loaded paint roller scroll up and down the wall, covering it with a lovely color inspired by Willie's one-time gardens. "I like this sage color," she added.

"Thank you. I think my Frank would have liked this color too," Willie replied, a little catch in her throat. All she could think about was getting her calm, peaceful life back. She never wanted to leave her little house again. She looked around the room with a half smile on her face. Eloise and Jack were doing their share of painting. Felicity, too, although that girl was messy for a ghost. She had paint spattered all over her coveralls, something no one else of the otherworldly persuasion seemed to be struggling with.

"When are you going to get the legacy paperwork out of its hiding place?" Eloise asked Willie.

"As soon as Esther and David get here. I don't want anyone finding fault with the papers or their authenticity. Is Ethel coming too?"

"Soon enough. She's been keeping an eye on Esther. We hope she wasn't in on Big John's shenanigans. She's been acting a little hinky since Clint was arrested and Big John had that stroke."

"Yes, no one saw *that* coming," Willie mused. "I guess Big John couldn't handle the shock of his son's arrest. How's he doing anyway?"

"No change. He's still not responding to any stimuli. He's been transferred to a nursing home, and the doctors aren't sure he'll ever recover or go home again. Seems he popped some big blood vessels in his brain and the damage is pretty extensive."

"Wowzer," was all Willie could think to say.

Eloise loaded the roller with paint again and floated it to another wall.

"Boy, that looks a lot less messy than the way I have to do it," Willie said. She looked down at her own coveralls and laughed at all the paint spatters down her front. "It's a good thing I'm wearing a bandanna, or there would be a mess in my new hairdo."

"Speaking of new hairdo, wasn't the wedding beautiful?" Felicity asked from across the room.

Jack added, "Meg looked beautiful—second, of course, to my Kai." He smiled wistfully.

Eloise nodded. "It was a beautiful wedding. Meg looked like the happiest woman on Earth."

"Yep, and Jace was over the moon," Willie chimed in. "Meg's new mother-in-law did an incredible job with everything. She even got my brother and his entire family here on short notice once she found out about them."

"How was it seeing Thomas after all those years?" Eloise asked. "And by the way, shame on you for never telling any of us about your family! We thought you were an orphan or something."

"Frank knew about them, and he knew it was painful for me, so we decided to keep it to ourselves. Come to find out, Tommy hadn't abandoned me after all. Our uncle was making sure Tommy never received a single one of my letters."

"When will you see him again?"

"Once the twins are settled and I have this house in shape, he and Dolly are going to come stay with me. After all, we've got about fifty years of catching up to do!"

"Lillian is scheduled for surgery on her shoulder next week. She and David seem to be getting along . . . for now," Eloise said with a smile. "When do you think Lisa and Ian are going to announce their wedding date?"

Just then, tires crunched over gravel as Esther's car came to a stop in the driveway. Eloise called out to the ghosts in the room. "All right, everyone, rollers and brushes down. We don't want to upset the apple cart for those who don't know about us."

Paint rollers and brushes quickly landed in the paint pans as Willie answered the front door. She stepped back to allow Esther and David to enter.

"Wow, you are moving right along." David nodded approvingly. "New paint and everything. When are you having the floors refinished?"

"Now that the ugly laminate has been pulled up, the floor guys are just waiting for us—I mean, me—to finish painting the walls. Then they'll come in and refinish the hardwoods."

Esther silently studied the changes since Clint had been removed from the premises. "Looks different," was all she said.

Willie felt sorry for her sister-in-law. Esther looked lost. Eloise and Esther floated near their sister as if to comfort her.

"Are you okay, Esther?" Willie asked. "I'm worried about you."

Esther took a deep breath. "Let's just get on with it."

David nodded. "Lead the way, Ms. Willie."

Everyone followed Willie into her once-beautiful sunroom. The laminate flooring was gone, exposing the intricate brick pattern of the floor Frank had laid in that room for her.

Willie picked up a metal tool and placed it in a small slit cut into one of the bricks. When it clicked into place, she pulled up.

A section of the brick floor lifted with a creak to reveal a hidden compartment containing a single metal box. Willie took the same tool and slid it into the lock on the box. It popped open to reveal a dusty, old red leather envelope satchel.

She lifted the package out and handed it to David. He carried the satchel over to a card table surrounded by four upturned five-gallon buckets. Willie had yet to move her furniture into place, and the makeshift table would have to do.

Carefully he laid the bundle on the tabletop and asked the women to take a seat.

Willie plopped down on one of the buckets.

Esther looked at the accommodations and said, "No thank you, I think I'll stay standing."

Sitting on one of the buckets, David carefully unwound the leather lace from around the package, lifted the flap, and pulled out a stack of heavy vellum sheets. He read the first three pages silently before he looked up again.

"Ladies, I need to take these papers and file them with the district probate court. It appears that Jessica, Lillian, Lisa, and Meg have inherited the entirety of Bridget Dougherty's estate, which includes the Golden Bear, plus a considerable amount of property throughout the state of Colorado, and a large sum of money. It's all in a trust being managed by a very old and prestigious law firm in Denver."

Esther said softly, "Can you explain why only the girls inherit the madam's estate?"

David looked down at the papers and turned back a few sheets before answering, "It is very clearly stated that only females of the bloodline can inherit any portion of the legacy, or any accumulated assets tied to said assets. If you and John—or you, Willie, and Frank —had produced female heirs, they would have inherited everything in the legacy. Since both couples had sons, the estate passes on to any women born in the following generation. In this case, Jessica, Lillian, Lisa, and Meg."

"I see." Those two fragile little words uttered by Esther had everyone, mortal and immortal alike, moving to her side at once. She stood weaving on her feet with two tears tracking down her pale cheeks. A moment later, an entire flood of tears began pouring from her. Then a broken, cracked laugh gurgled from her throat.

A chair appeared magically behind Esther. David sucked in a deep breath in surprise, then promptly eased Esther onto the seat. If he had known how the chair appeared, it certainly would have made him question his sanity.

Willowmina knelt in front of her distraught sister-in-law. She softly took one of her hands in her own and very gently ordered, "Esther, tell us what's wrong. We can't make anything right for you if we don't know."

Esther sucked in one breath and another. She tried in vain to hold back a sad little laugh. "No one can fix this. You see, that stupid, arrogant, greedy ass that I married . . ." Her words trailed off.

"Go on," Willie said gently.

Esther said bluntly, "Clint isn't mine."

"I know he's done horrible things," David said, "but how can you say that he isn't yours?"

"You don't understand. I didn't give birth to him." She looked into the eyes of the one person who would understand. "Willie, do you remember when I got close to term when I was pregnant?"

Willie nodded.

Esther continued, "I was sent by ambulance to Denver. Things were going horribly wrong."

"I remember you stayed in the hospital several days until Clint was born."

Esther nodded and her face crumpled into tears again.

David and Willie waited for her to regain some composure. They were afraid to move or even speak, afraid she might dissolve into deep despair or retreat into her usual rigid and unyielding self.

Esther took another deep breath. "I had a little girl." Her anguished smile would have melted stone. "In my heart, I think of her as my Bonnie Blue. That's what I would have named her."

Another tear trickled down her cheek as she looked deep into her past. "She was a pretty baby, but she had a bad heart and she only lived a day. Anyway, John swooped in and took over. I don't even know where my little girl rests. He just had them . . . dispose of her somewhere, and a week later he walked in and laid Clint in my arms."

"Where did he find a baby?" Willie asked.

Esther gave a miserable laugh. "It appears my loving husband had a mistress in Denver and she had just given birth a day before. John told me not to worry about the details. All I needed to know was that the baby was his, the mother didn't want him, and my name would appear on the birth certificate."

"Oh my. Esther, we never knew," Willie said and wiped away her own tears.

"No one did, except for John, me, and the other woman. I tried to be a good mother to little Clint, but as soon as he could ride a horse by himself, John took over and relegated me to the role of nanny and maid. He wouldn't let me do any mothering at all or have a say in anything to do with Clint." Again, Esther's gaze turned inward and she seemed to be far away. "I couldn't have any more babies," she whispered. "They had to take everything to save my life after . . . after my little Bonnie Blue was born. So, I became a convenience and a housekeeper to John."

"Oh, Esther, I'm so very sorry." It was all Willie could think to say.

Eloise and Ethel were devastated by the things they were hearing. Their older sister had always been less effusive in expressing her emotions, but this explained so much of her total rejection of affection.

Eloise looked at Ethel. "I want to hug her and we can't give her the love she so desperately needs."

Ethel looked ready to cry. "I know, so do I."

Eloise and Ethel might not have been able to give their sister a hug, but Willie sure could. She threw her arms around Esther and hugged her as tightly as she could. Esther absorbed all the soft kindness directed toward her for a moment or two and then pulled herself together and away from the tiny woman hugging her fiercely.

"I'm glad the girls will inherit everything in Ms. Dougherty's estate," she said. "I won't cause any trouble over it."

David interjected a thought at that moment. "Esther, do you want me to protect you and the ranch too?"

"What do you mean?"

"Well, the madam's estate is one thing. There's also the matter of the Garrison Ranch. When your husband dies, you stand to inherit his half of the ranch. But if Clint wants to make a fuss, he could challenge that and try to cut you out."

"Oh. I never thought about that. I guess I should check with our attorney . . ."

"You might be better off with your own attorney," David advised. "Your family attorney will have ties to Clint as well."

"I never thought of that either."

"Esther, if you want, I'll represent you at no charge."

"Oh, I couldn't ask you to do that."

"Do what? Represent you?"

"No, no, I want you to represent me. Just not at no charge." Esther had slipped back into the protection of her "I'm in charge" cloak.

"Very well. We'll work out a fee schedule. Give me a few days to get the legacy paperwork underway, then I'll give you a call." David returned to the makeshift table and carefully gathered the fragile documents into the red leather case. "Willie, I'll be in touch tomorrow."

After David and Esther left, the other occupants in the room—Eloise, Ethel, Jack, Felicity, and Willie—fell silent, thinking about all that had just transpired.

As the sound of gravel crunching beneath Esther's car faded away, Eloise was the first to speak. "My poor sister. I had no idea the things she's suffered."

Ethel sighed. "I wish there was something we could do to help her."

Eloise got that look on her face. "There might be. Maybe you, Willie, and I could figure something out."

Ethel looked shocked. "Not Willie," she whispered, forgetting for the moment that her dear friend had recently revealed her ability to see and hear the dearly departed. "She's been through so much. All she wants is a quiet life now, and I don't blame her."

Willie looked at the fearless foursome, transparent in the afternoon sun streaming through the window. As her dreams of living drama-free slipped away, she grinned.

"Well," she said—the other women looked up—"you know what they say. In for a penny, in for a pound."

M. Larson is a Colorado girl from the top of her head to the tips of her toes. She grew up on the Western Slope—for the most part. After all, she had a daddy with gypsy feet, and she married a sailor. Yet even while living as far west as Hawaii and as far east as Maine, her heart was always in the Colorado mountains.

After her husband retired from the Navy, they came home to stay in a high mountain valley. This is where she quilts, knits, crochets, and writes when she isn't at work or exploring the state she loves.

Be sure to check out the first book in the
Dearly Departed Series

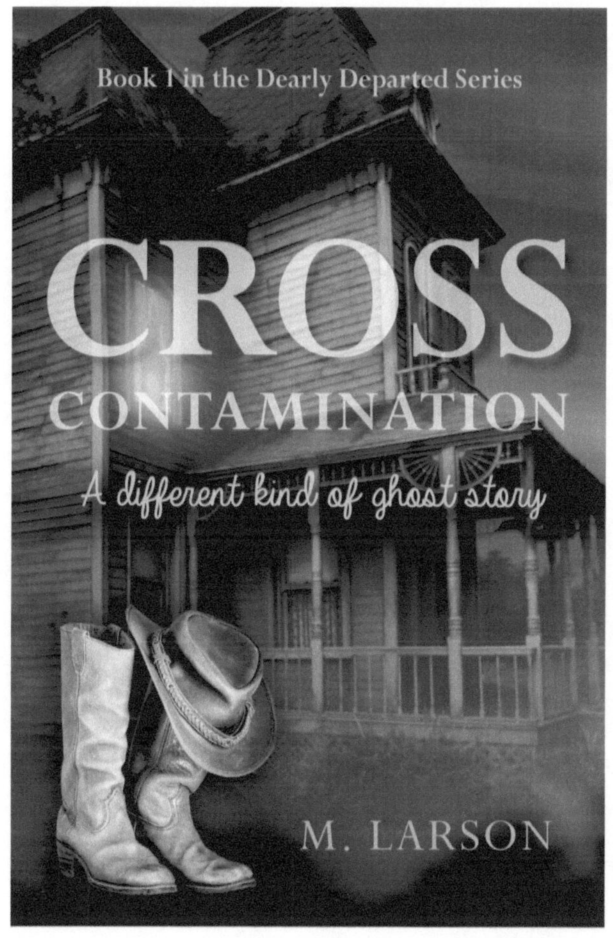

* 9 7 8 1 9 5 9 0 9 9 3 2 1 *